BARREN

Of Guards and Caretakers

◆ ◆

JON ANTHONY PERROTTI

Version M (masculine pronouns)

Text copyright © 2015 Jon Perrotti

All rights reserved.

ISBN 978-0-9980341-2-6

Cover illustration by Ray Lopez
Book design by Marie Stirk

Synopsis of Book 1: *Taking of Name*

Book 1 of the Barren trilogy is about a uedin, Elenn, who learns of his barren condition and must make peace with the fact that he carries no embryo and will never have passing-of-life, the glorious end that all uedin look forward to all their lives. Furthermore, the condition is likely to turn him into a kind of pathetic monster, deranged of mind, dangerous to others, and likely to meet a miserable demise in the desert when the condition reaches its full-blown manifestation. His struggle is not against persecution, since the uedin race is highly evolved and shows great compassion; it is simply a struggle to bear the burden of his unhappy fate. A medical breakthrough introduces a limited intervention, but Elenn is reluctant to accept it. It creates the pretense of normal life, arresting many of the symptoms of barren syndrome, but it does not address the central ordeal—it does not give fertility to a barren uedin, nor does it make him any more likely to ever know the passing-of-life. While Elenn wrestles with despair, various events shape his life and lead him to his ultimate choice to accept the treatment and live bravely with the knowledge of his condition and its implications. The following synopsis is provided so that readers may review the story with its various sub-plots in greater detail before starting Book 2.

In Part 1, *Last Unnamed Days*, the story opens with an un-named child-uedin who has finished with "exercises" outside the capital walls and is running back in to make curfew. He unknow-ingly skips past a deranged and suffering barren who is trying to make his way to the southeastern desert where we are told he is about to essentially commit suicide by subjecting himself to sun and exposure. The unidentified barren figure's brief ap-pearance at the beginning of the story foreshadows the trouble to come. The child-uedin continues along, pausing when he hears the sound of some teachers' voices doing "droning," another kind of exercise. He reenters the capital and runs to Quarterhouse, his domicile. There he ponders the upcoming Namestaking, an event which will give him a name and usher him into an adult world that will probably busy him with concerns and affairs that alien-ate him from Lern Beyana. That is, unless he becomes a server and is allowed to have a life of devotion and spiritual exercise. Be-fore he goes to bed, he talks with another unnamed child-uedin who is curious about his love of exercises, and they agree to meet after the Namesgiving ceremony. Early the next morning, the four old "ro" uedin, who were heard droning the night before, are on their way back from their all-night outing. They guess at the name of the server who has sung morning greeting and discuss a riddle poem. Domas, the youngest of the group of senior ue-din, is shown to be a scholar and a leader. An awkward reference to concerns over the "health" of the new generation upsets their otherwise predictable and game-like conversation. The next day, during the Names Eve Observances, the unnamed are given a speech about the responsibilities of having name. A practice run of the sourember smoke ritual is interrupted by a server who is "raving," or showing the signs of dementia and irrationality that signal the end of a uedin's life in the capital and his departure for the Lake of Ceulan and passing-of-life. Before he can be led away, he cries out something about trouble coming to the capital with the new generation. Domas gets the event back on track with a short speech to reassure the unnamed, and they all commence with academic drilling and quizzing about uedin history and literature. Late that night, a head caretaker, Benar, is up writing in his log and checking on some pickles that he is making. He thinks and worries to himself about the recent rise in barren syndrome in the capital. The consequent chapter skips ahead to the place where Benar takes a jar of the pickles to Domas and finds them discussing the interruption of the Names-Eve event. He tells them that on his way, he encountered some servers bidding goodbye to the ro-server who had been raving earlier that day and was now heading for his final pilgrimage. The next day, the Namesgiving Ceremony takes place with exercises, rituals, and quizzing. Finally, the taking of name actually commences, and when his turn comes, the child-uedin, who has been followed from the beginning of the story, chooses his two syllable blocks and receives his name, Elenn. The next day, Benar and Domas discuss name recurrences and, for the first time, the rise of the barren syndrome in the capital. When the time comes for the two newly-named to meet at the cold well, they learn each other's names; they are Elenn and Tilke. Then they go to the slopes for exercises. Elenn suggests that Tilke, who is much less namely than himself, consider server life, but Tilke says he wants to stay in Quarterhouse. Elenn admits that he wants to become a server himself, but he is afraid that he is too namely to become one.

In Part 2, *Newly-Named*, a half a year has passed since Names-giving, and the newly-named are on an outing to the lichen fields. Elenn tells Tilke that he has decided to join the servers at the central temple, and he wants Tilke to do the same thing. Discussing this, they trail behind the group. When they reach the lichen fields, after harvesting sacks of the lichen, they meet with the young guard Deben and start walking toward a spring where the others are thought to be relaxing and drinking water. Deben rushes ahead when he sees that some trouble is occurring at the spring. The two child-uedin catch up and find Deben talking to a naked and monstrous-looking uedin who is standing in the middle of the spring pool holding the carcass of a small wild dog that he has killed. It is a horrible scene, and Tilke tells Elenn that the uedin they are looking at is a barren. Some days later, Tilke is visiting a paper mill to determine if he might choose that work for his career, and his first impressions are very positive. Meanwhile, Elenn goes to the capital libraries to see if there is anything in the server archives about servers who struggled with nameliness. He finds an old journal which mentions a server whose name is written with the same characters as Tilke, but who apparently lost his passing-of-life in some mysterious way. Elenn, discouraged with his research, decides to do a mind-stilling exercise, but falls asleep. He has a terrible dream in which he is given the realization that he is barren. When he awakens, the realization does not dissipate, and he has a kind of emotional breakdown. He is met by Deben while trying to make his way out of the library. Deben cannot remember his name, and Elenn, collapsing in front of the guard, is too horrified by his realization to utter his own name. Later, in the infirmary, Domas talks with medic master Ferin about the barren taken into custody and about the syndrome in general. Then, Domas is visited by Elenn, who tells him that he has decided to join not the servers but the capital guards. When Elenn meets with Tilke the next time, we learn that Tilke also has changed his mind about his life choice of work. He had an interesting experience while spending time alone in the paper mill which made it evident that server life would suit him. When they meet, they learn the ironic truth: that Elenn has decided to join the guards while Tilke has decided to become a server. Both newly-named are upset about this twist.

In Part 3, *Apprenticeship*, the capital waits for the arrival of the Great Rains and the end of the novade. We learn that the barren uedin who was discovered at the lichen fields was apparently released and later found dead at the Haka Cliffs. Elenn is on duty with the guards when the Rains arrive. They monitor retaining walls of the streambeds as the tremendous storm comes. When a retaining wall at a certain spot fails, they are forced to break stone from the capital wall to create a barrier to erosion. A patch of ground collapses into the flooding river, and Elenn is swept under water. Catching a rock, he holds on, but seriously considers the option he has to let go and drown. He allows himself to be rescued, but feels some regret that he has missed an opportunity to die and escape his fate. After a number of days when the rains start to subside, Elenn receives an invitation to attend a celebration and view the wetuedin (amphibious infant uedin) at Quarterhouse. He also learns that his generation is going to be tested for barren syndrome. At the celebration, the masters feast, view the wetuedin, and share poetry. Udow compliments Elenn on his poem about the Lake of Ceulan. In the following chapter, Elenn is told not to report to his earlier assigned duty because he has to remain at the station where he and the other second-generation guards are to be tested for syndrome. When they are tested together in the station office, Elenn experiences some sensations at seeing the skullsap sample drawn from the necks of his comrades, and he is disturbed by his own arousal. The next night Deben calls him in to tell him privately that his results were positive; he wanted to let him know so that he could receive the official news with dignity. Elenn accepts this with great sorrow but is not surprised. That night he has a strange nightmare about Domas, and after awakening, he ponders what it means that he dreamt of destroying the uedin he admires the most in the capital. Thanks to Deben's advance warning, Elenn is able to remain calm when he is officially informed of his test results. Some days later, the guards are summoned in the middle of the night for an emergency at Quarterhouse. They go there to find that an attack by a barren has resulted in the death of a wetuedin. Elenn is asked to help move the body while others search the capital for the killer. Elenn is horrified to find that the smell emanating from the crushed skull of the wetuedin is enticing to him. While walking back to the station, he accidentally touches a finger to his mouth and is so intoxicated by the trace of wetuedin skullsap that he falls down. Ribol helps him back to the station where the superior guards assume that his collapse was due to being traumatized by the chain of events. Hela and Nemis rush in to report that the barren has killed himself by walking into a blazing kiln. Reacting physically, Elenn vomits. The story then jumps three years ahead, and we learn that Benar has become a caretaker to the barren. He is visited by Deben and they talk about the fact that

Elenn has grown large with the syndrome and might be at risk of derangement. Benar agrees to keep Deben informed. They also discuss Udow's murder by a barren. The barren was captured but never identified and ultimately released in the desert. They share a concern that the servers are not providing appropriate care for whatever barren uedin might be showing up in their midst.

In Part 4, *Purest Exercise*, Tilke is well into his experience with server life in the central temple, and the ritualized "meal of seeds" is described, along with a game he plays with a ro-server. While playing, Tilke ponders the depth of his relationship with Lern Beyana. Back at Flatpools, Elenn and Hela are asked to go to Redrock outvillage to help reinforce the crumbling gathering hall there. On the way, Elenn exhibits strange behavior that makes Hela think he could be showing some first signs of derangement. When they arrive at Redrock, they are welcomed warmly and invited to bathe in the hotsprings. Afterwards, they join a communal dinner in a large mining cave that is so dark that they have the entire experience in total darkness. The next day the guards tell the outvillagers about barren syndrome in the capital, and they hear that a barren once showed up in the outvillage. In the evening, Elenn tells the story of the vadime and the hailflower tree. Over the course of the following ten days of work, Elenn experiences a disturbing attraction to one of the outvillage workers. One afternoon, he has a fit of derangement. Tilke helps him cover it up by pretending that Elenn has stepped on a poison thistle. They take a walk, and as Elenn recovers, they have a heart-to-heart talk about Elenn's condition. Then unexpectedly, they encounter the three child-uedin, who want to show them the boiling muds. While looking at the boiling muds, they are attacked by a swarm of lethal wasps. Elenn saves himself and two of the unnamed by jumping with them into one of the mud pools, but Hela loses his life protecting the third unnamed. Elenn is deeply saddened by the loss of such a close friend and companion guard. Once Elenn returns to the capital, he replaces his mud-ruined robe and takes the new robe to Benar to dye for him. Benar accidentally shrinks the robe and must inform Elenn that he will have to sew another. In conversation that follows, Elenn admits his torment to Benar. Benar tells him about a new intervention being developed by the medic masters that will drain skullsap and arrest the symptoms of barren syndrome. Elenn is not sure what he thinks of this, afraid it would only perpetuate his troubled life with no passing-of-life to come. He decides to visit Domas to see if he can learn more. When he gets there, he sees that Domas is in an advanced stage of raving. Domas, because of recent nightmares, becomes terrified when he realizes that Elenn is barren, and Elenn leaves learning no more about the new possible treatment. A moon-cycle later, the availability of the experimental treatment is announced, and Elenn begins to notice some masters with bandages on their necks, others with straps. Henik and Wanba urge Elenn to get the implant. Wanba disapproves of Elenn's intention to forego the treatment and face the wilderness when his condition reaches its advance stage, but he agrees, with assurances from Henik, to let Elenn decide on his own. Leaving, Elenn sees Simol, who asks if he can go with him to chaperone the Bells unnamed on a play trip to the moss beds, and Elenn agrees to go. When they go to Bells to meet the group, they are told that one of the child-uedin is blind. Later, at the peat moss beds, Simol plays with the others while Elenn keeps company with the blind child-uedin. Elenn happens to see a uedin in the distance, and is able to determine that it is a barren uedin doing shifting exercises beautifully. He is deeply moved by the sight. Some days later, Domas makes a night-time departure from the capital to go on his pilgrimage to passing-of-life. He is bid farewell by Hera and Lemeh along with his caretaker Yenca. The next day, three uedin are described in their prospective scenes. Domas is walking through a field toward the hill country, bound for Lake Ceulan. Tilke is doing a deep and extended mind-stilling exercise in the temple. Elenn is preparing to attend Hela's memorial service, an event which will also include him being recognized for his part in saving the child-uedin at Redrock outvillage. He has received the implant and his neck is still healing. This signifies a major life decision that Elenn has made. He, Benar, and Simol laugh about the accident with the green dye. Deben joins them and comments on Elenn's neck strap, which Elenn seems to have made peace with. They proceed to Quarterhouse for the event, passing a blossoming hailflower tree on the way.

BOOK 2

OF GUARDS
AND CARETAKERS

Part 1

FEED OR BE FED ON

Counselors and Counselor-apprentices

YENCA LOOKED UP INTO THE canopy of mola bean trees. The dancing brilliance of sun behind the leaves made it difficult to focus. He was trying to see the newly-named apprentice who was somewhere up in the treetop, indiscernible in the swaying sparkle of sun and leaf. Beside Yenca stood the senior Quarterhouse caretaker, Master Benar, and two other newly-named apprentices, one of whom was blind. The Quarterhouse caretakers had accepted a blind apprentice from Bells. Yenca and Benar had brought the three apprentices with them on this short hike to harvest mola beans.

While they waited for the one apprentice to pick and drop down mola beans, Benar lectured the other two. He seemed to enjoy the opportunity to share his wisdom and experience with an admiring audience of newly-named apprentices. The blind one smiled courteously and faced in the general direction of Master Benar. The other, suppressing the urge to look up to see how high his fellow apprentice had climbed, likewise listened with deference.

"The best thing to do is be stern with them. I had one assigned to me who was very self-conscious when he received his neck strap and didn't want to go to his job in the grain house. I scolded him like a little wet-one." Benar smiled with self satisfaction. "He went back to work the next day. But you newly-named who come straight into the corps without ever working with child-uedin don't know how to use that kind of approach. You really are at a disadvantage there."

Yenca hollered up. *"How does it look? Are you all right up there?"* The apprentices finally shifted their attention away from Benar. It was a moment before the climber called down in response.

"Look out! Dropping more beans now!" announced a youthful voice from the treetops. There was a sound of objects hitting leaves as they fell through the branches. The giant pods fell from a spot quite apart from where they had been looking. He must have climbed across to the adjacent treetop.

The blind apprentice, carrying a large sack in one hand, followed with his free hand on the shoulder of the other newly-named. He went with his fellow apprentice, traipsing through the underbrush, then held the sack open while the others collected the dropped mola beans and dropped them in. The beans were nearly the size of their own forearms.

Benar tried to continue with his advice. "It would do you young caretakers well, even though you are training directly to work with the barren, to spend as much time as you can in and around Quarterhouse during your first novade here. You'll learn much from the regular caretakers and even from the unnamed themselves. . ."

"More falling!" came the warning from above. The four on the ground stepped back so as not to be struck. Beans bounced off branches on their way down.

"That's all," hollered the voice. *"The rest are not ripe—we'll have to come back in a few days. I'm coming down now."*

Benar seemed unconcerned and continued with his stories and advice. ". . .That one brings me gifts now. So you see, the fact that they have no passing-of-life ahead of them is not nearly the ordeal that we imagine it to be. They do fine once they've been given a little guidance."

Yenca silently disagreed and could not stand to let it go on any further. "Master Benar," he interrupted, searching his mind for a change of subject. "Did you hear anything about one of the ovens collapsing in the Quarterhouse kitchen yesterday?"

"Well, yes," said Benar quizzically, "I was the one who told you about the incident." There was a brief silence. Yenca had hoped Benar would take the bait and retell the whole thing.

"I suppose they'll have it rebuilt by the time we're ready to roast the mola." Yenca knew they had reassembled it immediately.

"How long do you roast the mola beans?" asked the blind apprentice.

"I don't know, I've never roasted mola before. Do you know, Master Benar?"

"It depends on what you're making." Benar was willing to take up the new subject. "If you want to grind them up for mola cakes you must roast them a whole day. If you're using them in a stew— and we usually use the fresh ones in stew—then you only need to roast them till the case curls away from the inside. Of course, you cook them a second time in the stew."

"Did you ever have mola stew at Bells, young Master Jutef?" asked Yenca. The blind apprentice was the stranger among them, since the other newly-named were Quarterhouse graduates. Being from Bells would have been enough to make him something of a novelty among the others. This, however, was completely eclipsed by the matter of his blindness, a condition that radically set him apart and gave him an extraordinary status.

"No. I don't think any of the Bells masters ever harvested mola beans. We had cakes, of course, which came from the distributors, but nothing ever made from fresh mola." Jutef continued holding the sack open wide for the others to put in more beans even though they had already picked up and put in all that had been dropped.

"Well, young master," said Benar, "You'll have your chance to taste mola stew tonight. It's a favorite at Quarterhouse this time of year."

One of the other apprentices took the sack from Jutef and guided Jutef's hand to his own shoulder so that he could lead as they started back.

"It wouldn't hurt any of you to learn to cook either," said Benar. "You are, after all, caretakers. Just because you've taken up the service to the barren doesn't mean the traditional caretaker skills won't be important to you. The more you help the regular caretaker masters, the better you'll fare in the long run."

It was a short hike back to the western gate of the capital. Yenca pursued his own thoughts and ignored Benar's ongoing chatter. They were soon back to the trail head which departed from West Road a short distance from the capital gate. Thick trees lined the road on both sides right up to the capital walls, and the morning chill lingered in the shade.

Inside, the activity of the Crafting District buzzed around them. A group of reed-craft masters worked together in the early sunlight weaving heavy tarps. Yenca thought about the fact that poor Jutef was caught in listening to Benar's rabble about all the essential things he thought they must know. Jutef couldn't see the reed-crafters or the crumbling storage huts or the bundles of freshly cut green reed ready to stack for drying under the lean-tos. If he could see it, thought Yenca, he would probably be interested. He had, after all, come from Bells, which is known for its weaving of tapestries. Would Benar be irritated if Yenca interrupted? Probably. He decided to speak anyhow.

"Young Master Jutef," he said, getting the newly-named's attention. Benar stopped and other apprentices likewise listened to hear what merited the interruption. "This area just inside the gate is the Crafting District. We're just walking past the reed-crafting masters. They're weavers, you know."

"Yes I know," answered Jutef. "I almost joined the reed crafters."

"Is that right?" said Benar with surprise. Yenca was surprised as well, and glad to see Benar found something interesting besides his own interminable advice.

"I already knew many of their techniques and patterns by feeling tarps. I never liked weaving tapestries much. . . I could never see the tapestries of course. The tarps I can feel. The patterns are very nice."

"Have you been here then?" asked Yenca. Perhaps Jutef would want to say hello to the reed-crafters.

"Yes, I was here more than once." He paused and added, "We compared tapestry and tarp patterns."

Yenca considered Jutef's words and asked, "Would you like to stop and offer politenesses to any of them?"

Jutef thought for a moment. "No thank you, Master Yenca." He shifted the bag of mola beans from one shoulder to the other. They continued walking.

"What made you decide to come to Quarterhouse instead of joining the reed-crafters, young master?" asked Benar without worrying whether the question was nosey or might put Jutef on the spot.

"It was not an easy decision," said Jutef. "When it came down to it, I suppose I just wanted one thing more than the other."

Yenca thought of his own decision to join the corps after Master Domas's passing. Domas had been his mentor when he had started as a teaching master, and Domas had groomed him for administrator duties at Quarterhouse. Though they had never spoken about it outright, they both had understood at the time that Domas also envisioned Yenca's participation on the masters council. Then Domas had fallen into an early ecstasy. He had left for his pilgrimage in the fifth year of the last novade. In the late stages of his ecstasy, Domas had been visited by a former student who was barren. Yenca remembered it well. Master Domas, wits dulled somewhat by the beginning of raving, had not realized the uedin's condition until the middle of the visit. Then he had become irrationally afraid. Yenca had caught some indication of Master Domas's phobia regarding the barren, but that incident had brought it to the forefront. It had become a puzzle to Yenca. Domas had never been fearful of anything. Every challenge was a problem to be solved, calmly and intelligently. What was it about uedin with barren syndrome that so disturbed him? He could only conclude that Domas feared that which undid his confidence. The syndrome was a problem which left Domas insufferably clueless. In ecstasy, his confoundedness had turned to terror.

After Domas left for his final pilgrimage, Yenca began to find the problem of the barren more and more compelling. It was as though he had inherited Domas's deep concern. He had planned to return to teaching after taking care of Domas in his ecstasy, but when it was over, after a brief period, Yenca had contacted Benar about joining the corps of caretakers in service to the barren—or "syndrome-afflicted," as they were now being called.

Now that all seemed like it had happened a long time ago, and here he was, experienced enough to be training apprentices. The corps was relatively new and had little tradition to fall back on when it came to care of the barren, but with some confidence in the medic masters and their use of catheters to alleviate the physical symptoms of the syndrome, the masters council had decided to let the corps recruit directly from the newly-named generation.

A quarter of the generation being considered for recruiting was itself barren. There would be an immediate need for great numbers of counselors, that much was certain. Meanwhile, the caretakers to the barren were looked upon by all the capital for reassurance, and there was tremendous pressure from the masters council and the medics to pretend that the catheters were doing the job and everything was going well. That was not the case. How much was enough for these newly-named caretaker apprentices to know?

Benar, quickly laying claim to the same noble intention that Jutef had brought to mind by saying he had chosen work with the barren over another option, was now in the mood to talk about his own virtue and dedication. "Bless Lern Beyana," he said, "I'm so glad I came into the service. The barren came to me, you know. I was counseling them before you newly-named even emerged. I have learned to know just what to say."

Just what to say, thought Yenca. Yes, you and most of the others in the corps have learned just what to say. Too bad it's not the truth you're telling. But he let Benar go on talking the rest of the way as they walked through the capital and back to Quarterhouse.

After supper that evening, Yenca found Jutef. He was exploring cabinets in the Quarterhouse caretakers' main den by feeling about with his hands.

"Master Jutef, there you are. Can I help you find something?"

"Oh no, Master Yenca," he had recognized Yenca's voice. "I'm just trying to orient myself."

"How did you like the mola stew?"

"Well," said Jutef, smiling, "I think I like mola cakes better than the stew."

"You might like it better the second time. Many foods are like that."

Jutef was no longer figuring out what was where and now stood politely facing his senior master.

"I was wondering, young master,. . ." began Yenca.

"Yes, master?"

"This morning in the Crafting District, you chose not to greet the reed-craft masters. Why not?"

Jutef's face took on a nervous expression. "Well," he said, bowing his head, "The reed-crafters were very accommodating when I visited them. I tried my hand at weaving reed, and I did very well. I think they imagined that I would be a good apprentice, and they were willing to give me whatever additional assistance I needed—being blind and all. . ."

"Yes, well, I'm sure they were sorry to miss having you," commented Yenca.

"The senior reed-crafters there were promising to work with me directly. When I told them I was going instead to be a caretaker for the barren, they didn't understand. I'm afraid I may have seemed ungrateful to them."

"And you said you just wanted one thing more than the other. May I ask what helped you decide?" Yenca realized this was a personal question.

Jutef hesitated. "Oh. . . I did very well at Bells, considering my blindness. But it was lonely."

Yenca didn't understand what he was getting at. "Did you think that you would be less lonely at Quarterhouse?"

"Less lonely. . .?" Jutef considered this. "Well, yes, Quarterhouse is a wonderful, welcoming community. But, well, I meant. . . because of working with the barren—other uedin who know what it feels like to be apart from normal uedin. Maybe that was not a good reason."

"If it was enough to help you decide, then it was a good enough reason," Yenca assured him. "But I don't think the barren are likely to feel 'alone' for much longer. You must be aware of the results from your generation's testing for syndrome."

"I don't believe there's been any announcement yet, has there?"

"No official announcement, but. . ." There was no point in pretense here. Yenca sighed and continued, "Everyone in the capital knows that a full fourth of your generation has tested barren. Surely the apprentices are talking about it."

Jutef hesitated. One of the lessons of his blindness was that there were always many, many things which were not going to be known to him. He had learned that it was best not to try to get to know them. Curiosity could be endless frustration to him. Yet it was always a great honor to be invited into confidence. "Yes," he finally answered cautiously, "I'm not always in on the gossip and rumors, but I did hear that the test results were alarming. So it's true?"

"The medics are not denying any of it."

"There's something else I overheard, Master Yenca. . ."

"What's that?"

"I heard some apprentices saying that there are still many syndrome uedin who seem to be getting larger. Of course, I can't see them, so I don't know."

Yenca was not expecting this to come up. "Did they talk about why that might be happening?" he asked.

"One apprentice—I don't know all the names yet—said the catheters weren't working."

It wasn't time to reveal the trouble to this young apprentice, decided Yenca, but in the future he would be a good one with whom to discuss the disturbing facts. "I'm not sure about it," Yenca answered, "but I don't think the catheters are defective in any way."

Mind-stilling Exercise is Interrupted

Elenn sat near the bank of the drystream that followed the north wall. He looked down past the jumble of boulders to a flat grassy spot in the streambed below. In a year it would flow again. It was close to the place in which he had been swept into the current during the last Great Rains. That had been the beginning of his compromise with himself, when, by holding on to one of those rocks, he had acted to preserve his own life even though he didn't want it. After that, if times came when he regretted his existence, he could only blame himself.

It was too hot to sit in the sun during the heat of the day, so he walked back to the shade of the capital wall. He found a smooth and level spot close to the wall and knelt, then sat back on his knees, bent forward and rested his chest against his thighs. He was taking the worm position to do a mind-stilling exercise. He felt the dry ground against his forehead.

It doesn't matter what I did then, or what I have done today, or what I may do tomorrow, he thought to himself. *It doesn't matter...*

Nor did it matter that his body was too large to assume the worm position properly, which made the pose painful to his knees and his ankles. He slowed his breathing. He was aware of an unpleasant feeling in his consciousness, a kind of edge. The peace of mind needed for a proper exercise required a strong-willed resignation, and this feeling of resistance was hard to put away. A senseless and aimless resentment was his constant irritant. The silence would melt it. It had worked before.

Elenn remained there long enough for the shadow of the capital wall to grow dark around him. He finally began to rest in a soothing state of forgetfulness. Time slipped away.

His consciousness was drawing down to a tiny range of thoughtless sensation. Worries collapsed one by one, now leaving only the rhythm of easy breath, a passive acceptance of the crunch of the weight of his body hunching forward toward gravity and the blurred gray of filtered light. The initial discomfort of his forehead against the ground and the strained position of his legs subsided; he was aware of nothing now except for the small space just in front of his eyes.

The scene around him was practically frozen as time passed. The wind that had been rustling in weeds along the dry stream now ceased completely. Elenn was oblivious of the tiny gnats rising in floating clusters from the damp gulch as evening set in.

When he felt the touch of a hand on his shoulder, he didn't immediately identify the sensation. He only felt a sudden stirring. The entirely unexpected image of an embryo suddenly flashed through his mind and interrupted his blank trance. It was a picture that resembled illustrations used in lessons that he recalled from his days at Quarterhouse. But it was different. The embryo image was only there for a second, but it appeared to be somehow starved, as if it were trapped in the skullwomb of a parent uedin whose body had ceased to function. His awakening consciousness jumped to a thought of Hela, swollen and dead from an attack of blue wasps at the mudpools of Redrock.

Elenn now knew that his mindstilling was interrupted. For a confused minute, two separate trains of thought competed for his attention, one puzzling over the dreamy image that had popped so oddly into his mind, and the other regarding with irritation the fact that his exercise had been broken. *The embryo in Hela's skullwomb must have lingered for at least a short while in a body that could no longer nourish it, he thought. What was that he had felt on his neck? Hela's embryo died inside him. Once Hela was dead, his body could not deliver skullsap any longer. For Elenn and the other barren like him, skullsap was always being produced for nothing.* He thought about the cavity of his skullwomb holding nothing but fluid which drained from his catheter into a pouch that he emptied every day in the bath. A feeling of sadness and painful longing rose up in him just as he felt something brush over his neck strap. By the time he registered the tinge of pain in the sensitive area around the catheter, Elenn knew what was happening, but he only gasped slightly and did nothing to stop it. In a moment he felt a mouth closing over the back of his neck. This was unthinkable. But a powerful will to submit to it rose up in him mysteriously. *Yes—receive it. Take my gift which has no other taker.* How could he be letting himself do this? He was amazed at his own willingness to allow it. In fact, he had never imagined anything so satisfying. Surprising himself, Elenn bowed his neck slightly more for the strange lips that were pursing around the duct.

His senses now began to awaken in waves. The weight and temperature of a hand on his back felt strange. A sting of pain at the spot where the catheter protruded from his neck was mixed with the weird stimulation of a wet and soft mouth against it. For a moment he opened his eyes, but the normal impulse to draw around and look at the invader was overcome by a feeling of dizzy pleasure; he closed his eyes again. Now he could hear the deep breathing and even smell the body scent along with the soapy fragrance of a recently laundered robe.

Elenn knew what this was, but he played a game with himself to keep his rational mind from reacting. He pretended that he wasn't aware that this was the dreadful behavior that some of the guards had been whispering about, always changing topic when Elenn entered the room. They referred to it as "feeding." The first few times Elenn had heard it mentioned, he had thought they were talking about the feeding of grain to wetuedin in the hatching pool at Quarterhouse. But it came up too many times, and it had been a very long time since there had been wetuedin in any of the pools. The new generation was already named and into their apprenticeship. He knew that this "feeding" was something else. Finally he had asked his counselor, Master Benar, to tell him the truth about this "feeding." Master Benar had been visibly uncomfortable at the very mention of the word and wouldn't tell him anything.

His head swimming, his whole body quivering, he lamely repeated the lie in his head: *I don't know what this is.* He couldn't allow himself to admit otherwise. This would be the undoing of his fragile dignity. It would ruin everything.

A deep, involuntary sigh came over his whole body. He felt as though the blood were draining from his face and fingers. As the frame of the other uedin drew back from Elenn, he collapsed onto his side, feeling only an exquisite emptiness. His legs unbent themselves from the worm position for the first time. He opened one eye and looked up at the blurry form gazing down on him. It was too dark to see the face, but he could tell by the sway and stumble that the uedin was experiencing a similar drunken rapture.

"What is your district of residence?" Ellen asked distractedly. The question was automatic, a result of being in the guards. He didn't care and wasn't sure why he was asking. He didn't want to know.

"No matter how much I tell myself not to," the stranger muttered as if he hadn't heard the question, "I can't help doing it again."

"What is 'it'? What did you do to me?" Elenn was still less than alert, but now at least aware enough to know that something abnormal and disturbing had just taken place. What was *it*? What did *it* mean? He was afraid that he knew the answer, and was only hoping that the other barren might understand something that he did not. Might he be able to offer some bit of explanation or reassurance? But the stranger was backing away, ignoring the question, speaking as if talking only to himself.

"It's because the passing-of-life is too wondrous for memory," he whispered. "Only when I forget can I even think that I might resist it at all."

"Passing-of-life?" said Elenn in hazy uncertainty, "But you're not even a ro-uedin. . ."

The other uedin turned and quickly fled away along the capital wall toward the north gate. Watching him run off, Elenn was too overwhelmed to notice that the stranger had no strap on his own neck.

Trouble Multiplying Itself

The outside entryway to the food storage was clear of servers, and no noise came from the temple kitchen. After waiting a few minutes to be sure no one was coming near, a tall uedin stirred in an overgrown corner of the dark, back interior yard of the temple. He stood in a tangle of vines that grew up and over the wall of the temple compound with their layers of new growth over the dead. He reached about his feet to locate what he had stashed there earlier.

Here it is. He picked up the bundle and pulled one edge of the rough fabric. The bundle fell open and he separated the two pieces of the server wrappings. He quickly undid the belt of the plain master's robe he was wearing, stepped out of it, and slipped anxiously into the server wrappings. Now folding the master's robe into the same kind of tight bundle, he felt the first relief at being home free. It was premature.

"Oh—is someone else out here, then?"

He gasped. The voice was right next to him!

"Someone here, then?"

He coughed to admit his presence and responded, "Yes, I was just checking to see if the. . . spill had been cleaned up from today." Now he could see the other server looking in his direction. It was a ro-server, wearing a baker's apron.

"Spill? Today?"

He slowly hid the bundled master's robe behind his back. He felt a little sick at his stomach, not just from fear, but from the awful displeasure of making up lies.

"Yes. We spilled some rye here today, and I couldn't remember if I'd gotten back to clean it up or not. Don't want ants showing up. . ." *Would this old ro-server question him or take his word?*

"But it's so dark. Of course you won't see it very well now, even if there was a spill. Why are you looking in the vineberries?"

"Yes, well. . ." He stammered. *What could he say now?*

"I don't remember your voice," the elder server went on, "You work in the day kitchen, do you?"

"You're right—can't see in the dark. I'll check again in the morning," he said, ignoring the question. "Good night, my fellow server."

"Wait! Could you step in with me so I can see your face? I'm just so curious—because I really don't remember your voice at all." The ro reached out and gently took the young server by the arm. "You know, we ro-servers have the hardest time keeping up with you young servers sometimes." He chuckled softly.

The younger server wanted to yank free and rush past him, but such an action would be unthinkably rude—it was out of the question. He might be able to entertain the old ro for a minute or two and then get on, but first he had to bury the bundled master's robe in under the mass of vines. Before he could attempt the maneuver, another voice called out from the entryway.

"Well, you sure are taking your time, now, aren't you, my fellow server? You said you were just coming out to take a pee. We've got two more batches of loaves—"

The ro shouted back, "One of the day workers is out here checking on a spill from today, but I don't recognize him. Come out here."

Oh, no! As a second figure came out the entryway with a small lantern and walked toward them, the captive looked about in desperation for a moment and then attempted to briskly throw the bundle into the vines. It hit against a thick, woody stem and bounced back.

"What's that?" asked the ro with innocent surprise. The server with the lantern approached just in time to provide light for the object, and the ro bent to have a closer look.

The other kitchen worker wore a jolly expression. "Day worker? Come back at night because he couldn't bear to be away from his job, then?" He looked very much in the mood for socializing.

When the ro reached for the bundle, the nervous young visitor snatched it from his reach, causing the ro to look up at him with genuine bewilderment.

"Now, what have you got there?" he asked a bit more insistently. His tone conveyed the authority of his elder status. He was not going to tolerate such brashness. Even if these young servers were fond of kidding about, he thought, they shouldn't be quite so brash with their elders.

"Got some kind of packet or something there?" asked the server with the lantern, grin changing into an inquisitive expression.

This is it. I am caught. There was nothing to do now but give up and see how things would go. He certainly had no intention of trying to create enough lies to get past these fellow servers. Lying was far too unpleasant and much too much work. The time had come to talk about what was happening to him. Maybe someone would be able to help him understand the situation better than he could by himself. He handed the bundle to the ro-server and tried to think of words for his confession.

The ro smiled politely as if he were being invited to admire some piece of interesting artwork or curio. "It must be something very special to be so beautifully wrapped," he said. But as he opened it to see, it was immediately clear that it was not a wrapped object, but rather a bundled garment.

"Isn't that a master's robe?" asked the lantern-bearing server with a look of surprise.

"Yes it is just that," said the ro. "Why do you have a master's robe, young server?" he asked with gentle patience.

The guilty one responded quietly, "I'm afraid my answer is going to be a problem," he said. "I'm in terrible violation of the rule."

The two now looked at him with sympathetic dismay.

"We'll have to wake up the superior," said the ro sadly.

The server who acted as personal assistant to the superior was a thin, bulgy-eyed uedin with a stutter. He looked uncomfortable about having to disturb the superior. His faced locked up for a moment every time he spoke.

"There is just one p-p-PROBLEM," said the assistant. "I will have to ask you to. . ."

"Yes?" said the offender, resigned to cooperate fully.

"Please, g-g-g—TELL ME YOUR NAME." The request came out with the force that sometimes follows a stutter and sounded doubly intrusive in such a tone.

"My name?" Servers generally discarded the use of their names. Being asked his name directly was a stark indication that etiquette was being put aside. The kitchen workers looked at each other momentarily, sharing sympathy for the young stranger. It was plain: server dignity was no longer his claim, and now he had to not only speak his name, but speak it in the context of this shameful predicament. "I'm Pavis. Third generation server, messenger office."

"So he's a messenger," said the ro to his fellow kitchen worker, "He's not a day worker in the kitchen after all." They nodded together at this new revelation.

"My fellow servers, you may return t-t-TO YOUR LABOR. I'll introduce this one to the superior. Thank you f-f-FOR YOUR HELP HERE." The assistant to the superior looked at Pavis with great concern.

The two seemed reluctant to leave and miss out on more details, but they raised hands to face in courtesy and then left.

Pavis looked after them as they departed. How could he allow himself to be such a disgrace to his fellows? The encounter he had had along the north wall with that guard was still fresh in his mind. A master guard—how reckless of him to engage with a guard!

But it *was* the passing-of-life that he experienced whenever he did that weird thing that he had seen masters doing. How he could experience it without going to Ceulan Lake was a mystery to him, but he felt strangely certain that the sensation was just that. His first experience had been almost a full year ago when he was picking up an order of tea bowls from Whiteroof. He had been unable to locate the particular pottery master whom he was supposed to meet for the transaction. While he was looking around, he accidentally witnessed one master submitting his neck to let another master have his skullsap. Pavis had been raised in the temple and everything outside its walls was foreign to him. What stunned him about this was that it was exactly the thing that had appeared in his dreams and floated into his mind at odd times. He had thought it was just a strange idea that had taken root in his imagination, but here were these two masters acting it out! It must be master's ritual, he reasoned. Had he been taught about it long ago and forgotten it so completely that it had not surfaced in his dreams until recently? But no—if this thing were well established, it surely would have been included in the lessons on master society during his orientation for messenger duty. It must be something new—a kind of fad. He wasn't sure how the masters had openings made in their necks that they kept under special patches that could be easily lifted away for the activity. These marvelous masters with their exposed names and loud voices were so bold and confident compared to the servers! How daring of them to discover this pleasure and invent a way to directly partake in it!

Such behavior was unthinkable for a server, but Pavis was irresistibly drawn back to it. Before long he had memorized the places on his route where masters with neck patches congregated, and after once getting up the nerve to join in, he was soon obsessed with finding opportunities for these intense and silent meetings. He discovered that he could borrow a master's robe from the laundry bins at Whiteroof without consequence, and that made it easy to blend in. Some of the masters had looked at him oddly when they saw that he did not have a neck patch himself, but there were rarely words spoken during these encounters. He worried that they might be displeased because he couldn't offer them his own neck, but the giving of skullsap seemed to bring as much of the sensation of passing-of-life as the receiving of it did. His elder servers had always taught him that he was lucky that he had taken leg from the small temple hatching pool and been spared the pains of life in the barbaric and frightening world outside the temple walls. His few years as a server messenger had gotten him used to the outside. Now he found himself wondering, "If I were a master, would I have my neck opened up like these others? Yes, I probably would." When he found himself wishing that he could be a master just for this purpose, he knew that the problem was seriously out of control. Servers had no business interacting with masters and joining in their worldly habits. It had to stop. It was becoming a torment. But poor Pavis couldn't help himself. And now it had come to this shameful predicament.

The superior appeared, looking a bit disheveled from having been called from his sleep.

"And, so you are. . . Server Pavis?" asked the superior. He spoke the name with reservation in his voice. This situation called for a dispensing with politeness, but he was too accustomed to server manners to blather out names casually.

"Yes, Superior. I'm here because I was caught with this master's robe. I'm guilty of getting involved with the masters' strange habits." Then Pavis added with a hint of desperation, "Please help me."

"First we'll have to establish consequences for violating the rule," the elder server spoke sternly. Then he looked up and added, "If you have a problem, I will try to help you as long as it may please the Soft One. If I can't help you, I'll refer you to my own superior in the second chamber."

Pavis raised hands to his face to express his gratitude. He was sure this wise server was going to be able to help him put this trouble behind him. He was filled with relief.

Three days later Pavis stood feeling exhausted and hopeless outside the doorway of yet another next rank of superior. He had been passed on at every level by increasingly detached and silent superior servers. He was now dealing with "high servers," assumed to be in very close communion with the Soft One, but none of them had any answers, only discomfort and referrals to other superiors. The kitchen workers he had surrendered to the first night had been very kind to him, but since then the amount of sympathy had decreased with every confession.

"Please go in now," said a very small and delicate-looking ro-server. Pavis entered the room. High servers seemed to favor these large, gloomy rooms with dim lighting. He found two superiors sitting quietly facing the empty space. One was very old, and the other was young, possibly even from his own generation. The younger, he assumed, must be the superior's assistant. He walked in and took a seat on the cushion that had been placed for him in front of them. He sat still and raised hands to face.

With higher rank, thought Pavis, the superiors became more odd and difficult to talk to. These two sat before him with their eyes closed as he waited a long time to be addressed. Finally the younger one leaned and whispered something into the ro's ear.

The ro-uedin raised his head but did not look at Pavis directly. He spoke quietly. "We understand you are seeking counsel. Tell us why you are here."

"I am Pavis," he volunteered. He noticed the younger server wince at the giving of name. He continued, speaking slowly, ". . . second-generation server, assigned to the messenger's office. I am regularly dispatched about the capital. I am a fast runner and careful with deliveries."

The ro-uedin leaned over again and whispered into the other server's ear. It was suddenly apparent that the ro was acting as advisor to the younger, and it was the *younger* who appeared to be the higher ranking. But why was this whispering necessary? Couldn't the young superior open his eyes and talk to him directly?

Pavis went on, "I violated rule by getting involved in one of the masters' vices. It has completely interfered with my duties as messenger and as server."

"Are you taking yeastdrink?" asked the ro advisor.

"No, it is not yeastdrink."

"Betting? Are you betting on games?"

"No, it is not betting. I have discovered a masters' habit that I didn't know existed, and yet it was something I was instantly eager to try."

"Tell us, what is this habit?"

"The masters take one another's skullsap into their mouths," said Pavis. "It gives the experience of passing-of-life."

The ro-server advisor looked up, and Pavis saw his eyes for the first time. He was obviously horrified by what Pavis had said. It was a look Pavis had now seen a few times. The young superior did not raise his head, but rather crouched sideways.

"You are wrong!" barked the advisor.

Pavis was stunned by the reaction. When he saw that the advisor was waiting for him to respond, he finally said in a meek and defensive voice, ". . . But it's true. Some of the masters even have permanent cavities opened in their necks which they keep protected with special patches. They lift the patches away for the passing-of—"

"It is *not* the passing-of-life!" growled the old advisor, trying to restrain his voice.

"I have experienced it many times now," said Pavis slowly, confused by the force of the assistant's reaction. "I wouldn't know what else to call it."

"It is *not* the passing-of-life!" repeated the advisor. "It is the *consumption* of life."

"I don't understand," said Pavis.

"Has no one explained this to you? Who did you see last? Who sent you to us?"

"Who?" *Did high servers actually use names themselves?*

"I wonder if it was Nekur. Unacceptable! Cowardice!" The ro-server advisor was rising to his feet. "Young server, please wait outside. I will be out in a few minutes to discuss this with you."

Pavis rose, bowed into his hands, and swiftly left. He was upset by the advisor's strong reaction. It *was* the passing-of-life! Anyone who experienced it would *agree* that it was! As he turned to wait outside the door, he saw the old advisor leaning over the young superior. He looked as though he was trying to console him.

After a short time, the ro-server advisor came out and looked at Pavis with great seriousness. "Follow me," he said, and he led Pavis to a smaller room full of stacked record books and supplies. Pavis was directed to take a seat.

"Young server, it is not just a master's vice that you are caught in," said the old uedin. "It is your physical condition that has led you into this behavior."

"My physical condition is good," protested Pavis. "I am the swiftest messenger on the temple staff. I'm very strong."

"Yes, well, that is surely a part of your condition." The ro looked as though he were pronouncing a dismal assessment. "Young server, it is very likely that you have barren syndrome."

"Barren?" Pavis looked at the ro with surprise. He hadn't heard mention of the barren since before he took his position as a messenger. "Just because I have taken part in that thing with the masters? Why should that make me barren?"

"You really don't understand. Doing that offensive thing didn't make you barren. It is your being barren that has made you do the thing. That's the only imaginable explanation."

Pavis felt anger well up in him. "You must be wrong! I want to speak to the next ranking superior!"

"There is no next-ranking superior!" the assistant practically shouted, "That was the Most High Server we were with just now!"

Pavis looked at him in confusion. That young uedin was the Most High Server of the Beyan Temple? But it didn't matter. What was this dreadful accusation? "Surely I'm not barren!" said Pavis. "I'm completely healthy! I'm not raving—I haven't hurt anyone!"

"But you are large. Your symptoms are just emerging."

"I don't understand this!" cried Pavis. Then, in a weak and broken voice, said, "What will this mean for me?"

"There is little we can do for you," said the ro solemnly. "We know that the masters have tried to contain this problem with their clever devices," he said, making a disgusted face, "but they obviously aren't working out as planned."

"Am I the only one in the temple?" Pavis asked, then added pathetically, ". . . if it is true?"

"No, there have been others."

"There *have been*? They're not here anymore?"

The ro-server softened somewhat as he explained the unpleasant matter to Pavis. "There is another element here, young server. The Soft One, as we know, is boundlessly compassionate—but she cannot endure a barren server in the temple. Anguish overcomes her."

Pavis tried to understand what he was being told. "Will I be sent away then?"

"That Nekur. . ." said the ro, mostly to himself, "he didn't prepare you at all, did he?" He reached out and placed his hand on Pavis's shoulder. "You will have to choose, young server. You may either leave the temple, or. . ." he paused before saying the words, "you may drink sleep medicine."

Pavis looked at him in disbelief. "Sleep medicine? You mean so that I will die?"

"As I said, you are free to leave the temple."

"Leave the temple or drink sleep medicine and die?" Pavis strained his mind to comprehend this judgment. "Where would I go?" he asked, "What would I do?"

"I have no idea," responded the ro-server somberly, "If you choose to leave, you will be the first server to do so since this current scourge began."

Back in the central chamber, the Most High Server was still sitting alone beside two cushions. The dim light created a shadowless, gray field of vision erasing the features of the room. He permitted his mind to bounce and trickle freely.

The server who'd been ushered before him hadn't seemed to be offensive in any way, but his speech was very loud and ignorant—

it was impossible to make it out. It hadn't been that long ago that he could communicate with the low-ranking servers, but now they had to be interpreted for him. The advising ro let him know that this one was a monstrosity to the Soft One, and as soon as the connection was made, he had felt her starting to sink into a churning misery. When the Soft One fell into great pain, he was pulled along into it. What would happen to the poor server? He could not tell if this flash of concern was coming from the Soft One or occurring in his own mind, but he knew, and he knew that she knew, the servers would never tell either of them any more about it. The servers were afraid of the Soft One's pain. That was really the only difference between him and the rest of them—he seemed more able to accept it. The Soft One had shared this truth with him—that resistance to a pain never eased the pain but only increased it. It was something he was unable to convey to the other servers. Such a thing had to be sensed.

Suddenly a memory from his childhood came to him. His little friend had told him, before he even began to consider entering the temple, that he was destined to be a server. They'd been on an outing when this friend had identified the characteristic that eventually came to define his unique position in the temple. At the time, the words had struck him in such a way as to leave him questioning whether he had been complimented or insulted. *"You have such an ease about you, Tilke. You'd be satisfied to stir paper pulp every day. You'd probably be satisfied to sit and peel greencones every day for the rest of your life. Do you know how special that is?"*

Tilke. That had been his name. When the name passed through his consciousness, he felt the Soft One react. She was uncomfortable with names, and seemed particularly disturbed by his own. He breathed deeply and allowed the displeasure to express itself and dissolve.

No, he hadn't known at the time how special it was to have a natural inclination to accept things. It seemed unfortunate to him that the only reasonable mode of responding to life must be deemed as "special." Yet, he understood the limitations of uedin, both master and servant. How could anyone face the unimaginable possibilities of pain and suffering without any resistance at all? The Soft One had permitted him to gain this much access to her experience, but there was still a point at which she shut him out in order to spare him.

He was starting to get some of the familiar sensation of sour discomfort that arose whenever he scrutinized or analyzed his connection with her. She didn't enjoy following him when he focused too much on "Lern Beyana"—that was the title that uedin thoughtlessly bestowed on her, unaware that such a fixed and twisted pronouncement of her identity served her no gratification.

Trouble is forever multiplying itself. When encountering trouble, accept it; when not directly encountering it, leave it alone. The Most High Server adjusted his mood with easy and relaxed skill. He felt his breath recover and focused on the pleasant feeling of cool air on his skin and the comfort of his legs pressing against the cushion. The surfaces of floor, ceiling, and walls blended together in the dim light. He gave his attention to breathing, feeling the cool air, the weight of his body. Yes, the Soft One liked this much better than all that spiraling.

Elenn Meets Yenca at the Fieldburning Festival

The yellow evening sun was quickly fading. A massive crowd was spread out in an area just beyond the Northroute Bridge where they could get a good view of the fire spectacle. Torches were lit, and singing and picnicking were well underway. Fieldburning took place every year after harvest.

Elenn was far from the crowd at a high place where the outfield workers were at work on the final touches of the fire beds. In recent days, by chopping and digging along peripheries, they had formed gigantic characters in the cultivated hillside for what would be a dazzling display in fire. This year the outfield workers had chosen to commemorate the poet Malta. The characters formed the words, "All Things in Correctness," the title of Malta's most famous poem, in an exact imitation of his own calligraphy. The creation, which was kept secret, had to be lit in multiple locations in order for the burning characters to be viewed together in their fullness.

Elenn, Nemis, and several other guards had hiked up to the location to offer their help. A thin and wrinkly elder master addressed them with a kind, gap-toothed smile. "Thank you, Master Guards, but we're well prepared this year. So nice and dry, this last year before the Great Rains—it's going to be a beautiful fire spectacle! Why don't you hurry on back down by the bridge where you can get a good look!"

Why not, thought Elenn. He looked to Nemis who gave him a little shrug. As long as the outfield worker masters didn't need any help, there was no harm in heading down. The outfield workers were so proud of their display that they even wanted the guards to see it from below. Elenn could make out one or two characters created by allowing tall stalks to remain in carefully shaped bands of ground while the surrounding areas were fully cleared, but there was no way to discern the whole message without getting a view from a distance.

They walked back down through the sloping field and along the outer bank of the drystream on their way to the gathering at the bridge. The sky was dark now, and suddenly the smell of smoke could be detected. The outfield worker masters were lighting square patches of fire in the outside sections on two sides and gradually working their way in. When the two sides came together the poet's message would be illuminated in flame.

There were a few other locations where the Fieldburning could be viewed in addition to Northroute Bridge. Elenn thought of the Quarterhouse teaching masters watching from the observation deck where there was a view of the northern hills opposite the hatching pool. He pictured them wide-eyed and animated, guessing which poet was due for the honor this year. He rarely received invitations to Quarterhouse anymore. The only Quarterhouse masters he had contact with were caretakers to barren, and they never invited their counselees into Quarterhouse activity. Generally, the caretakers to barren had less and less interaction with the other Quarterhouse masters other than taking meals and sharing facilities. Elenn's own counselor, Benar, was one exception. Benar told Elenn that he stopped in the kitchen every day to ask about the day's menu, and often checked in on the unnamed in early morning. Of course, it had been a while now that the new generation had received name and graduated to their apprenticeships; there wasn't any activity at Quarterhouse to check in on. He wondered if Benar would be back at Quarterhouse tonight or at the gathering at the bridge.

Elenn had no complaint about having Benar as his counselor. Elenn was not interested in talking a great deal about his condition, and Benar seemed contented with that. As often as not, their meetings consisted of Benar talking about his years as caretaker to the unnamed, complaining about the masters who had taken over his old job, or sometimes relating a funny incident, during which Benar himself always grew giddy in the retelling and would laugh at his own story. Benar was not a highly sophisticated master by Quarterhouse standards, but Elenn liked him very much. He found that Benar somehow fit much-needed encouragement and consolation between the lines. Elenn had gone to see him a few days after the incident that occurred when he was outside the wall for a mind-stilling. When he first started talking with Benar, he had been unable to confess what had occurred. But somehow Benar seemed to know without him telling. His eyes communicated recognition and comprehension. How could he know what Elenn had experienced? And yet, somehow it seemed that indeed he did know. There was neither shock nor curiosity. "We're all dealing with frightening prospects," he had said ambiguously, allowing that he might be talking about the high incidence of syndrome determined in the newly-named population, but then he shared a grave and intimate eye contact with Elenn, and Elenn felt that Benar was clearly referring to this awful, new problem of *feeding*. He appreciated Benar's sense of privacy. Benar was not always tactful or delicate in public discourse, but for all his social ineptitude, he appreciated Elenn's anxieties keenly.

Elenn and Nemis were nearing the bridge. Here and there, small groups of masters from every district were seated on blankets, sipping yeastdrink and eating colored salty biscuits, the traditional treat always prepared for Fieldburning. Someone was telling an apprentice about the fire characters in recent years. Unnamed were not allowed to attend the festivities, so most young apprentices were having their first experience of it. Even though the festivities took place far below the burning fields, the air was getting lightly smokey, introducing a lovely haze around the torchlight along with the agreeable smell of burned leaves and stalks.

At the foot of the bridge, Elenn saw Yenca, whose acquaintance he had first made when Yenca was caring for Domas in his ecstasy that time Elenn had made his last visit. Since Elenn had just been thinking about the caretakers to barren, he thought it somewhat coincidental to encounter Yenca here. Yenca's joining the caretakers to barren had been a surprising development to Elenn, who had remembered him as cross and unsympathetic. Now Yenca stood alone, gazing up at the burning patches on the hillside, his face lit by the distant flames. Elenn was not eager to talk with Yenca, but decided he should go say hello to him. He excused himself and separated from the other guards to approach Yenca.

Elenn tried to get Yenca's attention as he approached, but it was getting dark in addition to the smokey haze, and Yenca did not immediately recognize him. He held a hand up to shield his eyes from the distant firelight as Elenn approached.

"Master Yenca, it is Elenn, of the Flatpools guards. I haven't seen you since Master Jutef's induction to Quarterhouse. How are you, Master?"

Yenca made the connection and smiled back. "I'm well, thank you Master Elenn. Are you roaming about tonight like me?"

"I went up the hill with a few of the guards to help the outfield workers, but they didn't need us."

"The breeze is just right for Fieldburning," he said. His tone was friendly. "I think the outfield workers know their fire spectacle will be special this year. That's why they sent you down to where you could see it."

"I think you're right," said Elenn. "The old ro up there did seem pretty excited about it." Yenca was easier to talk to than he had anticipated. Perhaps it was because he was now a caretaker to barren and had a different attitude towards them.

"Did you get a look at the poet's tribute?" asked Yenca.

"I saw some of the formation for it, but I have no idea what it's going to say."

"Who's the poet this year?" Yenca asked teasingly.

Elenn smiled. "I really don't know, but from the look of the calligraphy I'd guess it's someone from the Post-Fasting Period." It felt good to be at such ease talking with Yenca.

"Well I'm not one of the old teaching masters who will stand in the toilet worrying about such things, but I am interested to see who they've chosen."

Elenn laughed. He didn't often laugh. "Take a guess. Why not?"

"Nebal?"

"Nebal. . . yes, could be him. If it's him, it's probably the first time. I don't think he's ever been given the tribute before."

"Or Ebo," added Yenca thoughtfully.

"Ebo didn't live in the Post-Fasting Period. Ebo was Clay-bridge."

"Oh, that's right. Isn't it strange how less important these things are to any of us who don't become teaching masters?"

"It's true. But I still treasure my Quarterhouse training." He realized as soon as he said it that Yenca might, in fact, have come in from another domicile, in which case his presumption of Quarterhouse's superiority might offend. "Pardon me, Master Yenca, I shouldn't presume. Did you come out of one of the other residences?"

"No, I came from Quarterhouse. So far, the young apprentice Jutef is our only caretaker to barren who's come in from another residence. Bells doesn't have any caretakers to barren."

"So we're both from Quarterhouse—that's good. I didn't want you to think I was another Quarterhouse snob."

"Don't worry," said Yenca with a laugh, "We're both Quarterhouse snobs!"

A group of young masters suddenly erupted into raucous laughter nearby. The yeastdrink was apparently flowing. A moment passed, and then Elenn spoke.

"To be honest with you, Master Yenca," he said, his tone more serious, "I never imagined that you would give up being a teaching master and become a caretaker to barren. Do you remember our first meeting?"

"Yes, I do," said Yenca thoughtfully, his smile fading.

"What do you remember about it?"

Yenca answered slowly, with a hint of reluctance in his voice. "You were the first uedin with syndrome that I ever encountered," he said, "but it was Master Domas's reaction that affected me the most."

Elenn gazed up toward the burning patterns on the hill. The flaming characters were coming closer together in brilliant fiery shapes against the black of the dark hillside. The poet's tribute would be readable soon.

"Master Domas fretted about your visit for days," said Yenca.

"He was upset at having been visited by a barren, wasn't he?" asked Elenn.

"He wouldn't settle down. And yet he didn't actually mention barren syndrome. He just talked about how you'd made your choice to join the guards, and you had to live with your choice, and that it was no longer his affair, it wasn't his fault if you were unhappy, and so on. He went on about that, repeating himself a hundred times."

"And he said no more about my being barren?"

"No. He said no more about it. But I believe he was expressing his anxiety about it in a confused way. I know he had anxiety about the rise of barren syndrome in the capital."

"How do you know that?"

"Because before Master Domas started to decline, he was very seriously involved in discussions about barren syndrome that were taking place on the council. He was very open and direct with me. He always told me everything about the council meetings and withheld none of his opinions about the other members. It was obvious that Master Domas was prepping me to get involved in council affairs. The syndrome issue was particularly important to him. It tormented him. He lamented about it until the day you came, and then never said another word about it again, even up to his departure."

Elenn was surprised to hear this. What did it mean? "Do you think Master Domas reached full ecstasy on the day I visited?" he asked.

Yenca looked back thoughtfully. "I would say he was entering into his ecstasy. But it was still quite a while before he left for his pilgrimage. I think Master Domas was very troubled about syndrome in the capital right up to the day you came. Then he expressed it all at once. After that he was able to let go of it," answered Yenca.

There was a phrase Elenn remembered from his unnamed days. Child-uedin were told that ros in ecstasy sometimes expressed anger or fear because to leave it unexpressed would mean poisoning their own passing-of-life. On the eve of their own Namesgiving, a raving server had somehow wandered from the temple and all the way up to the field behind Quarterhouse where they were having Namesgiving's Eve observances. Master Domas had spoken to all the unnamed about the ro being in a wonderful condition, and that if he didn't purge his bad dreams, he would be "holding on to the burning pan."

"Master Elenn, though I may have thought your visit was a bad idea at the time, I later felt that you helped Master Domas express a fear that needed to be expressed. Master Domas was quite happy when he left for his pilgrimage. He wasn't holding on to anything."

"I hope you're right," said Elenn. "Master Domas meant a great deal to me."

"He meant a great to me as well," said Yenca. "Master Domas had a tremendous mind, but he was deeply troubled with this problem that we are now facing." Now he looked intensely at Elenn. "You *do* understand, Master Elenn, that it is a problem we are all facing together, don't you?"

"Yes, Master Yenca," said Elenn, "I do understand that."

"Then you will forgive me for bringing up another difficult subject."

Elenn knew what he was going to talk about. "Is it something I can help you with?" he asked, hoping to deflect the inquiry.

"You can give me your thoughts. That will help me decide something."

"What is the difficult matter?"

"This thing the barren have begun to do, this 'feeding'. . ."

"I have no thoughts to offer you, Master Yenca." And he silently pleaded, *please don't ask me if I've done it.*

"It cannot be ignored, Master Ellen. It will bring disaster."

"What can I possibly say that would be any use to you? What is it you're trying to decide?"

"The barren must be brought into greater cooperation."

Elenn paused, then spoke solemnly. "Please understand something, Master Yenca. Feeding is not something the barren enter into willfully." Elenn wasn't sure himself whether this was true or not. Some of them seemed to have completely given themselves over to it. He could not deny that he had found it easier to discard fear and shame with each successive time he himself had allowed it to happen since the first mysterious incident that day on the bank of the drystream.

Yenca looked at him uneasily. "Of course not," he said. Elenn sensed that Yenca was disturbed by his response. No wonder. . . if he, a respected guard, had to comment defensively, Yenca probably figured that all the barren must be feeding. Perhaps it was true.

"When you say that the barren have to be brought into greater cooperation, are you proposing that the guards be involved? Why are you telling me?"

"You came to Master Jutef's induction at Quarterhouse, and you know he's apprenticing with us. I've had some discussions with young Master Jutef."

"And you have discussed the feeding with young master Jutef already—even though he is still an apprentice?"

"Master Jutef is remarkably astute and intuitive. He actually came up with a suggestion that I may propose to the masters council."

"What is that?"

"Jutef suggested a hood to be worn by the barren. It would be a hood to mark a commitment to the welfare of the capital. The barren would be asked to take the hood when they receive the surgery for their barren condition, and they would wear it over their heads for the rest of their lives."

The rest of their lives? How drastic! Already the barren were visible to everyone because there was no hiding their neckstraps. The thought of being even *more* visible in society was very disconcerting. But as Elenn thought about it more, he couldn't deny that it might be an effective solution. No barren could then take part in feeding without removing his hood. The question was, could they do it? Could the barren keep such a commitment? "I see the logic in young Master Jutef's idea. I don't know if it would work. . ."

"Master Elenn, will you come with me and lend your support to the idea before the masters council? Your opinion in this matter would be of great value. There is much discomfort about the syndrome now, and most of the masters on the council are not willing to look at these hard questions."

Elenn considered this request. He knew he was being asked because of his status as a guard, and it bothered him. He was no better than any barren cook or streetsweeper who was looked upon with a mixture of pity and discomfort. He didn't like the idea of speaking on behalf of anyone else but himself.

"I would definitely not want to speak at any masters council meeting," he said.

"At least come with me and let your presence at my side indicate your support."

Elenn paused for a long moment. "Let me think about it," he finally answered.

The two masters now looked up at the characters, which were by now burning in their full glory.

"*All Things in Correctness.* It's Malta," said Yenca.

"Good! Your Quarterhouse training is confirmed!" responded Elenn with a bit too much enthusiasm as he tried to recover the mood. They gazed up at the stunning fire display shining in the black hills above them.

Elenn didn't see the apprentice guard approaching from the side and was startled when he was addressed in an urgent voice.

"Master Elenn, come! Master Nemis needs your assistance on the inner bank!" At this, Elenn's attention returned, and he could hear the sound of tin clappers sounding an alarm somewhere over the din of the singing and chattering crowd.

"Excuse me, Master Yenca."

Yenca excused him with a nod. Elenn dashed off toward the bridge. He could see where a group of guard-issue lanterns burned some distance down on the inner bank of the drystream. He ran with the apprentice through the crowd and across the stone bridge.

As he approached Nemis and the other guards, he noticed that they were surrounding a tall figure wearing a server's wrappings. The uedin's hands kept moving reflexively up to his face in shame, but he stopped himself and struggled to keep his composure.

Elenn approached to hear Nemis addressing the server. "Are you lost?" Nemis asked. "Do you want us to take you back to the temple compound?"

Ippal was there too. He saw Elenn and came to inform him what was happening. "This server is very disoriented. We think he probably has the syndrome. The servers don't have their barren treated, you know. He doesn't have the implant."

Elenn moved closer.

"No, please don't take me back!"

"Come with us to the guard station," said Nemis calmly. "We'll get it all figured out."

"But I won't go back!" cried the server.

"Why, Server? Why don't you want to go back?"

"They'll kill me!"

"Now of course that's not true," said Nemis.

"They'll make me drink poison! It's what they ask us to do—to protect the Soft One!"

Elenn walked with the guards as they escorted the server back toward the bridge and through the north gate. Before passing through, he glanced back at the fire display. A part of the fire had already burned out, so that the characters now spelled out what looked like "ALL THINGS INCORRECT."

Pavis

When they reached the guard station, Nemis and Elenn dismissed the apprentices and took the server inside. Under lamplight, the server noticed right away that Elenn was wearing a neck strap.

"When did you have that done?" he asked. "Can I get mine done also?"

"Yes, you will have to. Now, what is your name—can you say it?"

"Of course I can say it. It's Pavis. Is the operation painful?"

"It's not too bad. The doctors will numb the area with some ointment." Elenn silently wondered if his childhood friend ever recalled his chosen name, Tilke. He often contemplated what Tilke's life was like inside the temple compound. He considered asking this Server Pavis if he had ever met a Tilke, but he felt sure that the servers knew nothing of one another's names.

"I am eager to have it done," said Pavis earnestly.

Nemis looked at the server uneasily. "Do you understand why the uedin with barren syndrome have that implant?"

The server looked confused. "Isn't it voluntary?"

"Well yes, it's voluntary. But it's done for a specific reason."

"Isn't it for neck sucking?" Pavis asked innocently. He looked at Nemis's unpleasant reaction and then turned his head to look at Elenn. "Isn't that what it's for?"

"No," said Elenn sternly. "It is not for that. That is actually something that we must not do. It overrides the whole purpose of the catheter implant."

"I don't understand."

"Didn't you say that a server assistant explained your barren syndrome to you?"

"Yes, he said that the syndrome caused barren uedin to do the neck sucking."

"It's true," said Elenn. "But there's more to it than that. The syndrome, besides making us barren, does cause that behavior that you're talking about, and it causes other trouble as well. It leads to derangement. We can end up doing horrible things."

"Like what?" asked Pavis.

Nemis spoke up. "Like the murder of wetuedin," he answered, "and attacks on our ro."

"The catheter implant is to stop those things from happening." Elenn looked directly at the server and spoke slowly so he would clearly understand. "It is not for feeding. You see, the excess skullsap that we barren produce creates an imbalance in us. The catheter is for expelling it. When one ingests skullsap, it recreates the imbalance and all the symptoms of barren syndrome."

Pavis looked as if he had been struck in the face. His confused look quickly changed to anger. He put his cup on the table and stood up.

"I know you are lying to me," he said angrily. "You're only telling me this to make me go back to the temple."

Nemis decided to let Elenn handle things. He made a deferential glance at his comrade guard, Master Elenn, the unofficial but unanimously recognized sergeant of all matters barren. It was a position Elenn was reluctantly learning to accept.

"We are not going to send you back to the temple if you don't want to go," said Elenn, "but everything I've said is true."

"Then why do the masters suck each other's necks?"

Nemis felt that this barren stranger and his crude way of referring to feeding were insulting to Elenn. "It's the disease," he said, trying to help.

"That doesn't make sense! If the medics give us a neckhole to leak out skullsap and stop the symptoms, there shouldn't be any more disease! The neckhole should be stopping the disease!"

"It does stop it," argued Nemis patiently.

"No it doesn't! If it does, why are there masters sucking on other masters' necks?"

"Please stop saying that!" shouted Nemis, showing irritation for the first time. "Only certain masters with barren syndrome are known to be doing that. They are being irresponsible."

"But there are *many* masters bearing their necks or putting their mouths to other necks!" cried Pavis.

"You must have seen the same few doing it multiple times," said Nemis. "What you are describing is not normal." Elenn could sense his comrade's frustration. This topic was not talked about among the guards—at least not when Elenn was around.

Pavis seemed to get angrier. "I may only be a message deliverer, but I am not a fool. Many masters are doing this. Even some of your own."

"What do you mean by that?" asked Nemis.

"There are guards doing this. I know because I had a guard master bear his neck to me once." Pavis gave Nemis a smug and victorious stare.

Nemis suppressed his impulse to look at Elenn. Instead, he looked at the floor, stunned. "I'm sure you're mistaken," he murmured unconvincingly.

Elenn tried not to let his shame be visible. He could see that Nemis was shocked by this statement. "Master Nemis," he said, "I know this is very uncomfortable for you. Please let me take over by myself. That might be best."

Nemis hesitated, as if afraid to leave the two barren alone. Then he quickly raised hands to face and dismissed himself. He was obviously being careful not to insult his fellow guard.

Elenn looked at Pavis. Pavis looked miserable. Who could blame him? How lost he must feel! He had found out about his barren status and been ejected from the community of servers all at once.

"It's very hard to accept all this," said Elenn, "but at least you can know that you will receive good treatment among the masters. The masters council has been very sympathetic. Perhaps it will be best if you take the robe of a master. I'm sure your experience as a messenger can be put to good use somewhere in the capital."

"I don't know anything about life on the outside," said Pavis.

"There's a corps of caretakers to the barren that's been in place for a few years now. You will have a counselor to help you."

"I don't need a caretaker," answered Pavis. "Caretakers are for child-uedin."

"I have found that the caretakers to barren are willing to leave us alone to whatever degree we request. I rarely have interaction with my own counselor. If nothing else they are helpful in practical matters."

Pavis said nothing. He was staring at the floor.

"Are you hungry?" asked Elenn.

Pavis looked at him with distress. His face began to tense up and then he bent forward again. His shoulders shuddered, and he began to sob. Elenn watched him crying with his face in his hands. The memory of his own painful process of acceptance came to him. He thought about the strange experience he had had in the desert with Hela, crying in despair as he pathetically attempted to chant the names of the Lern. His childhood longing to serve Lern Beyana was a distant memory now, but he imagined how painful it must be for an expelled server.

"It must be so hard for you to leave the service of Lern Beyana," said Elenn. "I once dreamed of becoming a server. Now I see that it was best that I never went to the temple."

Pavis remained bent over, crying.

Elenn continued, "You will make an adjustment to life with us masters. But the barren syndrome is a burden you will have to carry. It takes great discipline to put away the thought of losing ones passing-of-life. We are reminded of it constantly."

Pavis finally looked up from his hands. His eyes and face were red and swollen. He looked like he wanted to speak.

Elenn said, "It is very difficult for us, isn't it?" he asked, reaching his hand to the skull cap on the back of his own head, ". . . knowing that this is empty."

Still Pavis did not respond.

Elenn added, "If you like, I could recite the Names with you."

"I don't want to recite the names," said Pavis. "I don't care any-thing about Lern Beyana."

Elenn diverted his eyes from Pavis to excuse this rash com-ment.

Pavis continued, "I don't care about Lern Beyana, and I don't care if I never go on my pilgrimage," he said as tears returned.

"Of course you care," said Elenn, "How could you not care?" He reached his hand out comfortingly.

"I don't care about those things!" snapped Pavis and struck Elenn's hand away. "I only want to have masters bear their necks to me and bear mine to them!" he yelled.

Elenn's eyes grew wide in disbelief.

"That's all I want! I don't care about those other things!" Pavis repeated boldly.

"You can't mean that," said Elenn.

"Yes I do! That's all I want!" Pavis's defiant look then changed to pleading. "Please," he said, "you have the hole in your neck—bear it to me?"

Elenn was stunned and horrified.

"Please," continued Pavis eagerly and he reached for Elenn's shoulder. "Please let me put my mouth on your neck? Please?"

"No!" bellowed Elenn. He stood and walked to the door. "Mas-ter Nemis!" he called. He thought Nemis may have remained near the station house, but there was no answer.

Pavis stood and approached him desperately. "Please let me?" he begged.

"No, I will not! You must cooperate with us, or you will make your life more terrible than it already is!"

Pavis pushed past Elenn and ran out of the guard station. Elenn ran after him, but Pavis was amazingly fast.

"Master Pavis!" Elenn called after him, "come back!"

But Pavis was gone, borne off on his swift, message deliverer's legs into the night. And neither was it correct to call him *"Master Pavis."* Elenn reached for the mallet and began to strike the alarm block.

No, Pavis was not a master. He was no longer a server, but neither was he a master. *What was he?*

Jutef's Counsel

Jutef sat alone in the Quarterhouse pavilion. Propped against his leg was a bundle of fresh reeds tied with a length of torn cloth. One at a time, he pulled the reeds carefully from the bundle and wove them into a circular flat piece of basketry. He worked silently. He was getting used to working with reeds instead of the spun grass fiber he used to work with at Bells. Since coming to Quarterhouse, he found that weaving was a very relaxing pastime.

The other apprentices had invited him to go with them to the Fieldburning Festival. He had declined. In most instances, Jutef didn't mind being the odd one out and unable to participate in activities that required sight. But when his fellow apprentices invited him to go along to the Fieldburning, he could hear the awkward discomfort in their voices. They didn't want to have to lead him about. And for his part, Jutef had little interest in mingling with all of them while they drank the night away staring at the fire spectacle. There were things in which a blind uedin simply could not take part. A false attempt would only bring a greater feeling of isolation.

The voices of teaching masters up in the observation decks had ceased, and the Quarterhouse grounds were quiet. The only thing to indicate that it was a festival night was the hint of smoke in the air. Jutef's fingers nimbly bent the smooth reeds, one across another, making a slight rustling sound.

Suddenly he heard the light steps of someone walking without shoes. He didn't recognize the footsteps.

"Hello?" he spoke in a subdued voice, not wanting to sound overly startled. The footsteps stopped.

"Hello-o?" he spoke again. "Who's there?"

"Hello," said an unfamiliar voice. "What are you doing in the dark?"

"I am Jutef," he answered, thinking that the name would explain. "I'm just doing a bit of weaving here. And who is that one?"

"I am called Pavis."

Jutef imagined that it was a master from another district walking off a night of too much drink. "Lost your shoes, Master Pavis?" he asked, ". . . at the festival?"

The stranger didn't answer his question. Maybe he was a little ashamed of his drinking, thought Jutef. He did not, however, have any slur in his speech—though it did have an odd quality—some inflection he had not heard before.

"Are you a basketmaker?" asked Pavis.

"No," said Jutef, and placed his work on the ground beside him with a slight sigh. "I only do it for pleasure now. I was trained as a weaver at Bells, but I'm apprenticing with the Quarterhouse caretakers. I'm going to be a caretaker to syndrome uedin."

"Caretaker to syndrome uedin?"

"Yes. . . the barren."

After a pause, Pavis said, "I have heard of these caretakers." His tone was pensive. Jutef thought it was an odd thing to say. Who *hadn't* heard of the caretakers to barren?

"What have you heard?" asked Jutef with a joking tone in his voice, as if he might need to defend the caretakers to barren from some slander.

"Only that there are caretaker masters who work specifically with the barren," answered Pavis. There was no irony in his voice. "What exactly do you do for them?"

"I'm newly-named. My generation has been tested, and it appears that a full fourth of us have the syndrome. There is much work to be done. And the next generation will probably be tested very early, even before they take name. We will be involved in their care and education while they are yet unnamed. Those with the syndrome will grow up knowing that they will receive catheters along with their names. This has never been done before. There are sure to be many adjustments along the way."

"A full fourth of the newly-named?"

"You haven't heard about that?" said Jutef diplomatically. He felt sure that this master knew more than he wanted to admit and was only coaxing him to talk about the subject. "It's true. My generation, newly-named, has a one out of four occurrence." Jutef decided that having given this information, he was entitled to ask a few questions himself. "What is your vocation, Master Pavis?" he asked.

"I am a message deliverer," said Pavis slowly.

"Message deliverer?" Jutef knew that the distribution masters carried mail and packages to all parts of the capital, but he had not heard them called "message deliverers" before. "Do you work with the distribution masters?"

"I am not a master," answered Pavis.

"A young master? An apprentice, like myself?"

"No," he responded, offering no explanation. Jutef waited. Finally Pavis spoke. "You can't see me, can you, Master?"

"It's true," said Jutef, "I am blind."

"It's past midnight, but the lesser moon is bright now. If you could see me, you would see that I am wearing server's wrappings."

A server? Outside the temple and chatting with a master in the middle of the night? "You're a server?" he asked slowly, trying not to sound overly surprised.

"I *was*," answered Pavis. ". . .I left the compound."

"How—" said Jutef. "Why did you leave?"

"Because I am barren," said Pavis.

"Oh," said Jutef. He was beginning to realize the importance of the conversation he was having. "There has been much discussion among the caretakers about what happens to servers with the syndrome."

Pavis paused before responding. "I only know what happened to me. I did not know that there was anything wrong with me. As a message deliverer, I was about the capital more than a server would normally be. I started having strange experiences."

"Would you care to tell me about them? If you don't want to, I understand."

"I know you are kind. I would like to tell you," said Pavis. "I started to see masters with these patches on the backs of their necks."

"Yes, the neck straps that cover the catheters," said Jutef. "They have been in use for a few years now."

"Seeing them filled me with a strange sensation," said Pavis, "as though I had encountered such a thing in my dreams. I began to look for these masters."

Jutef was strangely thrilled about hearing this unique story. It was not something he could learn about in his regular training.

"Please go on," he said, "I will not hold anything you say to your discredit."

"I was so drawn to these masters," continued Pavis. "I didn't know they had any sort of disorder. In fact, I thought they were just a group of stylish masters who had begun to wear this ornament on their necks. I didn't even know their necks bore openings under the patches. But they did seem to be a special group of masters, unlike the others. I imagined them to be poets. And I began to wish that I had taken leg on the outside, so that I too could be a poet and live among them."

"Poets? How interesting," commented Jutef.

"Well, you masters love poetry, don't you? Poetry is a master's craft."

Jutef knew from his education that there were many server poets, but he chose not to lead the conversation away from Pavis's story.

Pavis continued, "Then one day a startling thing happened. I was sent to get teabowls. I saw some masters doing something strange."

Jutef knew what was coming.

"You saw some barren masters giving their necks to each other, didn't you?"

"Yes," said Pavis, "And I knew, when I saw, that I wanted to do it. And then when I did it, I knew what it was. The words came immediately into my head. Passing-of-life."

Jutef was astounded. "Passing-of life? You mean feeding?"

"You may not believe me," said Pavis, "but I had dreamt of this thing before. And in my dreams it *was* the passing-of-life. If you want to call it 'feeding,' go ahead, but for me it is the passing-of-life."

Jutef was puzzled, and then he was dumbfounded, and then he smiled despite himself. "Will you really call it the *passing-of-life*? That's an amazing thing indeed!" His feelings went from surprise to amusement. "I must tell Master Yenca about this notion. He's terribly concerned about all the feeding, but when he hears that you are calling it the *passing-of-life,*. . . Well, what will he think of that!" Jutef laughed hard, which sounded very loud and abrupt in the midst of the whispered conversation.

"What's wrong with that?" asked Pavis. "It's a wonderful thing."

Jutef immediately stopped smiling and responded seriously. "Well, it brings about barren syndrome's awful symptoms. You must know—derangement which seems like ro-uedin raving, but is much too early. Bulky frames, illness in the mind. Horrible things are connected with the symptoms of barren syndrome. Untreated syndrome uedin have done terrible things before they were given the catheters. That's why we worry about the servers. You servers won't allow testing for the syndrome. It makes no sense to us, but we honor your decision."

"Do you know what happens to a server who learns that he is barren? I can tell you what happened to me."

"Yes, please do tell me," said Jutef.

"I was invited to drink poison."

Jutef felt a great doubt come over him for the first time. This was a bit strange. Why would the servers refuse an available treatment for their syndrome-afflicted, and then ask them to kill themselves? It was unlike any uedin to think in such a cruel fashion, and servers were supposed to be more sensitive than masters. It even crossed his mind that the stranger was tricking him, that he wasn't wearing server's wrappings at all, and making this all up as a fabulous lie to test him somehow. An initiation prank for the apprentice, perhaps?

"May I feel the fabric of your sleeve, master?" he asked.

"I am not a master. Here," said Pavis, and he thrusted his arm forward putting his sleeved forearm into Jutef's hand.

Jutef felt the fabric. "No," he said, gaining understanding, "You are not a master." He doubted the story about barren servers being asked to drink poison, but it would take some time and discussion to separate out the facts.

"Will you help me, Master Jutef?" asked Pavis.

"What can I do for you?" asked Pavis.

"Be my counselor," said Pavis. "I trust you."

Jutef moved his hand from the stranger's sleeve to take his hand in his own and patted it. "Of course, I will," he said. The elder caretakers to barren had occasionally talked about how the early barren were not assigned to caretakers; rather they just found their way to them. He had considered that talk to be a sentimentality in which he would be unlikely to share. Now he understood how important the experience was, and it deepened his sense of purpose in being a caretaker to the barren. "I will counsel you the best I can," he said. He knew that it was now the middle of the night, for he could hear an owl's hooting in the distance. He would find a spot in the caretaker's den for this displaced server to sleep, and he would talk to Master Benar in the morning.

Yenca Receives a Letter from Elenn and Pays a Visit to Benar

Yenca entered the caretaker's common house brusquely, leaving the door tarp to wag on its cords. He had just returned from the infirmary where one of the barren was under surveillance. It was Master Inke, whom he did not know well at all. Inke had a perfectly well-functioning catheter, but he had been found in a deranged state wandering about in the drystreams. The medics knew that it was a result of feeding, and while they did not mention the word, nobody pretended to be ignorant of the facts.

They had chosen to call Yenca instead of Benar. Poor Master Benar would be offended if he knew this. He had to think of something to make sure Benar didn't think the medics preferred to talk to *him*. . . which, apparently they did, but. . . Maybe Yenca could say that the medics assumed Benar was busy dealing with that displaced server who had shown up some days earlier at the Field-burning ceremony. That, he had come to learn, was why Master Elenn had been called away suddenly that night when they were talking near the Northroute Bridge. The server was barren. Apparently, he ran away from the guard station later that night and had stumbled onto Jutef. Young Master Jutef, the blind apprentice, was proving to be an outstanding recruit. Yenca was planning to meet with him that evening. The news had spread very quickly that there was a barren server who had run away from the temple to seek refuge on the outside. There was a lot of fuss and rumor about what had transpired. Yes. If Benar were told that he wasn't called to deal with Inke because they all assumed he had an important role with the server, Benar would be flattered. That would work just fine; he would avoid offending Master Benar.

One of the other apprentices spoke and interrupted Yenca's thoughts.

"Master Yenca, a letter was delivered for you." He handed Yenca the folded paper. Yenca sat down and poured himself a cup of cold leftover tea from a pot brewed earlier in the day. He opened the letter.

Correspondence To Master Yenca, Quarterhouse Caretaker to Syndrome-afflicted.

Respectable Master Yenca, I beg your pardon for my hasty departure from our chance meeting at the Fieldburning Festival. I have thought more about your request that I accompany you when you make your proposal to the masters council. I have decided that I am in support of your proposal, and I will go with you and speak however necessary to help your cause. I wait for your instructions. Please respond when duties allow.

Lern Beyan kiman kiman uedin olor.
Elenn of Capital Guards, Flatpools District

Yenca read it over again to see if there were any subtleties to take in, but it was very simple and straightforward. The hand-writing was plain and void of decor, as one would expect of a guard. Master Elenn was in agreement. Yenca was glad. He took another swallow of the tea.

It was very important to know that Master Elenn was one uedin with barren syndrome who could be counted on after all. Whatever dishonorable activity some of the syndrome-afflict-ed indulged in, at least they could all be sure that Master Elenn would remain worthy of his guard's robe. Now the guards were busy with their own apprentices and preparations for the Great Rains, which was getting nearer every day. How fortunate that Elenn was volunteering his support.

Yenca decided to send a gift of appreciation to Elenn in re-sponse to the letter—perhaps some oilcakes from the Quarter-house kitchen. Benar always knew how to acquire goods from the kitchen. Since Benar was Elenn's counselor—an odd pairing, he had often thought—Benar might know what Elenn liked and have an idea better than oilcakes. Maybe Yenca could also take the opportunity to casually mention his visit to the infirmary and slip in the news about Inke. He put the letter away and headed for Benar's hut.

It was a short walk from the caretaker's common house to Benar's hut near the old Quarterhouse domicile where child-uedin lived for most of the novade. It wouldn't be long now before the Rains and another descent of wetuedin. With the thought of a new generation, Yenca couldn't feel any of the traditional excitement. There was too much dread in him about the inevitable disappointment in numbers and grave debates over how quickly to test for syndrome. This thought preoccupied him as he approached Benar's hut near the main kitchen.

He stood outside of the door tarp and called in.

"Master Benar? Are you home?"

There was a considerable pause. Yenca was about to turn and leave.

"Oh, who *is* it then?" came the response in a startlingly aggravated voice.

"Yenca here."

"Oh, preserve the Lern. . ." muttered Benar inside. Then Yenca heard a *trot-callump, trot-callump* odd manner of footsteps cross the floor on its way to the doorway.

The tarp was suddenly yanked aside, and Master Benar stood there with an expression of anger and exasperation. "What is it, Master Yenca?" he practically barked.

"Oh, Master Benar, I'm—, I'm very sorry if I've come at a bad time," stammered Yenca, completely taken aback.

Benar looked at him with most bizarre kind of confused horror, as if he had discovered a very large fly in his food. Yenca had no idea what to make of such a bizarre expression.

"I'll return at a different time," twitted Yenca.

"Come on," said Benar and turned to walk back in. That's when Yenca heard the trot-callump sound and looked down to see that Benar had a plyroot bucket on his foot.

"Master Benar, why do you have a plyroot bucket on your foot?" asked Yenca softly.

Benar turned around and looked at Yenca as if he were the stupidest uedin Benar had ever seen. "Because," he said in a strained and clipped voice, "the plyroot bucket is *stuck* on my foot, and I cannot *remove* it."

Yenca looked at Benar in dumb confoundedness for an instant, and then his face broke and his hand came up to his mouth as he was unable to suppress his laughter. Benar's face was suddenly forlorn, and his gaze sank away. He was too unhappy to answer this humiliation.

Yenca immediately corrected his behavior with a cough. "Please," he said, "let me help you. What happened?"

Benar sat down, closed his eyes, and shook his head as if he could not bear to go into detail. He sighed and said, "If you must know. . ."

"It's fine if you don't want to—"

"I will tell you," interrupted Benar. "I borrowed this bucket from the kitchen a long time ago. Sometimes I fill it with boiling water and carry it here to place on top of my bedding to warm it up before I go to bed. The problem is, I moved it to the floor and left it there. I didn't take it back right away. A few days later I threw the cold water out the window and tossed the bucket onto the floor. Well, as you know, plyroot gets soft when it has been wet for a long time, and the thing completely warped in on itself and then dried that way."

"Yes, I've seen that happen," offered Yenca dutifully, respecting Benar even as idiotic as he seemed, with a plyroot bucket stuck on his foot.

"I kept meaning to re-wet it, fix it, and take it back," continued Benar, "but I got busy, and it sat here for quite a while. Finally, since this happens to be the only plyroot bucket we have in the kitchen these days, some of the other caretaker masters started asking about it."

Yenca nodded politely.

"I should have just told them I had it. But I was a bit embarrassed about having kept it so long, and I acted as though I didn't know anything about it."

"I see," said Yenca, still not completely understanding, but sensing the complexity of the matter.

"So today I was going to soften it up, pull it back into shape, and quietly put it back in the kitchen. I brought a gourdful of water and soaked the bucket all around, but it was warped hard. I couldn't keep it pulled back with my hands. I used my foot to force it open to the right degree, but as soon as I took my foot out, it drew back again. I figured that if I kept my foot in there until it dried in the open position, then it would hold its proper shape. So I just kept my foot in there and took a little nap."

"And when you woke up, it was stuck," provided Yenca.

Benar looked at him again, this time without the anger. "It bent too much, curled around my foot, and then, in this dry air, hardened completely. I have been tugging at it for most of the afternoon. I tell you, I am quite defeated here."

"Couldn't you get more water?"

Benar quietly looked at Yenca, looked down at his foot, and then looked at Yenca again.

Yenca understood. Benar couldn't get more water without going over to the kitchen well with the stolen bucket on his foot. "Let me go for you," he said, "Is the gourd here?"

Benar pointed to it. "Master Yenca," he said quietly, "I would indeed greatly appreciate that favor."

Yenca took the gourd and left wordlessly. He walked back around the old Quarterhouse and into the kitchen, which he found fortunately empty. There was little activity in the kitchen during the pre-Rains season. He filled the gourd at the kitchen well and returned to Benar's hut.

By the time he got back, Benar had regained his composure and was smiling.

"I am going to owe you a great favor, Master Yenca," he said. "You have saved me considerable embarrassment."

"I'm happy to help, Master," said Yenca.

"I always seem to get myself into these awful fixes," said Benar.

"We'll have it off in no time," said Yenca as he knelt and poured a stream of water into Benar's bucket-boot.

"A great favor," pronounced Benar once more. "Now," he said with a sigh, "What was it you came to see me about?"

"There were a couple of things I wanted to discuss," said Yenca. "First of all, I want to send a small gift to Guardmaster Elenn. He is your charge; I'm sure you know him better than anyone. I was thinking of oilcakes. Does he like them? Or do you know what else he might like better?"

Benar's mood brightened more. Being the one in the know about any given topic was one of his favorite things. "Oilcakes? What is the occasion?"

"Oh, he's agreed to help me with a project of mine, and I want to express my appreciation." Yenca hoped Benar would not probe for details.

"Well, oilcakes, of course, is the specialty served when the masters celebrate the descent of wetuedin," he said. "It won't be long before he'll be eating oilcakes with us for that. How about a nice jar of yeastdrink? Master Elenn likes a bit of yeastdrink now and then. It would be good for him to relax with it more often."

"That is a very good idea," said Yenca. In fact, Yenca was not a fan of yeastdrink himself, but it did seem like a more substantial gift than oilcakes. "That's exactly what I'll give him. Thank you, Master Benar."

"Not at all," said Benar. "You have done much more for me by coming here this evening and helping me get this dreadful bucket off my foot."

The plyroot was softening now. Yenca braced it in his hands while Benar pulled his foot out with a jerk and a splash.

"Oh, thank you, thank you," said Benar. "And what was the other matter you wanted to discuss?"

"Yes," said Yenca, "well, I received a message to go to the infirmary this morning."

"The infirmary?"

"Yes. One of our afflicted was taken there. He was found raving somewhere in the drystream."

Benar was uncomfortable with this news. He nervously distracted himself with examining the bucket, still misshapen after all the trouble. "Who was it?" he asked in a low voice. "Was it one of mine?"

"No, Master. His name is Inke. That's all they had gotten from him. They don't know who his counselor is. He was very disoriented when they found him. You must know what it means."

"Yes," said Benar quietly. "I know what you're talking about. You don't have to say it."

"I'm glad you understand, Master."

"I'll bet he belongs to one of those Whiteroof caretakers. They still don't know what they're doing over there. Anyhow, the medics should have called for me. I'm the senior caretaker to barren. Why did they call *you*?"

"Well, there is the matter of the server with barren syndrome who showed up a few days ago. I'm sure they heard about him, and they probably thought you had your hands full dealing with him right now. What is that one's name again?"

"That one's name is Pavis," said Benar, "and he says he wishes to be called 'master' now, so we may be calling him *Master* Pavis."

"Oh," said Yenca with interest. "Well, I think the medics knew you would be occupied with him right now, and they decided not to call on you about this Inke." Benar seemed to accept this explanation. Yenca was curious now to know if Benar knew more than he about the barren server. "Where is, uh. . . Where is Master Pavis staying now?"

"He's with Master Jutef. He has asked young Master Jutef to be his caretaker. It will be a challenging arrangement, since Master Jutef is a generation younger than he, but young Master Jutef is a bright apprentice."

"So he's going to be third generation soon, like me. How is he going to take a master's assignment in the capital? Surely he won't have to find an apprenticeship like the newly-named, will he?"

"Apparently this Pavis delivered messages for the temple. He's swift about the capital and knows his way around all the smaller streets. We think the distribution masters will accept him."

"What is he like, Master Benar?" Yenca shared with all masters a curiosity about servers.

"He's very direct," said Benar. "He does not spiral at all. It's most noticeable."

"Ah, yes," said Yenca, imagining. Servers didn't spiral as much. It might be very refreshing to talk with "Master" Pavis.

"Now, what about this Master Inke?" asked Benar. "Did he hurt anyone or damage anything?"

"No, I don't believe so," said Yenca.

"Well then they might as well just release him. If they've had him since this morning, I'm sure he's recovered by now."

Yenca did not answer at first. He disagreed with Benar on this point. It was not enough to just release him. Inke had done no damage this time, but he was likely to do harm at some point if he had that kind of feeding habit.

"Master Benar, with all due respect, our afflicted must not be allowed to carry on with feeding."

"Why do you call it that, Master Yenca? That is a very unpleasant term."

"That is what the afflicted themselves call it."

"Well, they should avoid saying it that way. It is not like eating a bowl of yams, Master Yenca."

"Of course not, Master."

"I hate that term."

"I'm sorry Master Benar, I'll remember not to use it."

"At least not around me, if you can help it."

"Yes, Master."

"I don't know what can be done about the issue. I wish I knew."

Yenca decided to go ahead and tell Benar his plans to address the masters council about the hoods. "Young Master Jutef and I were discussing it."

"You were discussing this topic with an apprentice?" asked Benar with disapproval.

"Yes, Master Benar. They need to know what is happening. Actually, Master Jutef came up with a very excellent idea."

"Yes? What is that?"

"He said that it might work to ask the afflicted to wear hoods on their heads at all times and take an oath to keep them on."

Benar thought for a long moment about the idea. "Young Master Jutef thought of that?"

"Yes, Master. He suggested that the hood could become a symbol of their self-control, something to be respected as a sign of honor."

"Well, that's a very noble idea, and Master Jutef may be commended for thinking of it. But it will not work."

"Why do you say that, Master?"

"Because I know too many afflicted masters—one in particular—who is as decent and honorable as any master I have ever known. His decency and honor do not keep him out of trouble."

This was not what he had expected Benar to say. What disappointing news. But wasn't the hood idea at least worth considering? He lowered his eyes and looked at the misshapen plyroot bucket on the floor between them. He picked it up and tried to tug it into shape. It was going to take a lot of water and work to get it back the way it was supposed to be.

Part 2

THE BARREN
TAKE HOOD

Meeting of the Masters Council

Elenn gazed at the sky from below the eave of the guard station as he waited for Master Henik. There was no sign yet of cloud gathering. The council had considered saving the topic of barren feeding until after the Great Rains, but Yenca had convinced them to put it on the agenda right away.

Elenn would see Yenca and Benar at the council house, but he would attend in the company of Master Henik who was there to represent the guards and take back a report. Elenn had agreed to go with Yenca as a symbolic show of support, but plans had changed. The council actually contacted Flatpools and requested that he come because of his unique status as a guard who had the syndrome. Elenn knew he would be asked to speak.

In the many days since that conversation at the Fieldburning, Elenn had been thinking constantly about the hood proposal, and somehow the rumor of it had made its way to the guards. He had a strong feeling that the hood was going to mark a major change in his life. It could intensify his struggle, he knew, but it was necessary. Even during the brief interim since he had spoken with Yenca, he had found himself twice going to the drystream beds, a place where the barren could find opportunities for feeding. Both times he had imagined the powerful deterrent of the hood and its oath, and he had imagined that such a thing just might help him get a grip on the problem. He thought about how he could discuss the hood proposal without saying too much about his own habit.

Henik arrived with his usual brisk gait and his air of authority that had come from years of rank.

"Good afternoon, Master Elenn," he said, "I'm glad you are joining me today. Your unique status will have increasing importance to the guards." Henik liked to speak very directly.

"I'm glad to be of service, Master Henik," said Elenn. In truth, he was not particularly glad about playing such a role, but he had never lost his gratitude toward Henik for the time he had offered his support when Elenn was considering refusing the catheter implant.

"It is a busy time with the Great Rains coming, but at least we will begin to address some of the complicated matters we have before us."

"Yes, Master," responded Elenn. "Do you think it will be many more days before we see clouds?"

"Impossible to tell."

The two walked toward the council house. The dry heat and heavy silence reminded Elenn of his early days as an apprentice with the guards. The dust and wilted weeds were again as they had been back then. The two walked in silence into the central part of the capital.

When they arrived at the council house, a few ro council members were quietly whispering and nodding in private discussions in front of the building, and the noise of the assembly all talking amongst themselves came from inside. Elenn had never attended a council meeting before. He followed Henik in, and the two were seated near the front of the hall. Yenca and Benar were both sitting further down the row. Elenn was considering going over to greet them when the talking suddenly grew quiet and many masters' heads turned in the direction of the doorway. Master Jutef was arriving with his cautious, blind uedin's step. His presence was unusual because he was blind and stood out, and also because his robe identified him as an apprentice. It was all but unheard of for an apprentice to be seen at a masters council meeting. He had obviously been invited to take part in the discussion since it had been his idea to fit the barren with hoods. Elenn looked over to see Yenca and Benar observing Jutef's arrival as well, showing no sign of surprise on their faces.

One of the ro-uedin who had been talking outside now took a formal seated position on the platform in the front. He reached up with a wooden striker to hit the long metal bar suspended vertically from the ceiling, and it made a loud, deep bong. The assembly immediately began a recitation of the names as the few still standing made their way to their seats. The first part of the meeting went quickly. Bank reinforcements of the drystreams had been completed, and parts of the capital most susceptible to flooding would be watched carefully.

The presider cleared his throat to introduce the second item for discussion. "Today we will begin to address an issue that has complicated our operations for treating barren syndrome. Master Ferin, would you please introduce the subject."

Ferin of the medic masters rose from his seat and moved to the front of the room. He read from a prepared letter.

"A letter from the medic masters to the masters council. Esteemed council members and attending masters, thank you for allowing us to introduce a new topic during this time of preparation for the Rains. We recommend official recognition of an urgent problem about which many of you are already aware. During this novade, we medic masters have been called upon in unprecedented degree to deal with concerns regarding our masters with barren syndrome. Early on, we established a procedure for curbing the side effects with catheter implants. We knew that this would not cure the afflicted or restore their capacity for passing-of-life, but we thought it would at least eliminate the mental deterioration and abnormal growth patterns that plagued our afflicted and created so many problems early in the novade. Unfortunately, we have begun to notice a return of symptoms over the past year. It has come to our attention that the same craving that factored into the behavior of the afflicted prior to receiving implants seems to persist in many. We now know that this is expressed in a behavior undocumented in any of our medic archives, and to our knowledge never seen in uedin before this time. Our syndrome uedin have been interacting with one another to provide skullsap through a practice of direct consumption from the umbilical artery of one into the mouth of another. We believe that the composition of the skullsap changes when it cools below the temperature of the body, and the discharge that collects in the catheter pouch is not reconsumed by afflicted who experience craving because it is essentially what we may call 'dead.' However, skullsap drawn directly from artery to mouth without cooling retains the composition and potency that satisfies the syndrome uedin's craving. We do not know how this discovery was made within the syndrome population, but indications suggest that it has caught on with alarming speed. We urge the council to officially recognize this dangerous trend and direct action to curtail it at this critical time as we anticipate the descent of wetuedin."

Ferin rolled up the letter and put it into his sleeve. Then he looked up and faced the assembly. "I invite questions," he said.

For a long time, there seemed to be no questions, and Elenn thought how odd it was that this news was being received with so little reaction. Then he began to realize that the assembled uedin were quiet because they didn't know how to respond. All this was a revelation to them. He looked about and saw expressions of horrified disbelief. It was happening all around the capital, and these masters didn't even know it.

Finally, someone spoke. "Master Ferin, it was right for you to come to us with this issue," said a ro near the front, slowly getting on his feet to address Ferin. He spoke in a very slow and deliberate cadence. "In fact, I wish you had come to us sooner. This is a very grave situation. Here we are, about to welcome the descent of a new generation. We are greatly challenged by the simple fact that our newly-named are now known to have a very high occurrence of barren syndrome—is that not true?"

"Yes, Master, our tests are suggesting one in four."

"And are those one in four newly-named not being counseled and prepared to receive catheters and neckpatches?"

"That is correct."

"One in four of our newly-named are being counseled for implants, a generation is soon to come with some unknowable rate of incidence of the syndrome, and now we must face the possibility that this dreadful practice will nullify the effectiveness of our medic masters' only known treatment?"

Ferin remained calm in his response. "We are only here to report what we have observed at the infirmary, Master. It is up to the council to determine a course of action."

Another ro-master raised his hand. "Master Ferin, it seems to me that our situation comes down to one simple question. Is not the occurrence of this, this skullsap consumption. . . isn't it enough for us to say that the use of catheters and neckpatches is a failed intervention?"

"Failed?" said Ferin thoughtfully. He hadn't anticipated that this news would call into question the medical procedures that were already in place. "Well, I don't see how it would serve any purpose to stop using the implants, Master. Even if the catheter's effectiveness is bypassed by the afflicted, it can't hurt them."

"I'm afraid I disagree with you, Master Ferin," said the ro. "I believe it does hurt them, and it hurts the capital. The business you described is revolting. It is a horrible and reprehensible activity, Master Ferin. And it wouldn't be taking place if permanent holes were not being put into the necks of uedin. And if that procedure is not going to have its intended effect, but only allow this disgusting practice to catch on, then the procedure should stop. Shield the Lern! We cannot abide this!"

Elenn heard the fear and disgust in the ro's voice. He resisted the impulse to draw his hands to his face in shame. He looked at Master Ferin. A sensible and decent master, at this moment Ferin seemed to have no idea what to say in response. Perhaps he hadn't fully considered how upsetting his report might be. Medics were used to looking at things in terms of utility and practicality. They weren't as sensitive as, say, teaching masters. The masters in the assembly began talking to one another and it became noisy. Ferin looked confused about what to do. Elenn saw the relief on his face when Yenca stood to speak.

"Masters, please hear me! I have a proposal for the council!" called Yenca, and the hall quieted.

"Come and speak, Master Yenca," said Ferin, "Come up front."

Yenca rose and walked to the front of the assembly. "I am Yenca of Quarterhouse Caretakers, and I am one of the caretakers to syndrome-afflicted. Masters, it is understandable if you are alarmed after hearing what you've heard today. We are facing some serious challenges. But of course we must remain calm as we look for solutions together. Regarding these issues with the syndrome population, we caretakers are more familiar with them than anyone. And we have not backed away from our commitment. We at Quarterhouse have three new apprentices from the newly-named generation who are going to be caretakers to syndrome-afflicted. One of them is Master Jutef, sitting in the back there." Everyone in attendance had already noticed Jutef coming in, but many of them turned again to look at him. Jutef remained still, his sightless eyes directed nowhere. Yenca continued, "Young Master Jutef is an apprentice, but he has already contributed a valuable idea which addresses the very topic that Master Ferin just brought to our attention." There was silence in the hall as everyone waited to hear exactly what Jutef had come up with. "Master Jutef has suggested that we might ask the afflicted to start wearing hoods—hoods to deter them from the behavior that Master Ferin described to us. The hoods would be worn over their heads for the *rest of their lives* and *never removed*." Yenca paused here to let the idea sink in, then continued, "The hoods themselves would be looked upon with respect, as signs of the afflicted uedins' commitment to the welfare of the capital." There were looks of consideration and nods of approval as the assembled uedin comprehended the proposal.

Ferin spoke. "How would the hoods be any different from the strapping that we currently use to cover and protect the catheter implants? Undoing the strap is the same as removing a hood."

"The hoods would have a symbolic function. The afflicted would take an oath when they received hoods. They would understand that they are not only protecting themselves from symptoms of barren syndrome, they are honoring their fellow uedin and the whole capital by keeping their hoods in place."

"And when would the barren start wearing these hoods?" asked another member of the council. "Would we just start handing them out?"

"No," answered Yenca, "Some sort of ceremony is surely in order, to recognize the discipline that is being asked of them. There are many details to be worked out. I asked Master Jutef to come here today so that he could say more about his idea." He paused and looked again in the direction of Jutef, and then spoke to him directly. "Master Jutef, can you embellish your idea a little more for us? Have you thought any more about it?"

Jutef momentarily sat expressionless, as if he had not even heard his name mentioned. He was clearly deep in thought. Then he turned his head and looked in the general direction of Yenca and the council. He finally stood and opened his mouth to speak. "Yes, I have thought more about it. I have only one thing to say. I wish to disassociate myself completely from any plan to put hoods on the heads of the afflicted. I regret ever having shared such an idea."

There were immediate gasps and murmurings from the congregation. Yenca raised his hands to ask for silence. He turned toward Jutef with a troubled look on his face. "Master Jutef,... *Why?*"

Jutef, as young as he was, looked tired and mature beyond his years in this moment. The burden he had taken up as a caretaker to the barren seemed to melt together with the burden of his life-long blindness. He sighed, and started to speak, then sighed again. Finally he answered simply, ". . . It is too much to ask of them."

Elenn, from his place in the front row alongside Henik, was turned in his seat watching Jutef in the back. He noticed Jutef's exhausted look. Too much to ask? It sounded dangerously true. All he could think about was how Pavis had pleaded with him to give him his neck. The discipline and regard for the welfare of the capital that Yenca was talking about all made very good sense. But those who were not barren could never understand the strength of the desire experienced by those who were. Pavis was an embarrassment, but only because he was so open about what Elenn himself wrestled with in secret.

"Master Jutef, we are facing a level of barren syndrome that could destroy our society. We are facing real danger. We cannot allow the barren to fall into derangement," argued Yenca, admonishing his junior caretaker and trying to reason with him in this public meeting.

The other council members and attendants were not so interested in patient reasoning. They were appalled by Ferin's report. As protests and arguments commenced, Elenn found it difficult to stop the spiraling in his own mind, until Henik looked at him and said, "Master Elenn, it's time. You have to speak."

Elenn raised his hand, and the council facilitator silenced the assembly and beckoned him to the front. He knew as he stood that everyone would immediately see that he was barren, both from his size and from his neckstrap. He felt far from resolute, but he knew what he had to say.

"I am Elenn of the Quarterhouse Guards. I believe Master Jutef is distancing himself from his own idea because he is young, and still an apprentice, and he has the humility that one would expect for that position. Furthermore, he is now a caretaker to barren, and he is very committed to looking at the situation from a sympathetic point of view. So I want to commend Master Jutef on many levels, for bringing forth the idea, and then for being cautious about it. But I don't believe we can afford to delay action. It's true that the purpose of the catheters is being nullified because many of the barren have discovered this. . . *feeding* activity. . ." As he said the word, Elenn knew that the term 'feeding', the barrens' own word for it, was being used in front of the council for the first time. He momentarily looked downward with shame, but quickly took a breath and composed himself to continue. "I don't know if it is too much to ask, but I'm afraid we have no choice. If there is any question whether barren uedin are ready to take this oath and wear this hood, let me say that I will be the first."

As soon as he spoke it, Elenn realized that it wasn't completely true. Not because he wouldn't be the first, but because he did not mean to say that he was actually *ready*. Elenn was not ready, but he felt that the plan needed to proceed regardless of readiness or unreadiness. However, he had said, '*if there is any question whether barren uedin are ready. . . I will be the first.*' With that, he had framed himself as a heroic figure—a very risky display of nameliness. Once said, it was too late to explain himself; the re-action was immediate. The council jumped on the proposal. Re-actions were quickly affirmative, and the masters were all eager to press forward. There was a vote, and it was hurriedly decided that the caretaker masters would institute ceremonial oath-tak-ing and hood-wearing immediately for the barren population.

Elenn was uncomfortable with the lack of discussion. He wondered what he might have said to impress on the council that it was not an easy solution and might not even work. The council and the assembly were too eager to take decisive action. Their haste was accentuated by the manner in which they quickly moved on to the few remaining items on the meeting agenda. After some brief discussion about redigging gutters before the Rains and other incidental matters, the meeting was summarily brought to a close.

As everyone rose and began to talk to one another following the adjournment, Elenn saw many approving looks from members of the council as well as masters in the assembly, young and old. Their nods and smiles told Elenn that he had said exactly what they wanted to hear. They certainly did not want to hear what young Jutef had said—that it was too much to ask the barren to con-tain their nature under a hood that would never be taken off. He looked through the congratulatory faces, past Yenca's appreciation, past Henik's approval, to young Jutef, who remained seated in the back of the assembly with a somber expression on his face. Elenn thought back to the first time he encountered Jutef, when he was yet unnamed, on the outing to the peat moss beds. It was the time he had seen a barren uedin, one who was obvious in his condition because of his largeness, doing shifting exercises in the distance.

Jutef, a completely innocent child-uedin at the time, had been there with him, and since he could not see, Elenn had described the scene to him. Elenn never failed to recall the early connection when he heard talk about the new blind caretaker apprentice at Quarterhouse, but he had never really spoken to Jutef since his taking of name. He decided he would go and greet him now.

He approached the back of the council chamber where Jutef was sitting alone. Jutef turned his head, smiled, and faced him with an expression that asked who it was.

"One is Elenn," he said, using a word choice of youth. "Young master Jutef, it is very good to see you."

Jutef sighed and smiled. "Master Elenn," he said, "you gave a very good speech before the council."

"Do you remember me, young master?" asked Elenn.

"Oh yes. You kept me company at the moss beds when I couldn't run with the other child-uedin. There were two anteaters in the field that day. You told me about them—I feel like I saw them myself!" Jutef laughed.

Elenn paused to recall the day years ago at the moss beds. Jutef, he noted, had mixed up his childhood memories, as is often the case. It was not the anteaters that Elenn had described to Jutef those years ago—anteaters had appeared before they had reached the moss beds, and it was the other unnamed who had talked about them. Elenn hadn't spoken to the child-uedin until after they had reached the mossbeds and Nemis had gone to play with the other Bells unnamed. It was the uedin doing a shifting exercise in the distance that Elenn had described for the child-uedin back then when he was yet unnamed, censoring out, of course, that the shifter was a barren. Elenn chose not to correct him.

Now Jutef was a caretaker to the barren, and he had conceived of the whole matter of the hoods and then expressed his misgivings. Elenn quietly commented, "Master Jutef, your statement today gave me much to think about."

"Oh, Master Elenn, I hope you don't think I was disrespectful. . ."

"Not at all. I appreciate what you had to say."

"And that's exactly it—I *had* to say it."

"I understand. You had to say it because you are a caretaker. I had to say what I said because I am a guard."

"Well, it is hard for me to think about how it all came about. I had a simple idea and mentioned it to Master Yenca never imagining that it would take off like this. But now that it's been decided, I will do everything I can to support the new program. I'm sure it will work out." Elenn knew that Jutef was just saying this to be polite and supportive.

"Tell me one thing," said Elenn. "When did you decide that asking us to wear hoods for the rest of our lives was asking too much?"

Jutef paused, and then confessed, "It was after a discussion with Master Pavis."

"Just as I thought," said Elenn.

"Master Pavis is ignorant, but he's not stupid," said Jutef. "He told me that he didn't want to live without the passing-of-life. That is a very uedin thing to say, even though for him, passing-of-life is something very different from what we understand it to be."

"It's insanity to refer to feeding as the passing-of-life," commented Elenn.

"But you must have some idea what he's talking about. You've experienced it, haven't you, Master Elenn?"

Elenn realized that Jutef was asking him if he had taken part in feeding. He decided to be honest.

"Yes, I do have some idea what he's talking about. But it's not really the passing-of-life. It doesn't bring about new life."

"But for Pavis, and perhaps many like him, the experience is the closest thing to passing-of-life that they will ever know. Even if it destroys them, they don't want to give it up."

Elenn felt the first stirrings of a headache as he tried to understand Jutef's sympathy. "But they don't realize what will happen to them, or what trouble it will bring to the capital," he said.

Benar suddenly strutted up to them and butted in. "Young Master Jutef! You nearly wrecked the whole proposal with your backtracking! And the whole thing is your own idea! But you couldn't undo it—the council loved your idea. It's going to be a *lot* of work for us, though, and I'm sure you realize that. We will have come up with a good pattern for the hoods. One pattern that will go with every type of robe, otherwise, Shield the Lern, it would take much too long and be entirely too much work! It's going to be a lot of work no matter what. We'll get the apprentices to do a lot of it—well, not you, young Master Jutef, unless you want to, if you like sewing. I'm trying to imagine what might have an acceptable look. I just keep thinking of rain capes, which are hooded, but I think we're going to need a very different kind of hood. Speaking of rain capes, masters will be wearing them all over the capital soon enough. Maybe that's good, it means the afflicted won't stand out too much at the beginning. . ."

Elenn and Jutef were glad to let Benares babble on by himself.

Rain, Drink, and Wanba's Report

It was ten days into the Great Rains, Elenn's second experience of them. The initial few days of stormy downpour had kept the guards very busy, but no major problems had occurred. A light rain continued to fall, but the swollen streams were starting to subside, and the hatching pools were flooded to a suitable degree to accommodate the wetuedin which had already arrived in expected numbers. Everything had gone well, the wetuedins' arrival was at its tail end, and now that the capital celebrations were dying down, the guards were free to have their own little party. Elenn had received a fine jar of yeastdrink from Yenca after speaking up for the adoption of hoods at the council meeting, and he found it to be perfect timing for this occasion. He was sharing the jar with Deben and Nemis at the guard station. They were all a little drunk.

"Everything is luck," said Elenn, lazily tilting his head and appropriating his gaze toward the window and the gray, rainy view outside.

"Ha ha! That sounds like a verse for calligraphy!" said Nemis.

"Maybe I'll do it," growled Elenn jokingly, "Bring me some paper, ink, and a brush!"

Nemis egged him on. "Have a few more drinks, then the calligraphy! You won't get it right unless you're good and drunk!"

"No, no, no, no, no, no, *no!*" interrupted Deben, "You can't put that into calligraphy! It's nonsense!"

"Master Deben," pleaded Nemis, his head jerking around, "Let Master Elenn have his say. It's so rare that he ever says *anything!*"

"But everything is *not* luck!" Deben knocked on the table when he said the word 'not'.

"Oh yes it is," laughed Elenn, "It is, it is, it is. Everything is luck!" He lifted the jar and refilled all their cups.

"Master Elenn, better to say, 'Everything is choice,'" argued Deben, taking the cup and holding it in the air for a moment, regarding Elenn out of the corner of his eye as if challenging him to think about it.

Elenn's cavalier mood suddenly became serious. "Choice? What do you mean, '*choice*'? Do you think that young master Jutef chooses to be blind? Do you think I choose to be barren?"

"Luck, maybe," contributed Nemis, trying to keep the conversation from becoming unpleasant, "but not all bad luck. There is good luck too. Everything has gone beautifully with this Great Rains. The stream levees held, no damage anywhere in the capital, no roads washed out. We couldn't have chosen those things. Good luck!" He took a nice sip to affirm the good luck.

"That's not what I'm talking about. I'm talking about a different *everything*," argued Deben.

"I don't know *what* you're talking about," said Elenn, ". . . and you say *I* speak nonsense!"

Deben put down his cup and waved his hands to demand their attention. "Listen, listen! When you say, 'Everything is luck,' your *everything* is too unexplained. What is this 'everything'? You aren't referring to things you don't care about," he shook his head. "You're talking about things you *do* care about. You think the things you care about are all settled by luck. But I say, those very things you care about are really settled by choices you make."

"Until I have no choice, and that's when I stop caring. That's why I say luck sorts it all out."

Deben kept looking at Elenn as he spoke to Nemis. "Master Nemis, do you know that when Master Elenn first took name, he wanted to be a server?"

"Oh, I think that would have been bad luck," said Nemis, frowning and shaking his head.

Elenn protested in a voice that would not have sounded quite so pouty had he not been drinking. "Master Deben, you know that is *not* a subject I like to talk about."

"But it was something that really mattered, and it finally came down to *choice*, not luck."

"Master Deben, you don't know anything about that. Now, Master Deben, let's have another cup, and leave this talk alone before I take my jar of yeastdrink and leave you two alone."

"It's true, I don't know anything about it,. . ." started Deben.

"Will you let me have one more cup before you go?" interrupted Nemis.

". . . but can't we say that you made the better choice? Can't we say that?" insisted Deben.

"I don't know, I could be drinking poison instead of this yeastdrink," remarked Elenn sarcastically.

"That would not be lucky, Master Elenn, that would not be lucky!" Nemis shook his head again.

"It was something that you cared about, and there was a choice to be made, and you made the *better* choice!" declared Deben, as if making the final move to win a game of shell-toss.

"I didn't know at the time that it was going to be the better choice. I still think it's all just luck," said Elenn, squeezing his nose as a playful sign of mockery.

"All right, go ahead and do your calligraphy that says everything is luck."

"I don't want to do it anymore," quipped Elenn. "That is my *choice*!" All three laughed together at this.

"It's all right, Master Elenn," said Nemis consolingly, "You don't have to," then added jokingly, "We wouldn't want to have to look at it all the time anyhow!" And they laughed again.

"I feel *lucky* that I don't have to look at it," blurted Deben through his laughter.

"Is there any left?" asked Nemis, taking a peek into the jar.

Just then the door tarp was pulled aside and the sound of the rain was heard from outside. Master Wanba walked in wearing a raincape over his guard's garb.

"Having a little celebration?" asked Wanba.

"Yes, now that things are settling down. Will you join us for a cup?" asked Elenn. "Master Yenca of the caretakers gave me this yeastdrink. It's very good."

"You should try it, Master Wanba," said Deben.

"No thank you, I can't right now," said Wanba, "Who's on duty right now?"

"Masters Henik and Simol, and they have the apprentices with them," answered Deben, "I think they're over at Quarterhouse flatpool."

"No, they're not at the hatching pool. I just came from there. Is Master Ribol around?"

Elenn noticed that Wanba was looking very serious and somewhat distressed. "Master Wanba, has something happened?" he asked.

"Yes, I'm afraid something bad has happened. Something very ugly has happened."

Deben put down his cup and stood up, but he swayed as he stood.

"No, Master Deben, you're off duty and you've clearly had a bit of drink. But you could help me find the others. I'm sorry to spoil your party, masters."

"What happened at the hatching pool? Surely not an attack on wetuedin?" asked Elenn, remembering the horrible incident of a novade ago.

"No, not exactly an attack, but a kind of defilement. A uedin apparently waded into the pool last night, cut his own neck, and died there. His body wasn't seen in the muddy water and wasn't spotted until late this afternoon."

The news of this came like cold water over the guards, bringing them to instant sobriety.

"Shield the Lern," whispered Nemis.

"From his robe, we think he was a toolmaker master," added Wanba, "but we can't quickly identify him. The wetuedin have been nibbling at his flesh for many hours."

Elenn, Deben, and Nemis only stared at Wanba, speechless. Their were fathoming the horror of the situation.

"Because of the festivities over the past days, very few masters are attending to their regular jobs around the capital, so it isn't easy to go around and ask everyone who might be missing."

"You should start with the caretakers to the barren," said Elenn, "they may be able to help you determine who is missing."

Wanba looked surprised. "Why do you say that?"

"The body was large wasn't it?" asked Elenn.

"Yes, as a matter of fact, it was quite large," answered Wanba gravely.

Pavis Has a Difficult Morning

Pavis woke too early and couldn't get back to sleep. He wanted to sleep a little more before starting the day, and he dreaded hearing a server sing morning greeting from the temple compound. He lay on his bedding face down on the wheel-shaped pillow, eyes half-open to the pocket of darkness created in the space between his eyes and the bedding, listening to the faint whistle of air that went back and forth through the pillow straws. Since coming to live with masters, he found himself spiraling more than he ever had in his life. He couldn't stop asking himself questions. Was this the darkness that Master Jutef saw all the time? Since Jutef didn't know light, did he experience darkness at all? Would Pavis recognize the voice of the server who would soon be singing morning greeting? He didn't miss sleeping among servers, all in rows like bees in a hive. Yet there, he had slept easier, it seemed. Here, there were just five of them in the room, he along with four apprentices. He just had to get used to his new home with the distribution masters. Maybe it was good to live with the apprentices, even though they were a full generation younger than him. It was a chance to get used to master life along with them. The switch to life as a master was already easier than he had imagined it would be. It was just a different kind of game. In server life, you tried to disappear. In master life, you tried to build up a good name. That made all the difference. He found that some masters, like Master Jutef, were very much to his liking, while others he didn't like at all. That was new to him. Servers didn't distinguish themselves so much one from another, so they were neither likable nor unpleasant, they were just *there*. He didn't mind them, and they didn't mind him. Such a difference from life with masters! He couldn't try to disappear here. It didn't work. He was afraid they were going to not like him, especially because he had not belonged to them from Namesgiving. He thought about a conversation he had had many years ago when he was a child-uedin. He was talking to a few other child-uedin about the fact that someday they would be taking name. So long ago it had been, and yet he remembered it as though it were yesterday, remembered their little faces all looking exactly alike.

"If names aren't pleasing to the Soft One, why do we take names?" he had asked.

"Because that is the way to know who you are when you've done something wrong," was the answer one of his little fellow unnamed had given.

"So we'll hardly ever use our names, other than that?"

"Not unless you become a master," one of the others had said. They all knew that masters were rude-behaving uedin who do nothing but admire one another and boast about their master achievements, paying no attention to the Soft One at all.

Pavis remembered another asking, "Why are masters called 'masters'?" They all knew that servers were called "servers" because they serve the Soft One. Pavis couldn't remember if any answer came up for why masters were called "masters," but now, as he lay there spiraling, it occurred to him that masters were the true masters of the capital. Servers certainly did little to maintain the functioning of the capital. It seemed to him that all they did was fuss over their devoted attentions to the Soft One, and it also seemed to him that the Soft One, on the other hand, paid no attention to *them* at all. Pavis was not a server, not anymore. And neither did he have the great love for the capital that he needed to have in order to call himself a true master. What did it mean that he neither had the heart of a server nor the heart of a master? What was he? He had nothing to love but the passing-of-life. Master Jutef understood that about him.

A little tapping at the door tarp, and Jutef's voice, "Master Pavis, are you there?"

What? Was it Jutef's voice? At the very moment he was thinking about him?

Then unsettlingly, the tapping of the door tarp with a repeated "Master Pavis, are you there?" and the simultaneous sound of morning greeting being sung from the central temple.

Pavis was wide awake, but it was one of the apprentices, roused suddenly from sleep, who responded first. "What's going on? Who is that?" asked the disoriented apprentice from his bedding.

"It is me, Jutef of the Quarterhouse Caretakers." The morning greeting continued in the background. "I'm very sorry to disturb you all. I must speak with Master Pavis immediate—"

"I'm awake. Just a moment!" The morning greeting continued while Pavis extracted himself from his bedding and stood. In his undergarment, he stepped carefully across the floor around the apprentices, now all stirring and mumbling about being awoken in such a manner. He made his way to the door.

"Master Jutef, why are you here so early?" he asked, pulling the door tarp back, and then he saw that Jutef was not alone. "Who is with you?"

"Master Elenn is with me," said Jutef. "He came and woke me up just a bit ago and asked me to come with him to get you. He says there's something that you must see. He says it's very important."

"But why so early? It's barely dawn." Pavis rubbed his eyes.

"Please pardon the intrusion," said Elenn. "I had to come and get you early and show you what I must show you quickly, because I don't have permission."

Pavis comprehended Elenn's seriousness and asked, "What do you want to show me?"

"I can't take the time to explain it to you now. You'll understand when you see."

"Let me just put on my robe," said Pavis, and left them at the door for a minute while he went back to get dressed. He was at a loss as to what could be so urgent that it merited this breach of etiquette. He said nothing to the apprentices who were now only stretching and removing the top covers of their bedding.

The faint light of early morning barely reached the chilly streets of the capital. Elenn walked ahead, the other two behind, Jutef's hand on Pavis's shoulder. As they walked, the gray building fronts were silent on both sides, except for the occasional sound of someone lighting a stove or shuffling to the outhouse.

"Master Jutef, won't you tell me anything?" Pavis asked his counselor.

"I don't know any more than you do," said Jutef. "But if Master Elenn says there's something that you must see, I believe him."

"This is the way to the Flatpools District. Is he taking me to the guard station?" Pavis was worried that he was being detained for something. Might it be for partaking in passing-of-life? The whole capital seemed to be upset about it in recent days. They were going to ask all the barren to wear hoods and promise never to partake in passing-of-life. Pavis could hardly believe that it was Jutef himself who had dreamt up the idea. Pavis felt sure the plan would fail, and he had shared that opinion with Jutef in no uncertain terms.

Jutef didn't say anything about the direction they were going, but it gradually became apparent that they were going not to the guard station, but to Quarterhouse. Pavis did not like being led through the capital this way. It might have been all right for a child-uedin or a newly-named, but it was not a respectful way to treat an adult uedin. Pavis began to think that he was being treated rudely, either because he had come from server status and was thought of as an outsider, or because he had once begged Elenn to bare his neck to him. He grew increasingly impatient and frustrated.

Finally, as they were entering the Quarterhouse grounds and approaching the hatching pool, Pavis exclaimed, "What? Are you bringing me here to see the wet-uedin? I've already seen them! And what is your point?"

"No, I didn't wake you up to show you the wet-uedin," said Elenn sternly, "Come. You'll see soon enough." He led them up to the observation deck and across to the granary. A guard was sitting on a stool by the granary door. He stood up when he saw them approach.

"Master Elenn?" called the guard.

"Yes," answered Elenn. "Thank you, Master Ribol, I am much in your debt."

"Don't mention it," answered Ribol. "And don't worry, I won't say anything." He opened the door to the granary. It was completely dark inside.

Ribol went in and reached for the shelf to find one of the special lanterns used for nighttime viewing of the wet-uedin. They followed him in. Before Ribol lit the lantern, Pavis could already see dimly that the grain sacks had been piled up on one side to make room for a figure that was on the floor with a sheet of wax-cloth covering it from head to toe.

When Jutef heard the sound of the lantern catching a light, he asked, "What is it?"

"It's a body," said Pavis, "It's a dead body."

"Take a good look, Master Pavis," said Elenn quietly, as he removed the wax-cloth. "This is what I wanted you to see."

The body was slightly larger than Elenn or Pavis. Because it was lying face up, you couldn't see whether a neckstrap was still attached or whether it had come off, but it was obviously the body of a barren uedin. The skin had the whitish hue of dead flesh, except for a birthmark on the shoulder. Its extremities—fingers, toes, nose, lips, ears—were partially eaten away. What remained of its face was swollen and looked very unnatural. A deep gash was open on its neck, exposing muscle and veins, but washed completely clean with no trace of blood.

"Shield the Lern," whispered Pavis, "What happened to him?"

"What do you see?" asked Jutef, but Pavis didn't answer, waiting for Elenn to speak.

Elenn explained, "Yesterday, at about this same time in the morning, this uedin entered the hatching pool, waded among the wet-uedin—who have been here but eight days—and cut his own throat. We don't know why he did it. We don't know why he chose to die in this place of new life. The wet-uedin ate his fingers and lips. When they take leg and grow to maturity, they will have to deal with the knowledge of this ugly thing happening to them at the beginning of their life and their generation. The right decision might be to hide it from them, but that decision can't be made without informing the council, and at that point it will be debated openly and will then be impossible to keep the word of it from spreading."

"But what does this have to do with me?" asked Pavis.

"Can't you see he was barren!" shouted Elenn. "He was barren, and he had been feeding, and he was deranged! This is what comes from feeding! Feeding is not the passing-of-life! You have to stop! But first, you have to *want* to stop!"

Pavis turned and sideswiped Jutef as he rushed out of the granary. He ran to the railing and faced the still, dark surface of the pool. Jutef tried to follow him, taking careful steps out about midway across the deck.

"Master Pavis, are you there?" called Jutef.

"I will wear your hood," said Pavis.

"What did you say?"

"I will wear your hood! I will wear it!" cried Pavis. He had recognized the birthmark on the dead uedin's shoulder from some past encounter, some past experience of what he had, up till now, been calling "passing-of-life." He couldn't call it that anymore. He had just been thinking that he had nothing to love but the passing-of-life. Now he understood that he really had nothing to love at all.

The Taking of Hood

The sky full of beautiful, bright clouds did not match the mood of the day. Elenn had known that the hood-taking ceremony contrived by the masters council would not be a festive occasion, but he was not expecting it to be so somber. He also knew that the caretakers to the barren were upset because they were not consulted as much as they thought they should have been about how to inform the sizable new generation of barren about their condition. The masters council had more or less taken over all decisions and matters related to the syndrome-afflicted, and they had dictated how the ceremony should proceed as well. He caught the face of Pavis in the crowd, and Pavis had the same defeated look that he had had the morning they had made him look at the dead toolmaker uedin who had killed himself in the hatching pool at Quarterhouse. But the dismal look on Pavis's face was completely overshadowed by the looks on the faces of the young uedin who had just learned of their condition and were now assembled to be put into hoods. They hugely outnumbered all the other barren uedin. They all had bandages on their necks where catheters had just been implanted. In Elenn's eyes, they looked incredibly young and vulnerable, having barely received name. In very short order they had learned that they were barren, would never have passing-of-life, that they had to have the implants in for the duration of their lives lest they become deranged, and that there was a problem with barren consuming skullsap from one another which now was going to require them to wear permanent hoods. The looks in their eyes made it painfully clear to see that they were completely terrified.

Elenn had initially asked to be excused from speaking at the ceremony. Although he had agreed to be the first to take hood, he didn't think it was necessary that he be a spokesman, and he didn't know what he could say to make the situation look any less dreary than it was. But Jutef had made it clear that he was not willing to speak, and the council did not press Jutef greatly, owing to the fact that he was only an apprentice caretaker. Instead they recruited Elenn, insisting that he only need basically repeat what he had said at the masters council meeting. He had the impression that they only wanted him to speak because he was barren. He had planned what he was going to say. He wanted to prepare the newly-named for the temptation they would face. That was something the masters council could not appreciate and had no way of knowing how to address. All day, Elenn had been bracing himself to speak the hard truth, but now the look of panic on the faces of the young barren masters completely threw him off. He had no idea what was the right thing to say to them in the state they were in.

How strange it was that the servers were nowhere to be seen. The word from the temple, he had learned from Benar, was that the servers saw no reason to take part in the ceremony because they had had the good fortune of not having any among them who showed symptoms of barren syndrome. They had, however, asked that any newly-named who were determined to have the syndrome be discouraged from considering server community; the masters were better prepared to look out for their welfare. Elenn had asked Benar if there had ever been any communication with the servers about Pavis and his claims, but Benar said that no official inquiries had been made. Whatever the reason, it now appeared that server involvement in capital ceremonies was being suppressed. There would be no server shiftings, no sourember smoke.

There was no obligatory silence either, but Elenn noticed that the crowd was silent anyway. It didn't have the feel of a ceremony; the only thing that indicated ceremony was the fact that nearly everyone there was wearing ceremonial turquoise vestments. Elenn was one of only two wearing the green of the guards, the other being Nemis who was there on duty. The crowd was mostly made up of these newly-named who had just learned of their condition, and very few of them were even capable of putting up a brave front. They waited in silence. It had been decided that the event would be only attended by those who would actually be receiving hood, with the exception of the caretakers and members of the masters council. The notion that the whole capital should be there to witness and support them had been determined by the council to be unwarranted.

Elenn noticed a stirring in the crowd to his left and turned to see Benar coming through with some apprentices. Benar led them as they carried large baskets containing white bundles. All around them, uedin were trying to get a look at the hoods. Benar was turning around to tell the apprentices, "Don't slow down, just keep following me." He walked past Elenn as if he didn't see him, and seemed not to even hear when Elenn said, "Greetings, Master Benar!" Elenn watched him as he kept right on going, but decided not to call to him again. But what was that peculiar smell? Was that coming from Benar? Elenn couldn't place it, but it was vaguely familiar.

A drum was struck to silence the crowd, and the fact that the crowd was already silent gave it a disturbing irrelevance. A ro-ue-din took his place in front of the crowd to address them. Elenn recognized his face from the masters council but had never spoken to him before and didn't know him at all.

"Young masters and masters," he called out. His voice was not strong, but because of the quiet, everyone could hear him. "I am Embal of the masters council. It is very good that you are all here today to take this important step that will safeguard the future of the capital. A very great responsibility is yours to bear.

"To begin today, I want you to think about the wet-uedin who have arrived with this last Great Rains. If you have not been to see the wetuedin at any of the domicile hatching pools, I urge you to go to one of them and see our beautiful new wet-uedin. Seeing them will inspire you to have courage and strength, and that is just what you will need to carry out your duty to the capital." He paused to get a sense of how his listeners were regarding him. Elenn looked around also, particularly interested in seeing what kind of looks the young masters with bandaged necks had on their faces. They were listening as if their lives were at stake.

Embal continued, "What you must understand is that it is not what you must *do* for the welfare of the capital; it is what you must *not* do. You have been told about the activity that some uedin with barren syndrome have engaged in for the sake of some sort of sensation, some sort of satisfying effect. You also know that it nullifies the catheter intervention, and it leads to derange-ment. For these reasons you must never do it. But most of all, you must never do it because it is an offense to uedin society, and an offense, surely, to Lern Beyana."

Elenn noticed many of the young masters nodding in agree-ment, which only struck him as very sad. The newly-named with syndrome had no idea what Embal was talking about—they had never experienced it. Embal himself had no idea what he was talking about. These young masters could not begin to know what kind of temptation they were going to face. It was an un-bearable desire they would be up against. Elenn could not stop thinking about how Pavis had referred to it as "passing-of-life."

"Today you will swear an oath on your honor as uedin, and you will promise that once you have taken the hood to stop you from bearing your necks to one another, you will never remove the hood. You will work, eat, and sleep with your hoods on your heads. This will save you, and this will save the capital. This is the single most important thing in your life now. Do you understand?"

Many of the young barren were nodding, and some spoke out, *"Yes!"*, but Elenn felt sick thinking about the torment that awaited these innocents. Jutef sprang to mind, and he thought how lucky Jutef was to not have to speak to these poor newly-named being given a burden quite beyond their understanding. Was Jutef even now regretting ever having mentioned his idea of barren taking hood? And yet, what other choice did they have?

Embal glanced over to Elenn to signal to him that he was about to introduce him.

"Now I am going to introduce Master Elenn of the Flatpools District Guards. He spoke very excellently to the council in favor of hoods for all uedin with syndrome and so helped us come to this important task." He raised hands to face to defer to Elenn who now walked to the front of the crowd. Seeing all eyes on him, Elenn felt like he wanted to run away.

"I am Elenn, third generation, of Flatpools District Guards. I am one of you. I am barren. I spoke to the masters council to advocate for this thing that we are doing today, this taking of hood. I said then, and I still believe that it is the only way to try to save us from ourselves and save the capital. I will be the first to receive hood." Elenn looked at the glum faces in front of him. The points he had intended to include in his speech, he knew, were completely out of the question. He would not be able to warn them that many of them would fail, many would not be able to resist temptation, and there would be those among them who would probably become deranged. Their faces showed that they were already too afraid and too overwhelmed.

"When I spoke at the masters council, there was no way for me to tell myself that I had the right to represent you. No barren uedin asked me to represent him. In fact, there was no discussion among those of us with syndrome as to whether we felt prepared to make this commitment or not. I had to speak only from my own experience. Believe me, I would not have gone along with the idea if I had not struggled—and failed, many times—to stop myself from doing this thing that many of you newly-named have only just learned about. . ." Elenn wasn't sure if it was wise to admit that he had done the unacceptable thing that they were all there to suppress, but he felt lost. What could he possibly say that might prepare them for their future? He just wanted his speech to be over. He would simply share some empty words and let things move on so that they could get their hoods. What was the main point he had made at the masters council meeting?

"We have to accept hoods because the alternative is unacceptable," he said, thinking that that was basically the statement that had impressed the masters council. But now he was speaking to the barren themselves, and it rang hollow. It did not address their fears. Just finish up then, he thought. "As hard as it may be, as much as we may have to struggle, we must keep our hoods on our heads at all times. Let's be strong, remembering that we resist temptation not only for ourselves, but for the whole capital." As he finished this short speech, he was completely disappointed in himself, having failed to say anything that might impart courage or hope. Unfortunately, he had nothing else to offer. So he raised his hands in gratitude for the attention of his listeners, and stepped away. As he walked to the side, he saw many newly-named uedin hanging their heads, others looking desperate, eyes glancing back and forth. He felt it would have been better if he had not spoken at all.

Meanwhile, Yenca left Jutef alone and went to help Benar who was getting ready to distribute the hoods. Benar was busily pointing, putting his hand on the shoulder of an apprentice and giving him a little shove in another direction, shaking his head, and saying, "No, no, no, not yet, no one is to put anything on yet!" The apprentices positioned themselves in the front with the baskets around them. Benar walked forward in dramatic, carefully measured steps. He was obviously trying to convey the sense of ceremony.

He stopped, cleared his throat, and addressed the crowd in his most dignified voice. "I'm Master Benar," he said, "Senior

Caretaker to the Syndrome-Afflicted. Greetings and congratulations!" Elenn thought it was odd to say "congratulations" on this occasion. He was quite surprised by Benar's confident tone. "It looks like there may be a few third or fourth generation masters out there," Benar continued, "So some of you may remember me from Quarterhouse. I was a caretaker to the unnamed there for many novades. Now I'm the senior caretaker to the barren, so if you don't know me yet, well, you should try to remember who I am." He suddenly cracked a smile, as if slipping out of character, but then quickly resumed his lofty tone. "Now. We are about to distribute the hoods. Your caretaker apprentices will hand them to you as you come up to receive them. Please come one row at a time, move toward the center from both sides. . ." Benar paused and stared ahead at the crowd, trying to picture how they would move toward the center. Then he snapped back to attention, saying, "Yes, from both sides toward the center, and proceed forward slowly to receive your hood. Do not unfold them, whatever you do, until everyone has returned to his place and is holding his bundled hood." Benar gazed at the apprentices holding the large basket of bundled hoods. "I know you're going to want to look at it, but just hold on!" he said in a scolding voice.

Just as Benar said this unceremonial choice of words, "just hold on", Elenn suddenly thought of the smell he had smelled on Benar earlier. It was sourembers! Benar must have partaken in sourember smoke on his own before the ceremony. Yes, that sounded like something Benar would do! He was probably disappointed that that had been excluded from the ceremony and decided to have his own little sourember ritual. It all made sense. Benar definitely seemed to have had a good whiff of it.

Benar held his hands up graciously and looked slowly back and forth to see that the crowd was paying attention and ready to proceed. He then called out with exaggerated piety, *"Lehera Beyana yana ya. . ."* To which the crowd automatically repeated, *"Lehera Beyana yana ya. . ."* He hesitated, smiled, and continued, *"Lerna Beyana ulrana uedina,"* and the crowd responded. Benar's lead recitations grew increasingly sing-song, to the point that some of the older members of the masters council looked back and forth at each other uncomfortably. The young newly-named, however, did not have enough experience with recitations of names to know that this sing-song recitation was irregular. Many of them even mimicked him when they repeated. He took them through a full recitation of the names. After it concluded, he gestured for the apprentices to step forward with the baskets and invited the front row to come.

The apprentice caretakers motioned the crowd to step apart and form an aisle from the front to the back. Then they ushered the front row inward and forward. Each took a small, tightly wrapped bundle from the baskets much as they had once taken name blocks at their Namesgiving. They circled around, allowing others to come forward. Benar stood for the entire time watching the ushering process and the movement of uedin, totally engrossed in the circulation of the crowd. He looked quite pleased when they were all back in position and facing him. He smiled at them with delight.

"Now, masters and young masters, I would like to open this one to show you how it is constructed and say a few words about how to take care of it. So please don't unfold anything until I tell you to." He certainly sounded like one who had spent years as caretaker to the unnamed, telling them to behave themselves. He loosened the bundle and held up the hood. It was smaller than Elenn had imagined it would be. It obviously wasn't the kind of hood that drapes loosely over the head like the ones on rain capes. "Now see how this comes together," Benar continued, displaying the hood in his hand, "It's attached at the neck in the front, and it has these pieces that cover the shoulders and form flaps in the front and the back. The flaps are to fit under your robe. They will fit under any master's robe." Now Benar was really admiring the hood, acting as if it were a fashionable thing. "Since you must wear them all the time, it wouldn't do to have them hanging in your eyes, so they have been sewn to fit snugly on your head. They're telling you that you must never take them off, but you'll need to take them off when you take a bath, and that would be a good time to give them a washing." Benar held it up again and turned slowly from side to side to give everyone a good look, even though they would be unfolding their own very short-ly. Then he called Elenn forward. "Master Elenn, you have asked to be the first one to take hood. Please come up and we'll show everyone how it is properly worn." Elenn walked to the front to stand beside Benar. He had not imagined it happening this way, but of course, he had to cooperate. "Go ahead, Master Elenn," Be-nar said, "*Unfold your hood!*"

As Elenn loosened the bundle to unfold his hood, he felt a strange combination of emotions. It was going to mark him as barren at all times and no matter where he went. At the same time, he knew he was betting on his best hope for himself by put-ting on this hood. It was pride and shame, two opposite emotions, coming together with the taking of hood.

"And so you shall take hood, putting it over your head like this," said Benar ceremoniously, and then reached out his hand and said to Elenn, "May I?" Elenn handed the unfolded hood to Benar, who then raised it up and lowered it over Elenn's head. Unfortunately, Benar had it turning the wrong way. He had it nearly all the way down Elenn's head when he realized it was backwards. Elenn's face was covered with the white cloth and his skullwomb and neckstrap showed in the exposed back where his face was supposed to be. The crowd immediately started laughing. Elenn took ahold of the open edge in the back with one hand and squeezed the fabric by his nose with the other hand and rotated the hood, dragging it over his nose, till his face appeared in the front. The crowd laughed all the more. Benar worried that he had embarrassed Elenn. He looked at him apologetically. Elenn looked back at him and smiled broadly.

"Thank you, Master Benar," he said, "I couldn't have done it better myself." The crowd did not hear him because they were laughing, but Benar heard him and smiled back with affection.

Benar raised his hands once again to quiet the crowd, and Elenn turned toward them with his hands crossed over his chest, and, in a loud voice, said the words of the oath that had been decided by the council: *"I swear on my honor as a uedin to wear this hood for the rest of my life, and by doing so, bring no trouble to the capital or to Lern Beyana."*

Then Benar instructed them, "Now all of you, please unfold your hoods, and when you hear the drum, you may put them on." He waited and watched while the masters and young masters loosened their bundles and unfolded their hoods. The drummer, after getting the cue from Benar, produced a loud and lively rhythm which he kept up while they adjusted the hoods over their heads. When the drum stopped, Elenn led them in their oath, calling out, "Now repeat as I say the oath again: *I swear on my honor as a uedin. . ."*

The barren crowd repeated in unison, "I SWEAR ON MY HONOR AS A UEDIN. . ."

Elenn continued, "*To wear this hood for the rest of my life,. . ."*

"TO WEAR THIS HOOD FOR THE REST OF MY LIFE,. . ."

"*and by doing so, bring no trouble. . ."*

" AND BY DOING SO, BRING NO TROUBLE. . ."

"*to the capital or to Lern Beyana."*

"TO THE CAPITAL OR TO LERN BEYANA."

Elenn was glad to see that the hoods were made to fit closely and did not hide their faces at all. He looked out at the multitude of faces framed in hoods, and saw that they were much more relaxed and many were smiling. What did it matter if the very first time he had had his hood on, it was on backwards? Benar's silliness had helped everyone to relax just a little. Embal was now coming back to make a closing address, but Elenn didn't mind whatever it was he was going to say. They had their hoods on, and the hardest part of the ceremony was over. It was unpleasant to think about whether future generations of uedin would require hoods, thought Elenn, but since it was very possible that they would, perhaps he should suggest to the masters council that sourembers must be included in future hood-taking ceremonies.

Inspection at Murro

The following moon cycles went remarkably well. Since the majority of those wearing hoods were young masters, the whole capital was especially sympathetic and respectful. Elenn was only slightly more self-conscious than he had been before, since he was used to being noticed for his size and his neckstrap. The white hood somehow symbolized his best intentions, and he was able to wear it without embarrassment. Likewise, he felt none of the shame by association when he saw other barren as he had felt before they were in hood. Any of that was nullified by seeing so many young and innocent masters wearing the hood of the barren. Sometimes he even forgot that he had it on.

So it was the day that Nemis came up to Elenn with a bit of pleasant news. Elenn had cooking duty, and he was peeling yams when Nemis came to find him.

"Master Elenn, I just spoke with Master Wanba, and he told me that he's going to assign you and me to go inspect the grainhouses at Murro."

"Murro?" he asked, "That's south of the capital. Why are Flatpools guards involved?"

"I wondered the same thing. The Southgate District guards have always inspected the grainhouses, but Master Wanba told me that guard districts all around the capital have decided to start trading duties. I think some of the guardmasters in districts with no hatching pools are eager to see the wetuedin. Flatpools Station has been given the inspection of the grainhouses at Murro, and Master Wanba is going to let us do it."

It was at that moment that Elenn suddenly became aware again that he was wearing a hood. Was Master Wanba doing him a favor because he had played a part in the adoption of hoods for the barren? Most everyone in the capital had seen the grainhouses at one point or another. It was not a long hike. But it had been many years since Elenn had been there. They were beautiful and interesting. Some grain was still stored there, but Murro was mostly kept up as an architectural treasure. It didn't matter if Wanba was giving him special treatment. He wanted to go.

"When?" Elenn asked.

"Wanba will be talking with you directly about it, but I'm pretty sure they want us to go the sooner the better. I have an idea. Why don't we camp there for a night?"

Elenn was touched by this friendly suggestion. "That's a great idea!" he said.

Later that day, Wanba did call Elenn and tell him about the assignment. Elenn politely accepted the assignment and carefully avoided giving any hint that he suspected he might be receiving special treatment. He then found Nemis and made plans for their trip.

"I have cleaning duty the day after tomorrow," said Nemis. "I'll be done by mid-day. Why don't we go then?"

"That sounds good," said Elenn. "We'll have tomorrow to get the inspection details and pack what we need."

"Shall we go right after mid-day meal then?"

"Yes. And we'll let Master Wanba know that we're going to camp for a night."

"There's only one moon up now, and it's well into waning. The stars are going to be fantastic. Do you know that's my hobby—looking at stars?"

"No, I didn't know that," said Elenn. "Maybe you'll be able to show me some constellations."

"I will!" said Nemis.

Two days later, the comrade guards tied on packs and walked through the capital's Central District toward Southgate. They were certainly noticed, wearing guard's garb and carrying packs, not to mention Elenn's hood. They walked past the bartering yards, the plaza in front of the central temple, and the sunken court of the cold well. Nemis greeted some familiar masters and stopped to tell them that he and Elenn were on their way to an inspection at Murro, and how they were looking forward to camping there. They made a courtesy stop at the Southgate District Station to extend regards on behalf of Flatpools and review the written instructions they had received. By the time they passed through the South Gate, it was late afternoon. They lingered at the Clay Bridge, which showed no signs of damage from the recent Great Rains. Their shadows were long as they followed the road on through the grassy plain on their way to Murro.

When they reached Murro, the grainhouses appeared tall and grand against the flat landscape. The sun was setting, and its golden light put one face of the structures in beautiful clarity and left the other side in dark shadow. They could quickly see that some damage had indeed come to one of the grainhouses. A section of its roof was caved in on the north side. They agreed to check it out thoroughly when they inspected all the grainhouses in the morning. Their current priority was to find a spot to camp and put down their packs. Since there was no sign of rain or high wind, they would camp in the open as they had planned.

By the time they settled in and had a meal of cold yams and melonseed buns, it was dark. A single crescent moon brought hardly any moonlight to the night landscape. The silhouettes of the grainhouses were only visible because of the sheet of stars behind them.

Finally, they put out their blankets, lay on their backs, and started looking up at the night sky for recognizable constellations. Elenn was not surprised that Nemis knew the constellations much better than he did.

"There's the Sourberry. I always spot that right away," said Nemis.

"I always spot the Broom, but I'm not seeing it anywhere right now. . ." said Elenn.

"It's the wrong time of year," said Nemis, "You'll see it before the next cold season."

"Come to think of it, that's when I've always seen it."

"Oh, there's Alka!"

"Where's Alka? I've looked for Alka, but I didn't know where to look."

"You see the stem of the Sourberry? Follow from the stem down, and you see those two little bright ones? That's Mouse. You know that. Now, from the lower star of Mouse, go down at about a forty-five degree angle until you see those four making a trapezoid."

"I think I've seen that before, but I didn't know it was Alka."

"Yes, that's Alka."

They gazed at the constellation for a long moment, and then Elenn asked, "Do you remember studying about the great hero Alka?"

"Yes. I know he was the first uedin to write down the ancient codes. Up to that point, ancient codes were all in oral tradition, right?"

"Yes. I don't think historians know much more than that about who Alka actually was," said Elenn. "But all the myths and legends around him are really fascinating."

"I know they used to say that he wrote with both hands and both feet," said Nemis, "Is that what you're talking about?"

"Well, yes, that's one of the legends. One has to wonder where such stories come from. What if he really wrote with both hands and both feet?" he said jokingly.

Nemis started laughing. "I can just picture it," he said. After a short pause he laughed again and said, "Now if he could copy four different codes at the same time, *that* would be even *more* amazing!"

Elenn laughed, and then contributed, "It's very interesting, though. That's how historians know that the original codes were augmented with new codes. One of the codes is a tribute to Alka. From seeing that, it is evident that the writer only knew legend about Alka and didn't realize that he was creating a landmark for code scholars. Alka copied down an oral tradition that predated him. A reference to himself couldn't have been contained in the oral tradition."

"Is that right? How interesting! You know a lot about Alka, don't you."

"Well, you know the constellations very well."

"Tell me one of the other myths about Alka."

"Well, I should tell you the one about the constellation we're looking at, and how it got to be named Alka. It's the myth about him going to the Lake of Ceulan."

"That was Alka? I thought that was someone else."

"No, that was Alka. The legend says that when Alka was very young, he followed the 'broken box' to the Lake of Ceulan. The 'broken box' was the old name for the Alka constellation. The association of the 'broken box' with Alka gradually caused a name shift, and the constellation is now just known as Alka."

"I never knew that," said Nemis. "So we're looking at the Broken Box."

"We are," said Elenn.

"I wonder if we'd get to Ceulan Lake if we followed it," joked Nemis.

It took about one second for Elenn to feel the sorrow. He would never go to the Lake of Ceulan. But he didn't want his sorrow to spoil the moment, so he put it out of his mind.

"The legend says that when he got close to the Lake of Ceulan, he met a talking dragonfly."

"Now I'd like to meet one of those," said Nemis and laughed. "Did the talking dragonfly give Alka the oral codes? Is that how he got them?"

"You're teasing me, aren't you, Master Nemis?"

"But I do want to know what the dragonfly said," said Nemis.

"The dragonfly told Alka that he had to do one thing before he could see the lake. The dragonfly told him to reach down and scoop up a handful of pebbles, which he did. Then the Dragonfly told him he had to count the pebbles in his hand. If he had an odd number of pebbles, he would be allowed to see the Lake of Ceulan. If he had an even number of pebbles, he was not allowed. So Alka sang as he counted, and it went like this:

> *One, two, I love to play games*
> *Three, four, I love to play games*
> *Five, six, I love to play games*
> *Seven, eight—I've lost!"*

"Hah! Wonderful!. . ." said Nemis.

"The dragonfly liked his song so much that he let him through, even though his number was even."

"And then he saw the lake?"

"He saw the lake and talked to the wetuedin,"

"Who could also talk, of course," said Nemis.

"Of course. And they told him that they were very happy to see him so they could know what they would become someday. And that's the end of the myth."

"So the moral of the story is that one can lose and still win. Alka failed the challenge but got to see the lake because of his song. Thank you. I knew there was a myth about someone going to the Lake of Ceulan, but I didn't know it was Alka. And I didn't know our modern Alka constellation was once called the Broken Box and was connected with the myth like that."

"Can you show me another one?" asked Elenn.

"All right. You see there over by the corner of the grainhouse roof? You see that crooked row of stars? That's the Crow. And up from that. . ."

Elenn let Nemis continue to point out constellations even though he doubted he would remember any of them. Gradually Nemis grew quiet, and Elenn knew that he was asleep. Elenn was ready to sleep, but he could not. He was remembering the time he had camped with Hela on the way to Redrock Outvillage. He often thought about Hela and how kind he had been during that particularly difficult time of Elenn's life. Because of his accidental death, Hela was denied passing-of-life, just as Elenn was. Hela never knew that they shared this fate. Elenn thought also about how he had experienced some early derangement on the trip to Redrock. He was grateful for the catheter that had made it possible for him to live without the inevitability of that. He was also grateful for his hood, which he now slept in. The hood would protect him from himself. He put his hand up to his head to feel the fabric covering his ear, and slowly drifted off to sleep.

The next day they woke early and inspected all the grainhouses. The one with the collapsed section of roof would require the most time and attention. They would save it for last.

The grainhouses were all identical. They were massive pyramidal structures with very thick walls of log and mortar leading to a flat top. The lower logs of the exterior were carved with a decorative motif that was bold and primitive, having irregularities in its spacing and shapes that weren't seen anymore in uedin decor.

The first one that they entered had some large bales of grain in it, wrapped in woven covers and painted with a layer of tar to resist pests. After that, they found only one other grainhouse actually containing grain along with plows and farming tools. Mostly the interiors were vast and empty, with shafts of sunlight coming through windows near the ceiling of each story. The upper floors were reached by traversing the interior perimeter on a series of ramps that each led to landings at each corner, gradually reaching an opening to the next floor. The top story contained the same system of ramps.

"Why do you suppose they built ramps on the top floor, going up to nowhere?" asked Nemis.

"Maybe at one time they thought they might build a fourth level," suggested Elenn.

Finally, they inspected the grainhouse with the damaged roof. When they got to the third floor, it was considerably brighter than any of the other interior spaces they had seen because of the additional sunlight coming in through the gap where the section of roofing had fallen in. What they also noticed was that the set of ramps led directly to the corner closest to the gap. This provided them with a perfect opportunity to inspect the damage up close.

As Elenn and Nemis approached the top of the last ramp going up, they saw something that excited them. Through the opening in the roof, it was possible to see a view of the landscape.

"I wonder if you can see the capital!" said Nemis, and they hurried to look out. Sure enough, if you looked westward, you could see the southeast corner of the walled capital, and its southern face with the Clay Bridge some distance in front of it. From the hills beyond, small streams which looked as though they were not yet dry, seemed to wind around the capital in ribbons.

"It's beautiful!" said Nemis.

"Yes! And how green everything is since the Great Rains! I bet the slopes are even green, but you can't see them from here," said Elenn.

"Can you make out the Flatpools District?" asked Nemis.

"No. There aren't any high buildings in that part of the capital. But you can see Bells," said Elenn.

"This is a view very few uedin have ever seen," commented Nemis.

"It's marvelous. We should tell the other guards to come and see it before the roof is fixed."

"It's almost a shame to fix the roof and close this up," said Nemis with earnest. "I wonder if there's any way they could build a window or a balcony up here."

"A roof-top deck would be wonderful. Then you would be able to see not only the capital but the Haka Cliffs and the southeastern desert. . . you can't see it from this angle now. But I don't know if the masters council would approve making changes to the basic architecture."

"No? It's just one of the many grainhouses."

"Still, I think it would be a very long debate. But it's good idea. Maybe you can see what Master Wanba thinks about it."

"I think I will," said Nemis. They remained there a long while, enjoying the rare view.

They had just turned around and were starting down the ramps again, when some kind of very large flying bug whirred past Nemis's head and startled him. He drew back hard and lost his balance, slipping completely off the ramp. Elenn immediately reached out and grabbed his wrist. The full body weight of Nemis pulled Elenn forward, but he heaved and slowly pulled Nemis up and back onto the ramp.

Nemis was clearly shaken. He was colorless and took a while to catch his breath. He could have easily fallen the considerable height from the ceiling to the floor and broken his neck. He looked at Elenn with a shocked looked on his face. "You're very strong!" he said. "I think you just saved my life!"

"I never saw a bug like that before," said Elenn.

"Thank you, Master Elenn. I do think you may have just saved my life."

Elenn slowly comprehended what had just happened. It was because of his overgrown size as a barren that he was able to grab Nemis and pull him up. If he had been a smaller uedin, a *normal* uedin, Nemis's weight probably would have pulled him over. It was the first time his condition had ever resulted in something good.

Nemis had to calm down and steady himself before he was able to make his way down the ramp. "If they do build a window or an observation deck," he said with conviction, "they definitely will need to put some kind of railing on these ramps."

They made their way down and out of the grainhouse. They sat in the building's shade for a while and wrote some notes for the inspection paperwork, then gathered their packs and started back toward the capital. On the way back, Nemis talked about the fact that the grainhouses of Murro would have a huge renewed popularity if a balcony or deck were put in to allow uedin to view the capital. While he talked, Elenn was distracted by his own thoughts about being large and having body strength that ordinary uedin don't have.

When they neared the Clay Bridge, Nemis said, "I noticed when I was looking out from the top of the grainhouse that many of the streams are not dry yet. Do you think there still might be a running stream under the Clay Bridge? I'd love to drink water from under the Clay Bridge!"

"Let's take a look," said Elenn.

They got to the bridge and looked over the side.

"I don't think there's any stream left. Just mud," said Elenn.

Nemis looked down and said, "Hey, look! Somebody's down there!"

Elenn looked down. There were two uedin coming out from underneath the bridge. They were wearing hoods.

Nemis called, "Hey!" and they both looked up. Elenn immediately recognized one of them as Pavis.

"Any water in the stream?" yelled Nemis.

"Just mud!" yelled up Pavis.

"How did you get down there?" yelled Nemis.

"A path! By that corner!" yelled Pavis, pointing to one of the corners on the capital side of the bridge.

"We're coming down!" yelled Nemis.

Elenn and Nemis finished walking across the bridge and found the path. Not exactly a path, it was more of a passageway formed by erosion from the recent rains, probably something that would have to be repaired. They made their way down and went over to the other two uedin.

Pavis looked surprised when he saw Elenn's face. "Master Elenn," he said, "What are you doing here?" The other hooded uedin was young, one of the second-generation newly-named barren. He looked very flustered, as though he had been caught.

"This is Master Nemis," Elenn said to Pavis and the young master. "We are just getting back from a guard assignment to inspect the grainhouses at Murro, for damage."

"Master Nemis, good to meet you," said Pavis, but his tone was not very friendly. "Masters Elenn and Nemis, this is young Master Tono. He's a cook. Young Master Tono, this is Master Elenn, and Master Nemis."

Tono raised hands to face politely. "Good to meet you, masters," he said, recovering. "Master Elenn, you spoke at the ceremony and were the first to put on your hood. It is my honor meeting you."

"Thank you," said Elenn, returning the gesture. "Master Benar got a laugh out of us at the ceremony, didn't he?"

"We all like him," said Tono. "We're glad he's the senior caretaker."

"Did you find any damage to the grainhouses?" asked Pavis.

"One of them has damage to the roof, and if you go up the ramps on the inside, you can see the capital from the hole in the roof!" said Nemis with excitement.

"That sounds interesting," said Pavis. "Tono lives in the Southgate District, and he was just showing me the Clay Bridge. I had never seen it before."

"What brought you down to this side of the capital?" asked Nemis.

"I'm with the distribution masters," answered Pavis. "I go all over the capital with deliveries." Elenn felt sure that Pavis was covering something up, and he had a pretty good idea what it was. It had been just a matter of one shorter moon cycle since the ceremony of the taking of hood. Was the plan failing already? And yet, Elenn did not feel at all inclined to judge Pavis for his weakness. He pitied him. He thought that Pavis was probably destined for derangement, and Elenn knew how horrible that would be.

"Young master Tono," said Elenn, "have you been given a counselor? To help with matters related to the syndrome?"

"Yes, I have, but I haven't met him yet," said Tono, "and I can't remember his name." Not remembering his counselor's name seemed very unlikely to Elenn, but he did not press the issue.

They looked at the muddy stream bed for a few minutes, then made their way back up to the bridge and walked together back to the capital gate, passing through and continuing part way into the Southgate District. While they walked, Nemis mostly talked about his idea for an observation deck at Murro and how he planned to share his idea with his supervisor and perhaps make a proposal to the masters council.

When Tono reached his lane and said his goodbyes, Elenn said to him, "When you meet with your new counselor, you should definitely tell him about meeting Master Pavis and myself."

"I definitely will," said Tono, with a bit of awkwardness.

Yenca Meets with Master Wanba

When Yenca arrived at the Flatpools District guard station, Wanba was expecting him, but he didn't know why Yenca had requested the meeting. He thought it might have something to do with Elenn. He asked the other guards to leave him alone with Yenca.

"Please come in and sit down, Master Yenca. Is there something we can help you with?" asked Wanba, pouring tea.

"I wanted to talk to you about the hood-taking ceremony," said Yenca.

"I had a chance to talk to Master Embal. He said it did not go quite as planned, but he was satisfied with it."

"Yes, I think the ceremony went well enough."

"It's been a full cycle of the lesser moon. How are they doing with the hoods?"

"That's what I wanted to talk to you about," said Yenca. "We knew from the beginning that there would be some masters who would not be able to keep their oath."

"It's to be expected," said Wanba, "but I understand, it's very serious."

"Some of us caretakers were discussing our concerns, and the question came up of whether the guards might be able to help us keep track of problems as they arise, so that we can respond to them."

"Are you asking if the guards could keep track of syndrome uedin?" asked Wanba with objection already evident in his voice. Yenca noticed that he politely referred to the barren as 'syndrome uedin' in order to emphasize his courteous regard for them, and thus set up an argument that it would be inappropriate to subject them to monitoring.

"I don't mean keep close track of them," said Yenca defensively, "Just keep an eye on them and let us know when you encounter a problem."

"I'm afraid that's impossible, Master Yenca. I'm sure the guards of this or any other district will not want to monitor our masters with hoods. There is nothing in the codes about any of this, and the masters council has not asked us to do anything but respond to barren in derangement." Yenca noticed that now Wanba called them "barren" instead of "syndrome uedin."

"And we will indeed have many barren in derangement, I'm afraid, if we don't control the situation," said Yenca, trying to convey that guard involvement might be necessary.

"But what exactly are we supposed to do if we see them feeding on each other?" argued Wanba, "Demand their names?"

"I think if they just know they are being seen, it will deter them."

"It didn't deter the third and fourth generation barren before they took hood. There were cases when other masters—not only guards but other masters from all walks—came upon them while they were feeding on each other, and they didn't even stop."

"That was before they received hoods. They have a better understanding now of what is expected of them."

"I'm sorry, Master Yenca. You have a very challenging situation. But the guards will not agree to monitor the barren unless they are required to do so by the masters council. And if you propose it to the masters council, we will not be in support of your proposal."

"Master Wanba," said Yenca, hoping for a compromise, "aren't there other guards like Master Elenn, who are wearing the hood?"

Wanba looked down in thought. This did have something to do with Elenn after all. "Yes, there are," he said. "Only Master Elenn here at Flatpools, but each district seems to have one or two others."

"Could we have your permission to recruit those guards with syndrome from around the capital and ask them to monitor their own?"

Wanba's face changed somewhat when he heard this suggestion. It might be the best way for the guards to deal with the situation. If the masters council plan to counter the barren problem with hoods didn't work out, the guards would surely get dragged into it whether they liked it or not. Better to let those guards with barren syndrome have the responsibility from the start.

"That would be worth consideration," answered Wanba finally. "I will get in touch with some of the senior guards from other districts and see what they think."

"That would be very much appreciated!" said Yenca. He smiled at Wanba, but Wanba did not return his smile.

Hood Squadron is Formed

Elenn had no idea why he was called to a meeting at the Central District guard station. Though the Central District was in the very middle of the capital, its guard station was smaller than Flatpools, probably because the district was mostly taken up by the temple compound which was not under master jurisdiction. As soon as he got there, he saw the familiar faces of caretakers Benar and Yenca, as well as senior Flatpools guards Wanba and Henik. There were also a number of senior guards from other districts and caretakers whom he didn't know, as well as three like him who wore both guard's garb and hoods. The three hooded guards looked like second generation young masters. In a short moment, it began to make sense to him. In the same way that he had been urged to speak to the masters council because he was a guard with the syndrome, guards with hoods were now being obviously recruited for some special assignment.

Benar looked up and smiled at him, and Elenn raised hands to face for half a second to briefly greet him, but took a seat next to Henik. After Elenn was seated, another one wearing guard's garb and hood, who looked to be third generation, arrived with the same confused look that Elenn had had a moment earlier, and he was followed by yet another older-looking one who showed the same reaction. Six barren guards had been assembled. Elenn had heard before that he was not alone—that there were other barren guards in the capital—they had just never been easily identifiable without hoods. His interest level rose considerably.

A ro guard, probably the most senior in the room, finally addressed the assembled group. "Master guards and master caretakers, thank you for coming. Today we are going to hear from senior caretaker Master Benar about a joint venture between guards and caretakers that will require your participation. But first, let us all introduce ourselves. My name is Amit, and I am senior guard here at Central District." He raised hands to face in a full but brusk greeting and then directed his eyes to the next uedin sitting beside him to give his name. As the self-introductions continued around the circle, Elenn tried to concentrate on paying attention to names so that he could remember them, but he couldn't help thinking about what the joint venture was going to be. The first thing that popped into his head was the experience he had had with Nemis at Murro. He had understood for the first time that day just how beneficial his barren strength could be. Might they be asked to do something which made use of their physical strength? The introductions were done, and Amit invited Benar to speak. Benar looked a little nervous.

"Well, as I just told you, I'm Benar, senior caretaker to masters with syndrome, and I want to tell you right away that we're here because of a very small problem that we want to address, and we would like to ask for the help of some of you guardmasters. It's a problem with our hooded masters—not all of them, of course, just a few of them, certainly not any of yourselves. You know that it wasn't very long ago that our masters with the syndrome, including you, as we can see, were given hoods to make sure that they didn't do anything that would bypass the medical implants—catheters, that is—that were developed last novade to alleviate symptoms." Benar's eyes darted about as he spoke. He was trying very hard to be friendly. "Yes, that hood idea came from one of our own apprentice caretakers at Quarterhouse. Anyway, putting on those hoods came along with an oath, as you know, that you would not take it off. Well, you take it off just when you take a bath. But otherwise, you wear it all the time, even when you're sleeping. And I hope the hoods have not been too hard to get used to. I think they were designed very well to not get in the way of your daily activities. Well, the problem is a small one, as I said, and we feel sure that it only affects a handful of our syndrome masters. But the thing is, a few of the poor masters have such a hard time keeping their oath. And that's why we want to ask you hooded guards to help them. Help them keep their oath by giving them gentle reminders and encouragement when you see them."

One of the younger hooded guards raised his hand. "Do you mean that we'll join you when you meet with other hooded masters to help encourage them?" he asked.

"Well, not exactly. . ." said Benar, looking at Yenca. "We just want you to keep an eye out for them and encourage them, remind them of their oath, whenever you see them about the capital. Now there may be some whom we know to be having a particularly hard time with their oath, and we'll let you know who they are so that you can watch for them."

Elenn raised his hand. "Will we be able to speak directly with the ones you tell us to look out for? We won't be spying on them, will we?"

"Oh, no, you won't be spying on them. You'll just be keeping an eye out for them. But maybe it's better that they don't know they're being singled out, since that could make them very uncomfortable, don't you agree, Master Yenca?"

Yenca nodded. He looked as though he wanted to take over and explain to everyone what was really expected, but he respectfully deferred to Benar. Benar continued, "Other than the ones that we bring to your attention, it's probably not likely that you'll ever encounter a hooded master who you think is at risk of removing his hood, but if you do, you can talk to us about it, and we'll all try to figure out who it is so that we can help him."

It sounded to Elenn as though they were indeed going to be spying on some of the hooded masters. He thought of when he saw Pavis under the Clay Bridge with that young apprentice.

"Now this next thing is what's going to take some getting used to. We've already met with your senior guard masters, and they've agreed to some changes that are going to affect you right from the start. You won't be working with your fellow guards at your different districts anymore. You'll be working with each other in teams of two. That may be a hard adjustment for some of you. But the good news is, you will have a very easy task, because most of the time you'll just be walking around the capital together, keeping an eye on our hooded masters."

Elenn did not like this development at all. He did not want to work apart from his comrades at Flatpools. But the presence of Wanba and Henik made it clear he wasn't going to have a choice.

"Master Yenca here is one of our third generation caretakers to syndrome masters," said Benar, "and now he's going to give you more details about how you'll be paired up and assigned."

Yenca stood with some notes in his hand. "There are six of you guards with hoods. Masters Umat and Cebik from Northgate District, Master Elenn from Flatpools, Master Nula from Crafting, and Masters Onnek and Posha from Southgate. You will all sleep and take morning and evening meals in your home districts. During the day you will all move throughout the capital depending on where you are needed. Partner assignments will be as follows: Masters Umat and Cebik will work together and report to the Bells caretakers. Masters Elenn and Nula will work together and report to the Quarterhouse caretakers. Masters Onnek and Posha will work together and report to the Whiteroof caretakers." Yenca continued with details about the general recommended routine. Elenn looked at the other hooded guards. Which one was Nula? Nula and he were the odd ones out, so it made sense that the only one looking around like himself must be Nula. He made eye contact and nodded to him. Nula nodded back. He was second generation, one novade younger than Elenn.

When Yenca was finished, Amit spoke again about the importance of their dedication to the assignment, emphasizing that it was a serious guard duty and a great responsibility. Then the senior guards, including Wanba and Henik, left the meeting, and the others broke up into groups. Elenn joined Nula with Benar and Yenca. They talked informally. Nula was somewhat familiar with Quarterhouse. They agreed that they would check in at the Quarterhouse library attached to the main domicile in between the larger meetings of the squadron. The wetuedin were still a few moon cycles away from even taking leg, so it would be some time before the Quarterhouse library would be busy again and they would need to consider a new location.

Later, after the meeting was over, Elenn and Nula walked together from the Central District station to the temple courtyard and talked there. Nula was very reserved.

"You grew up at Crafting?" asked Elenn.

"Yes."

"How did you end up in the guards?"

"My advisor suggested it after I took name. I wasn't good at any of the artisan trades."

"Have they been good to you at the Crafting District guard station?"

"Yes."

Elenn waited for him to ask about his own experience at Flatpools, but Nula didn't ask. Elenn figured that he was young and not used to carrying on conversation.

"Has it been hard for you to adjust to having the hood?"

"I don't like it, but I accept it," said Nula. Hearing this answer, Elenn got the feeling that Nula had probably never had any feeding encounter, perhaps had not yet even experienced the temptation to do so.

"Have you ever seen what happens when one of us goes into derangement?" asked Elenn.

"No," answered Nula.

"Well, as a guard, I'm sure you will," said Elenn, "It's just a matter of time."

"Do you mean that you think there will be some who will take off their hoods and do that. . . thing?"

"You mean feeding."

"Well, they didn't call it that when they informed me that I had the syndrome."

"What did they call it?"

"They just called it consuming skullsap."

"Oh. Well anyhow, yes, I am afraid there will be some who will take off their hoods to do that. That's why we've been given this job."

"I think it's horrible. I can't believe that uedin would do that."

Elenn didn't comment. Just wait, he thought, until you find that you are racked with the desire to do it yourself. He asked Nula, "When did they inform you that you had the syndrome?"

"Just a few days before the ceremony when we were given these hoods," said Nula. "They called us all together. There were about twenty of us in the Crafting District. They explained what barren syndrome was, and they told us that we had tested positive. Then they told us that we would all be getting catheters put in our necks, but that many masters with syndrome have a problem with consuming skullsap from one another, so we would have to wear hoods to keep us from doing it."

"Do you understand why the catheters are necessary?"

"Yes, it's because we would eventually become deranged from our own skullsap. I didn't really understand, though, why anyone would consume skullsap from another uedin."

"Because we are addicted to it," explained Elenn, "We gradually become addicted to it after we reach adulthood."

"We are addicted to it, but it causes our derangement," said Nula.

"Yes, exactly."

"What stops anyone from consuming the skullsap that comes out of his own catheter?"

"It changes after it exits the body," said Elenn. "It doesn't satisfy the addiction anymore."

"But if one uedin with syndrome takes it directly from the neck of another,. . ."

"That's right. It doesn't change if it goes directly from neck to mouth, because it acts as though it's still in the body."

Nula looked unhappy thinking about this.

"Master Nula," said Elenn, "I know that when the caretakers talk about us, they try not to use the word 'barren'. I use it. I hope you won't mind."

"No, that's fine," said Nula. "I understand. We're barren."

Elenn and Ribol Talk in the Bathhouse

When Elenn went to take a bath, he saw there was already a fire going in the small fire cubby on the outside wall of the bathhouse. Somebody was already in there. Given a choice, he would prefer to take a bath alone, but he wouldn't postpone a bath out of embarrassment any more. It had been five years since he had had the catheter implant. When he first had it and had to learn to wash around the catheter and clean the pouch that held expired skullsap, he had been too self-conscious to share the bath with anyone and had carefully chosen odd hours so that he could take his bath alone. But over time, he had relaxed about it somewhat. He wondered who was inside.

When he moved the door tarp and entered, he saw Ribol's head sticking out of the surface of the hot pool that was built into the floor.

"Hello Master Ribol," said Elenn. "Is it all right if I wash up in here?"

"Oh, yeah, I'm already done, I'm just having a little soak," said Ribol.

Elenn removed his footwear, went in, took off his garb, and hung it on a peg. Ribol scootched his legs aside for Elenn to get a bucket of the hot water. Then Elenn went to the corner, sat on a small bath stool, and pulled off his hood. As soon as the hood came off, the air felt good against his head. He placed the hood on the wet floor beside him and poured some of the hot water over his shoulders and head.

"Hot water feels pretty good, don't it?" said Ribol.

"It sure does," said Elenn, as he commenced to wash himself from his feet up. When he got to his neck, he undid the neckstrap and disconnected the pouch. He reached over to hold the pouch carefully over the floor drain while he squeezed out the cool, grayish fluid that had accumulated since the day before. Then he washed out the pouch with the remainder of hot water that was in the bucket. He emptied the bucket out carefully around the drain to wash it down and stepped over to refill it.

"Excuse me again," he said while dunking the bucket in the hot water a second time, and he lifted it back to his corner. While he was delicately washing around the catheter implant, he saw Ribol stealing a peek out of the corner of his eye.

Elenn felt bold. "You want to see it?" he asked, and stepped over and knelt beside Ribol so that Ribol could see the implant in his neck.

Ribol leaned over a little bit to get a good look. "You 'din with that syndrome have a tough time, don't you. It must be so hard dealing with that. I don't how I'd get along if I had that. I respect all of you." Then he added, "It must have hurt pretty bad when they put that in your neck."

"It did at first. It doesn't hurt at all anymore," said Elenn.

"I'd say the hurt of putting that in is sure worth it," said Ribol, "cause at least it ain't like it used to be. I'll never forget Master Leci, that's for sure."

Master Leci? Elenn did not recall ever hearing of him. "Who was Master Leci?" he asked.

"That's right. Nobody even remembers Master Leci. But I do. See, I think maybe we were so little when he left, my generation, we were just too small to remember. And the next generation up was probably just newly-named, and they were apprentices, and they just didn't talk about it. And the older tutors and caretakers at Quarterhouse just didn't even want to think about it, so they probably didn't talk about it either. So everyone just forgot him!"

"He was a Quarterhouse tutor? Or a caretaker?" asked Elenn, getting very curious.

"Master Leci was a tutor. He taught us how to get dressed by ourselves. And you probably think that's such an easy thing to do, but I was very little, and I had a very hard time with it. All the other child-uedin had it all learned up, and they had all moved on to learn other things. But oh, I just couldn't get that sorted out, all the pulling and turning sleeves right-side out, and making sure it's not backwards. Oh, I dreaded having to practice that with Master Leci. I really was scared I wasn't ever going to get it, that I was different from the other child-uedin, and oh, let me tell you, I was a very little little child-uedin, and that was the beginning a very hard early childhood for me."

"Was he stern with you?" asked Elenn.

"Oh, no, he was so patient, you can't even imagine. He got me through it. Oh, I loved Master Leci. Loved him more than I ever loved any master."

"Was he a ro-master?" asked Elenn.

"No! He was young! I remember his face, and he wasn't a ro at all, no, Master Leci was pretty young. That's how I figured it out."

"What's that?" asked Elenn.

"Before I finished learning how to talk, Master Leci just disappeared. And I missed him so bad, I was terribly upset. And it took me years and years to figure out what happened to him. When I asked about him, it made me so angry when my tutors and caretakers would say, 'Who was Master Leci? Oh, you must be thinking about someone else. That must have been Master So-and-So that taught you how to put your clothes on,' and I knew they were just telling me that because I was too small. It wasn't till after I became a guard and had to try to help out 'din like you all. I understood that barren—oh I'm sorry I mean uedin with syndrome—"

"It's all right, I use the word 'barren,'" said Elenn, "Go on."

"Well, I understood that they go through these changes, and they go like they're raving even though they're not really raving, and then, in the end, they go out in the desert, and the sun kills them. Oh, it must be so horrible—I can't imagine it. And I know, I just know, that that's what happened to Master Leci. And it breaks my heart."

Elenn choked up, hearing this. A storm of thoughts and feelings came up for him. He didn't know what to say. Maybe it was best that catheters had been invented to help the barren, and maybe it was best that they were wearing hoods now to keep them from derangement. His work with this new syndrome squad was very important work, and the few on the squad were really the right ones to be doing it. But how could they do it on their own?

He was thinking about this when Ribol said, "So yes, I really do care about you 'din with the syndrome, and I can't tell you how I hope you and those guards on the squad do a fine job with it."

Elenn swallowed. "Well, we'll do the very best job we can do, Master Ribol. Thank you for telling me about Master Leci."

Ribol changed the subject. "Did you know I cut two of my fingers off one time?"

"Is that right?" said Elenn.

Ribol held up his hand and said, "Yeah, they grew back."

"You must have been young."

"Yeah, I was just an apprentice. If it had happened when I was any older, probably wouldn't have grown back," he said.

"How did that happen?" asked Elenn.

"Master Henik and I had a big pile of fern-root. We took it over to the Quarterhouse kitchen to grind it up."

"You and Master Henik are same generation, aren't you?" asked Elenn.

"Yeah. We're seventh gen. The biggest one—five hundred and eighty."

Same as Master Benar, thought Elenn. "So you two were apprentices together?"

"Yeah. We had this big pile of fern-root, and we were running it through the grinder real fast. Master Henik was turning the crank, and I was feeding the fern-root into the grinder. We started going faster and faster, having fun seeing how fast we could go, and I wasn't careful enough, and I got my hand caught. Lost two fingers."

"How long did it take for them to grow back?"

"Oh it took about a year," said Ribol. "I was so glad they grew back. Wasn't sure if I'd get them back or not. They're just a little bit smaller than my other fingers." He held his hand up for Elenn to see.

"Ah, yes, I can see." Elenn smiled at Ribol, and then went back to his corner to wash his hood.

"Master Henik told me you was on special duty now, looking after other 'din with the syndrome. I guess that's a good thing, you all can look after one another."

"I hope it's a good thing. I don't know what to expect. We haven't had these hoods long enough to know for sure whether they're going to fix things or not."

"They should have made you leader of that squadron. You was the one that talked to the masters council, and you put on the hood before anybody else, right?"

"Oh, I don't need to be the leader. There are just six of us, and we report to the caretakers. They can tell us what to do."

"That is exactly how I feel about being a leader, too," said Ribol, rising to get out of the hot pool. "That's why I never went after any kind of rank. There's always some 'din that wants to be in command. Let him, that's what I say!" He got out and reached for his towel, then began to dry off. Elenn noticed the sag of his belly, showing his age. He seemed older than Benar and Henik, both in appearance and in manner. He already had the air of a kindly old ro.

"Well, Master Ribol, I do agree with you. And I don't intend to take on any more responsibility than I'm asked to take," said Elenn. In his mind, though, he was still thinking about how hard the work of the syndrome squadron was going to be. Just how much would they be expected to police the barren? And how bad could it get?

While Ribol got dressed, Elenn rubbed the cloth sides of his hood against each other with a bit of soap to wash it and then rinsed it. He walked over, pushed the door tarp open and laid the wet hood on the bathhouse stoop in the sun to dry. He turned around and saw that Ribol was dressed and on his way out.

"It was good talking to you, Master Elenn. I hope everything goes well for you," he said.

"Thank you, Master Ribol. Have a nice day, and I'll see you at evening meal."

Ribol left, and Elenn went in and stepped into the hot pool. He lowered himself down and leaned back against the wall of the pool. Then he stared blankly at the steam-softened view of the empty bathhouse interior. The more he thought about it, the more he started to think that the situation with hoods was probably going to get very bad. They would need a lot of help. The caretakers wanted to coach them, but would the caretakers be ready to get directly involved in confrontations when barren were actually feeding? They wouldn't want to cross that line, they would be afraid of losing the trust of their counselees. And the other guards who weren't barren would be very unprepared to step in. The squadron would need support from other barren masters who were willing to get involved, those who didn't get caught up in the feeding. But how would the squadron enlist their help? Well, it was too early to start worrying about that. They didn't even know how much of a hard time the barren were going to have with keeping their hoods in place. Elenn told himself this, and that maybe it wasn't going to be such a bad situation, he just had to wait and see. Don't worry about disaster before it strikes. He slid his bottom away from the wall of the hot pool and dunked his head in the hot water.

Elenn and Nula Remind Hoodwearers to Keep their Oath

For the first moon cycle after the squadron was formed, Elenn was relieved to find that the masters with hoods were very glad to have their presence and encouragement. Also, Nula relaxed considerably and seemed to embrace the work. He even started repeating the same line that Elenn used when they met masters with hoods—"Just coming around to say be strong and remember your oath." Nula used the exact words. Elenn got in the habit of letting Nula say it, since most of the hooded were of his generation. He was finding it sufficient to concentrate on the success of the squadron in general and didn't find it necessary to be in the forefront.

It was a second-generation master with a hood whom they saw in the Northgate District one day, pushing a cart of firewood. They noticed how he stopped immediately and put down the cart as soon as he saw them.

The young hooded one greeted them by saying, "Such a nice day, lovely clouds!" He was not shy.

"Just coming around to say be strong and remember your oath," said Nula to the young master.

"Oh I am, I am," he said. "And I'm glad to see you. I'm sure any master with a hood is glad to see you. We know about the hood squad. We admire you."

Elenn was fascinated with the name *"hood squad."* The squadron members had not come up with the name "hood squad" themselves. . . Elenn didn't know where it had started. "Not all masters with hoods are glad to see us," said Elenn. "But thank you for your kind words. How do you know about the squadron?" he asked.

"Our counselors told us you came together to help us keep our oath," said the young worker. "I'm very honored to meet you in person."

"What is your name, young master?" asked Elenn.

"I'm Serka. Second-generation outfield worker."

"Thank you for your support," said Elenn.

"Oh, I want to support you however I can," said Serka. "There are three of us with hoods in the western outfield. We all hope you'll come to the outfield sometime, we would be very glad to see any of you from the *squadron*." Elenn couldn't help noticing that the young master didn't say "hood squad" and knew that it was because Elenn himself had used "squadron." The young master was deeply respectful, and Elenn and Nula both felt his respect.

"We should go and visit them sometime, Master Elenn," said Nula, politely acknowledging Serka's invitation.

"Maybe we will. For now, please pass on our message. Tell your fellow workers to be strong and remember their oath," said Elenn, good-naturedly saying what he thought Serka would like to hear.

"I will. I can't wait to tell them I saw you!"

"But most importantly, to be strong and remember the oath," said Nula with innocence.

"Do you all have good counselors?" asked Elenn.

"Yes, we do, here in Northgate."

"I'm glad to hear it," said Elenn. "Well, have a good day."

"See you again!" said Serka.

Elenn and Nula spent the rest of the day in the north part of the capital. Besides looking out for masters with hoods in the busier neighborhoods around Bells, they also walked through empty places, like the old drying barns which weren't being used during the early green season, and even the drystreams outside the north wall, although the area was still muddy. Elenn was optimistic that he wouldn't find anyone there, and he was happy when he did not. Nula understood without being told that when they check the empty places they were making sure that no barren were feeding there. He dreaded the day when they might actually come upon such a scene.

Later, that evening, Elenn stopped for a brief chat with Master Benar. Benar sat and peeled fieldpears while he listened to Elenn talk about how things were going with the squadron.

". . . And young Master Nula is taking to it very well. I'm glad to be working with him."

"Well, he seems like a fine young guard,"

"He is a. . ." Elenn was going to say the word "delight," but he thought that wouldn't sound proper. ". . .fine young guard, indeed."

"You may need to give him some direction. I know his counselor, Master Yinob. He is one of those overly soft-hearted caretakers," said Benar, eyebrows raised.

"But I'm sure he's a very good counselor," said Elenn. He was glad that Nula had a soft-hearted caretaker for his counselor.

"Well, it's important to be kind and caring," said Benar, "as long as you don't neglect to give good guidance."

Elenn liked Benar, but when he said things like that, Elenn was even less inclined to share too much about what he was going through on a personal level. He was not going to say anything more about young Master Nula.

Benar and Yenca Watch Wet-uedin Taking Leg

Nearly a year had passed since the Great Rains. Since Benar and Yenca were syndrome caretakers, they didn't often go to the hatching pool and didn't get to watch the wet-uedin develop. When they heard that some of them were starting to take leg, they decided to take a walk and see them together.

On the way, Benar said, "Now, we're not going to talk about syndrome stuff. I want to put all that out of my mind and just pay attention to the wet ones taking leg."

"That sounds just fine to me," said Yenca.

"Oh, it seems like such a long time since I've been here," said Benar when they neared the hatching pool observation deck. "It used to be all the time when I was a caretaker to the unnamed."

"I've only been here a few times, myself," said Yenca. He hadn't even been a caretaker until he had nearly completed his apprenticeship with Domas, and then it was straight into the corps for syndrome uedin.

"Oh, wait till you see them," said Benar. "They are so remarkable. You'll never forget it if you get to see one come out of the water for the first time."

"I hope I get to see that," said Yenca as they climbed the stairs up to the deck.

There were quite a few Quarterhouse caretakers on the deck, but no tutors. Only caretakers were allowed to be there during the taking of leg. It was no good to have crowds with noise. With just the caretakers there to do their important work, it was very quiet.

"We're lucky they let us come in, even though we're syndrome caretakers, not caretakers to the unnamed," whispered Yenca to Benar.

"I would have never stood for it if they had tried to keep us out!" Benar whispered back with a grin.

There were thick woven mats laid on rocks near the edge of the hatching pool, and caretakers huddled around the recently emerged baby-uedin with bowls of mashed grain, water, and piles of small wet blankets. Wet ones needed to have their skin kept wet for their first few days. From one group, Yenca could hear the sound of a funny little voice crying.

"Don't worry about the crying," Benar said, still whispering, "That's the first thing they do when they come out."

In the shallows all around the pool, the little ones rested with their bellies down, heads poking up out of the water, with little mounds of bubbles in front of their mouths and noses as they adjusted to breathing with lungs. Some of them had whitish remnants of fin and webbing clinging to them, especially around their hands and feet.

"Come on. Let's go across to that side. I think we might get a good look at a baby-uedin." They walked across to the far side of the deck and looked down at two caretakers fussing over a small one. Benar and Yenca could see it clearly. It was just as Yenca had envisioned, a fully developed child-uedin, just smaller and plumper, with a very indistinct look on its face.

"It's beautiful," said Yenca.

"Isn't it?" agreed Benar.

They watched it for a long time. For a moment, it looked as though the baby-uedin had spotted them and was looking right back, but then it kept moving its gaze around to everything.

Suddenly there was a little cry from the periphery. Benar patted Yenca's shoulder quickly and said, "Come, come, come, come, come!" They tip-toed excitedly over to the midsection of the rail and looked down. Two caretakers were already moving towards the wet one with mats. It was a baby-uedin, propping itself up on its arms and trying to kick its way up and out of the water. It cried and gasped as its mound of bubbles trailed down its side. The caretakers put a mat right up to its chest, each took an arm, and they pulled it out of the water and up onto the mat. Then one steadied it there while the other arranged other mats for them to sit around it. As soon as they were situated, they bent down, gently placed a wet blanket over its legs, and started saying something quietly into the baby-uedin's ears.

"What are they doing?"

"They're whispering the Names," said Benar. "The first thing a wet one hears when it takes leg is the Names of the Lern."

"I didn't know that," said Yenca. He was deeply touched. "It's a wonderful thing we're seeing right now, isn't it?"

"I told you. You'll never forget seeing this," said Benar, almost inaudibly.

Again, they remained there standing still and watching for a long time. They thought maybe they might see another one coming out of the pool, but it remained quiet, and finally, the afternoon light reminded them that it was time to head back and start preparing the evening meal.

Walking back, Yenca thanked Benar. "I know I am a caretaker, but I probably wouldn't have gone if you had not invited me to come with you."

"I think it's something all caretakers should see," said Benar.

"It is a joyous occasion," agreed Yenca, although it wasn't so simple to put away worries. Even while he had been looking down at the new baby-uedin, his mind couldn't fend off thoughts about the syndrome. He knew that many of the new generation were probably going to end up being barren—that seemed to be the trend. More sorrow, more struggle, more challenge.

Tell or Be Told On

Young guardmaster Nula had come to accept his duty as a member of the squadron to support the keeping of the hood oath, and he very much liked working with Master Elenn. Master Elenn was the first uedin of an older generation with whom he had ever formed a close friendship. In Nula's mind, Master Elenn seemed to be resigned to his life with barren syndrome, able to cope with it with great strength of character, and very serious about keeping his oath. Nula wished that he could be exactly the same way. Nula definitely took the oath seriously, but little by little he was understanding how hard it was going to be. The daily routine of traversing the capital to remind barren masters to keep their oath was getting complicated. In the first place, it had become very clear that not everyone with a hood on wanted to hear the message of encouragement. Secondly, as Nula experienced his first stirrings of temptation, he felt like a fraud. He had already seen hooded masters of his own generation loitering in places where Master Elenn said that feeding was probably taking place, and seeing them opened up the idea that he too could choose to have the experience if he wanted it. He didn't want it, but it frightened him that it was a possibility, and sometimes he dreamt about being in tempting situations. Whenever he had a dream like that, it bothered him greatly, and he wanted to ask

Master Elenn about it, but he was too embarrassed. Even though Master Elenn was very open with him, he was not ready to admit that he felt temptation.

They were checking out the area around the western gate not far from Crafting, where Nula had grown up. According to Elenn, the area near the edge of the woods was once frequented by barren before the taking of hood, and he suspected that it was still visited by some who were seeking to feed. They had made it a custom to talk loudly whenever approaching a spot where feeding might be taking place, so that they could give the offenders a fair warning of their presence.

"Before the taking of hoods, there were some who came here to give their necks to each other," Elenn spoke in a fairly loud voice so that anyone within earshot of them could hear him. Then he added quietly to Nula, "I know because I was one of them." Elenn had told Nula rather early in their partnering together that he felt it would serve them best if he communicated as openly as possible, and Nula was no longer surprised by such admissions of past feeding.

"Anyone here?" he called out, resuming his loud voice.

"Anyone here?" called Nula.

Two unhooded masters called from a short distance off the side of the West Road. "Hello!" one of them hollered. Elenn and Nula headed toward them. They were both holding small baskets of mushrooms. As they got closer, Nula could clearly see what was going on. They were normally hooded masters who had their hoods off and were trying to pretend that they were not barren by standing a little bit back in the woods and facing carefully toward the guards to avoid letting their neckstraps be seen. They were clearly second and third generation, the larger one being the older. Their sizes and ages mirrored Elenn and Nula. Nula wondered if it embarrassed Elenn as it did him.

"We're just out here picking mushrooms," said the older one.

"I'm guardmaster Elenn, and this is guardmaster Nula," said Elenn. He waited for them to offer their names.

"We're from Whiteroof. We just came out to get some of these mushrooms," said the older one, trying to avoid giving his name.

Nula let Elenn determine their course of action. He had noticed that there were times when Elenn would turn a blind eye toward two barren who were obviously feeding, and other times he would confront them. This time, Elenn seemed intent on intervening. Perhaps he didn't like the fact that an older master was initiating a younger master. It seemed to Nula that they had seen that third generation master's face before around the capital in places where it wasn't clear that he had any business.

"What are your names, please?" asked Elenn directly.

Both of the strangers looked back at him with resentment. They were caught, and they were very unhappy about it. "Must you really require our names?" asked the older one.

"Just tell us to remember our oath and then leave us alone," said the younger one. Nula thought that was a very rude thing to say, but he still felt sorry for both of them.

"You are third generation, same as me," said Elenn to the older one, "It is our job to show an example to the newly-named. Tell me your name. Your counselor needs to know what you are doing."

"My counselor only needs to know what I choose to tell him," said the larger uedin.

"That's not the way it works anymore. Our numbers in the capital are too high, and mass derangement is a real danger if the hood statute fails. The caretakers are in a very critical position, and they need to know what is happening. Please tell me your name."

"I am. . . Teku," answered the larger master. Nula wouldn't ordinarily think that any master would actually lie about his own name, but at this point, he had so little trust or respect left that he immediately suspected that Teku was not his real name.

"And what is your work in the capital, Master Teku?" Elenn asked.

"We are both groundskeepers at Whiteroof," he answered.

"Put your hoods back on. We're following you back to Whiteroof," said Elenn.

"Please don't!" yelled the younger one.

"That's really not necessary," said the older one.

"What is *your* name, young master?" asked Elenn.

The younger master reached down to the ground and retrieved his hood. He looked off to the side trying to avoid eye contact. He didn't want to give his name either. He acted as though he were taking his time to get his hood on correctly, then suddenly started running toward the capital gate. Nula ran after him. His training with the Crafting guards had included a good deal of running, and he was easily able to overtake the young offender. He felt quite confident in his ability to apprehend him as well, until the young master, apparently in a panic, kicked Nula hard in the leg in his effort to resist being held. Nula felt a moment of anger, but the pain in his shin was no match to the obvious terror that this young uedin felt, and Nula only wanted to keep him from running away so that they could do their job. Nula quickly grabbed his arm, pulled it behind his back, and got him into a tight arm-lock. When the young offender squirmed against the arm-lock, even to the point of injuring his own shoulder joint, Nula pulled him tight and held on.

"I'll tell you! I'll tell you my name!" he cried.

"Shhh," said Nula. He was listening to hear what Elenn and the other barren were saying.

"Don't you see what you're doing? You're making criminals out of us!" The larger barren yelled.

"Don't you see what *you're* doing? You're headed for disaster!" shouted Elenn.

"No," answered the barren. "Disaster came when I was born."

As Nula held on, the younger barren seemed to submit as he too concentrated on hearing the exchange.

"Let's go," Elenn said. "We're going to Whiteroof, if that's where you say you're from."

There was no response, and Nula craned his neck to get a look at what was going on. The barren took two steps toward Elenn and then dashed off in the opposite direction down the West Road that led deeper into the woods. At first, it looked like Elenn was going to chase him, but then he just stopped and let him go. He turned and looked toward Nula.

"I've got the other oath-breaker in a good hold, if you want to go after him!" Nula shouted.

"I don't think we can help that one right now," answered Elenn starting toward them, "But we can help the younger one."

"You let *him* go! Why won't you let *me* go?!" complained the young master under Nula's grip. Nula could smell his breath. He was fascinated by the scent.

"We can't let you go until you at least talk to us," said Elenn as he approached.

"Please! Please don't make me tell my counselor!" He began to cry like an unnamed.

"What is your name, young master? We are only trying to help you," said Elenn. He now put his hand on the young master's shoulder and gestured to Nula to keep him tight in the arm-lock.

The hooded youth turned and looked at Elenn. "If I tell you my real name, will you promise not to report me?"

"Now, you know that you have to be reported. Your counselor needs to know about your trouble. You can cooperate and walk calmly with us, for your own good, or we can drag you to the Crafting District station. What is the name of that third-generation master? You're going to have to tell us."

"I don't know his name!" cried the young master. "Please let go of my arm. I'll walk with you. I'll tell you everything I know."

"Don't try to run again," said Elenn. "There are two of us, and we will not let you get away."

"I won't run. Let go of my arm, and I'll tell you everything. I'll do whatever you say." Elenn nodded for Nula to release the arm-lock.

"Start with your name and your work in the capital," said Elenn.

"I'm Chibo, and I'm an apprentice groundskeeper at Whiteroof. But the other master I was with is not from Whiteroof. I don't know anything about him. He approached me a few days ago at the drystream north of the capital where I was getting a cart of gravel. Well, we approached each other. I knew that some masters were feeding at the drystream up there—Whiteroof didn't even need the gravel. We gave our necks to each other there. It was my first time. It was scary. . . but I liked it. I wanted to meet him again. We were going to meet at the same place, but when we went there the next time, some other hooded guards, just like you two, were there to tell us to keep our oath. So we left, and he told me to meet him here outside the western gate. He said to bring a basket so that we could say we were here to pick mushrooms. He never told me his name, and I didn't ask for it. I didn't tell him my name either."

"And the two of you met here and gave each other your necks? Was this your second time?" asked Elenn.

The young Chibo had an unpleasant look on his face, showing that he wasn't enjoying these questions. "No, I did it one time in between—with a second generation master I saw at the bartering yards. I led him to an alley in the Central District. This time with the older master was my third time. I know I'll never be able to stop."

"You must!" snapped Elenn. "If you don't, you'll become deranged! You know that!"

"I know it, but I don't think I'll be able to stop myself," said the young master miserably.

"Your counselor will help you," said Elenn, unmoved.

Nula had hardly spoken through the whole encounter. He was very upset by the whole thing. He was upset because he didn't like getting other masters in trouble. But there was something else on top of that. While he had had this apprentice groundskeeper in an armlock, he had held him tight from behind with his face practically rubbing in the young uedin's neckstrap. He found it terribly arousing. Now he was trying to act with a guard's authority alongside Master Elenn, but he could not put the conflict out of his mind. He and Master Elenn were going to march this Chibo all the way to Whiteroof to report his behavior to his counselor, even while Nula himself secretly felt a powerful desire to do the same thing that Chibo had done.

They went through the western gate and started through the Crafting District. Nula could see that the young groundskeeper was exhausted and docile. He was not going to make a run for it. He walked alongside them, hanging his head. He clearly didn't want to see other masters' faces when they saw him being escorted, a hooded master escorted by two hooded guards. It made it very obvious to everyone that he had been caught feeding. Nula imagined his shame and felt sorry for him.

The march through the streets at the height of mid-day activity only grew more and more uncomfortable as they made their way through the capital. Nula knew that Elenn felt uncomfortable too, because he gradually opted for the back streets to avoid drawing attention. Nula tried to reassure himself that they were doing an important job. As unpleasant a situation as it was, they had no choice but to accompany this young master Chibo back to report his behavior to his caretaker. It was for his own good, and the future of the capital would be at risk if they let such things go without taking action. This was what it meant to do the job of the squadron. It was their duty.

When they reached Whiteroof, Chibo stopped walking suddenly and looked at them both with tears in his eyes. "Please," he begged, "Please don't make me tell Master Yuri. I don't want to tell him." He started crying again.

Elenn was stern with him, "Young master, get a hold of yourself. There is no avoiding this. It is for your own good. Let's get it over with."

Chibo walked them to a row of huts behind the main domicile of Whiteroof where baby uedin could be heard crying inside. A middle-aged caretaker was sweeping outside one of the huts. He looked at the two guards escorting Chibo to him and stopped sweeping. He regarded them all with a very serious look in his eyes, and then dropped his broom and held open his arms. Chibo ran to him, put his arms around him, and fell to his knees, sobbing.

"Master Yuri, I'm so sorry!" he said with his sobbing voice trembling, "I know I've disappointed you!" His shoulders shook with his crying.

"It's all right, young Master Chibo," said the counselor tenderly, patting Chibo on the back, "It's going to be all right."

"I'm sorry," Chibo continued, crying with his face buried in Yuri's caretaker robe. Nula could not stand to see it. He turned his back and looked in the opposite direction, taking a deep breath to try to suppress the emotion he was feeling.

Elenn spoke to the caretaker. "I'm Elenn of Flatpools, and this is Master Nula from Crafting District. You are Master Yuri?"

"Yes, I am Whitehouse caretaker Yuri," answered the master, raising one hand to face as the other hand held the shoulder of young Chibo. "Thank you for bringing young Master Chibo back to me. You don't have to explain anything. I understand everything."

"I felt that it was very important for you to know what was happening. A third generation master was with young Master Chibo. It is a very dangerous situation."

"Yes, I understand. You did the right thing." He looked down at his counselee. "Young Master Chibo," he said, "It is good that it happened this way. We will get control of this problem."

"I can't stop myself," said Chibo, his voice muffled in Yuri's robe.

Yuri looked down with a face that reflected both sadness and kindness, saying, "Yes you can. You can, and you will."

"Thank you for your service, Master Yuri," said Elenn. He raised hands to face, and Nula turned to do likewise.

"Thank you, Masters," said Yuri. "Thank both of you for your important service to the capital."

To Nula, Elenn seemed to receive this compliment with the proud bearing of a guard, but Nula was too conflicted to consider that the work of the squadron was indeed an important service to the capital. All he could think about was how it felt like a terrible lie to report another young master for something that he himself might not have the strength to resist. He felt unworthy to wear his guard's robe.

Outfield Workers

Serka was standing and sharpening a scythe to use in the flax-fields when one of the older workers came to tell him that two hood squadron guardmasters had arrived at the workhouse and were asking for him. He was completely surprised by this news. He had met two hood squad guards while delivering a cart of firewood, a gift from Master Tamo to someone Tamo knew who lived in the Northgate District. Master Tamo was one of the elders of the workhouse and had many friends in the capital. It had been Serka's first time encountering the hood squad, and he had been very impressed by them. When he told them to come visit him and his other two hooded friends at the western outfields, he had wondered to himself if they might actually do it. And here they were, coming to visit! He put down the scythe and sharpening stone.

"Where are they? Did they just get here?"

"They're talking with Master Ghera in the kitchen. They said they're here specifically to visit you. Do you know them?"

What were their names, what were their names? Serka could not remember. The one his age was Nu-something. *Nuren? Nulo?* As for the older one's name, he had no idea. "I don't really know them, but I met them when I was taking Master Tamo's firewood to Northgate." Serka was following the older outfield worker to the workhouse, but he was too excited to walk. "Do you mind if I run ahead?" he asked.

"Go ahead, but there's no rush. They just got here."

Serka ran toward the workhouse. He couldn't believe the two hood squad guards were actually there. He would have to get Leol and Jeber, the other outfield workers who were, just like him, second generation and in hoods. When he had gotten back from the capital that day and told them about meeting hood squad guards at Northgate, they had been jealous. He wondered if the guards would stay overnight. Maybe they could all have an outdoor fire and stay up late talking. He ran straight to the workhouse kitchen. He heard them laughing just as he got there.

". . .and that whole batch of soap got thrown out because it smelled so bad!" Ghera was telling them one of his many stories. He liked to talk. "Oh, here's young Master Serka now," he said, seeing Serka arrive, all out of breath.

"Hello!. . ." he bent over a little to catch his breath, "Welcome!"

"Young Master Serka, you told us to come visit you, so here we are!" said Elenn with a smile.

"Hello, Master Serka," said Nula.

"Master Elenn and Master Nula told me that you met them up in the capital."

That's what their names were! Elenn and Nula! Serka was so glad that Master Ghera had said the names. "Yes, we met at Northgate!" answered Serka, still out of breath.

"I believe you said there were other hooded masters here?" asked Elenn.

"Yes. Master Leol and Master Jeber are here too. There are three of us. We're all second generation."

"They are all very good young uedin," said Ghera to Elenn, "all three of them."

"Master Ghera, may I go and get Masters Leol and Jeber right now?"

"No, let them finish their chores. They'll see the guardmasters at evening meal. Master Elenn and Master Nula are going to be spending the night with us."

"Great!" said Serka, thrilled with the news.

"Have you finished your chores yet?"

"I have to finish sharpening a scythe for Master Orbof, and I have to feed the silkworms."

"Well, go on and finish that. I'm going to get some bedding ready for the guardmasters."

"Can we have an outdoor fire tonight? Please?"

"You'll have to ask Master Tamo," said Ghera.

"He'll let me. If I tell him that the guardmasters are here for the night."

"He might, if you get your chores done first," answered Ghera.

"I'll see you later then, Master Elenn and Master Nula. I'm so glad you've come! We'll have an outdoor fire!" said Serka.

"All right! See you later on!" said Elenn.

"Can I help you with your chores?" asked Nula. "I've never seen silkworms."

"Would it be okay, Master Ghera?" asked Serka.

"I suppose it's all right," said Ghera. "As long as you get it done."

"May I, Master Elenn?" Nula asked his senior guard.

Elenn thought momentarily about letting the two hooded young masters go together. He didn't think he needed to worry about them tempting one another. They were both very dedicated to the oath, from what he could see.

"Go ahead," Elenn answered. "I'll stay here and see if there's anything I can do to lend a hand."

The two young masters went back to the tool shed where Serka had left the scythe and sharpening stone on the ground.

"Tell me about life with the guardmasters," said Serka, picking up the stone and scythe.

"I thought I would just be doing normal things around the capital, helping out with normal duties or when accidents happened. I'm from Crafting. I had no idea I'd be all over the capital, doing this sort of thing," said Nula.

"Well, we didn't know we even had syndrome when we chose assignments," said Serka.

"When I joined the guards, I thought the hardest thing would be the physical work, but it's not."

"You *do* like being on the squadron, don't you? Isn't it exciting?"

"It's very difficult," said Nula. "We are starting to have to argue with masters who don't want to keep the oath."

"There are masters who come right out an say they don't want to keep the oath?"

"They don't say it to everybody, but they don't want to, and they let us know."

"They must be third or fourth generation masters, right?"

"Some second generation masters don't want to keep the oath either," said Nula.

"Second generation masters—like us?"

"Some of them don't want to keep the oath. Every day we're seeing more and more signs that masters are breaking their oath. And there are only six guards on the squadron, trying to keep watch over the whole capital."

"I didn't know hooded masters were breaking the oath. That's terrible," said Serka.

"It's a terrible problem," said Nula. He didn't know what else to say about it though. It wasn't a job for masters who weren't barren, and it wasn't a job for masters who weren't guards. The six masters in the squadron were the only ones who could do it. Serka was now running the sharpening stone back and forth along the blade of the scythe.

"Can I try that?" he asked, changing the subject.

"Sure. Here, hold the scythe like this," Serka positioned the implement in Nula's hand so that he would have the best angle for sharpening. Nula took over the sharpening for a little while. After they finished sharpening the scythe and testing it out in some weeds, Serka put the scythe away in the corner of the toolshed and picked through a small box of short-blade knives to find two good ones for Nula and him to use for something.

"Come on," said Serka. "We're going to get some mulberry leaves for the silkworms." He led Nula to a small grove of mulberry bushes and showed him how to cut the right size of tiny branches that could easily be bunched together and held in one hand.

While they were cutting mulberry twigs, Serka finally spoke again, saying, "I just can't understand why any barren uedin would not want to keep his oath."

"I think they just give up on it," said Nula.

"What do you mean? How can they give up on it? Don't they care if they become deranged?"

"I don't know. Maybe they know but they can't help themselves."

"Well I think it's just terrible," said Serka.

"It *is* terrible. I've come close to seeing it first hand."

"What have you seen?"

"I've seen masters that were supposed to have hoods on, and they didn't. Once I saw two barren masters who had just finished doing that thing, consuming skullsap."

"You mean *feeding*."

"Yes. Master Elenn told me that they had just done it. He could tell by the looks on their faces."

"What did they look like?"

"They looked normal to me, but Master Elenn said he could tell by their looks," said Nula.

"You said that there were even second generation uedin, like us, doing it?"

"We saw one not long ago. It was very sad, though."

"Why?"

"We made him take us to his counselor, and he was so ashamed, he started crying."

"Crying?"

"He did. He was crying like an unnamed."

"You're right, that is pretty sad," agreed Serka. "but he broke the oath, didn't he?"

"He definitely did," said Nula. He secretly wanted to ask, *Have you never felt temptation?* But if he asked that, Serka would know that he himself had indeed felt temptation before, and he didn't want anyone to know that. He hadn't even talked to his own counselor about that yet.

"Well, I think you're very lucky," said Serka. "It must be such an honor to be a guard on the hood squadron. And you're lucky that you have Master Elenn to explain everything."

"I do feel lucky to work with Master Elenn," said Nula.

When they both had large bundles of mulberry twigs, Serka took Nula to a small cabin that stood behind the workhouse. Inside were the lidded crates that held the silkworms. Serka let Nula look at them up close, and then they distributed the mulberry leaves and left them alone.

Later, Serka introduced Elenn and Nula to Leol and Jeber when they arrived for the evening meal. The large room adjacent to the kitchen had an odd collection of tables and mismatched chairs where workers were now sitting down for their meal. Leol and Jeber were a little more reserved than Serka. They seemed very glad to meet the guards, but they didn't talk a lot. When the elder Tamo came to their table to greet the guests, Serka asked him immediately, "Can we have an outdoor fire tonight after we do clean-up?"

"Wait a minute, young master," said Tamo. "I haven't even met our guests yet." He turned to Elenn and Nula. "I am Tamo, senior worker here. Master Ghera tells me you're from Flatpools District?"

"I am," said Elenn. "I'm Elenn, third generation. Young Master Nula is from Crafting."

"Oh, you're from Crafting?" said Tamo to Nula. "Right inside the gate here?"

"Yes, well, I joined the Crafting District Guards, but now I work with Master Elenn on the squadron, and we report to Quarterhouse caretakers at Flatpools."

"I see. Well, you have very important work. And young Master Serka met you in the capital?"

"When I delivered firewood for you to Northgate," said Serka to Tamo.

"Yes, that's right. I do remember you telling us that you'd met two guards."

"We were glad to meet a young master who is so dedicated to our oath," said Elenn.

"These three are all very good young workers," said Tamo, looking around at the three hooded youths. "We were worried when we got the test results back from the capital infirmary, but we're very proud of them now that they've taken hood."

"Master Tamo, can we have an outdoor fire tonight? We all finished our chores."

"Did someone feed the silkworms?" asked Tamo.

"Yes, I did," said Serka, "Master Nula had never seen silkworms before."

"All right, but be very careful with the fire. We don't want any accidents," said Tamo, "And you will help with clean-up here before you go."

"I'll keep company with the young masters," said Elenn. "I'll make sure they're careful with the fire."

"That sounds like a very good idea," said Tamo, giving a nod of approval to Elenn.

After finishing their meal of vegetables and flatbread and taking care of kitchen clean-up, Serka, Jeber, and Leol took Nula and Elenn to a fire pit a short distance from the workhouse. Leol carried a fire pot with a coal from the kitchen stove. It was getting dark, but in the distance they could still see the edge of the forest that grew outside the western gate with a band of trees along the capital wall. Elenn sat on a bench and let the young masters build the fire. They quickly had it burning, and before long it was dark all around as they circled the bright fire.

"Do you go into the capital much?" Elenn asked the young worker masters.

"All the time," said Jeber. "We go to the bartering yards with Master Yinat at least twice a moon cycle."

"And we go to see our counselors," added Serka.

"You all have different counselors?" asked Elenn.

"Yes. But they're all at Bells. We go at the same time."

"When you go to the capital, do you usually go through the western gate?"

"Usually, but sometimes if we don't want to go through the Central District, we take the road that follows the drystream along the capital wall and then go in the north gate."

Either way was a problem, thought Elenn. The barren liked to meet each other in the woods outside the western gate, but they also were known to loiter around the drystreams.

"Well, it's good that you go to see your counselors at the same time," said Elenn. "Try to go together whenever you go into the capital."

"Why, Master Elenn?" asked Serka. Nula thought that Serka should have been able to figure it out for himself, but apparently he wanted Master Elenn to spell it out for him.

"There are masters there who can't keep their oath," said Elenn.

"Oh." Serka made an unpleasant face.

"Why can't they keep the oath, Master Elenn?" asked Jeber.

"Well, you know some uedin are better at certain things. Some are very strong when it comes to self-control. Others aren't so strong."

"Master Elenn, did you know when you became a guard that you were going to be strong? I mean, strong about keeping the oath?" asked Leol. Nula was especially interested to hear how Elenn would respond to this.

Elenn was not quite prepared for such a question. He felt that he needed to answer with honesty. He remembered when he had spoken at the hood-taking ceremony. He wasn't able to talk about the difficulty of resisting temptation. Now was a time when the least he could do was not lie to them.

"When I became a guard, I had no idea how weak I would be," he said solemnly.

"Weak? But you're not weak at all," said Nula. "You were the first to take hood."

"Was that you, Master Elenn? Was that you that had your hood put on backwards?"

"Yes, that was me," said Elenn with a chuckle.

"You say you're weak," argued Leol, "but you've never done that *feeding* thing, right?"

Elenn looked around the circle at the fire-lit faces of the young masters. They all wanted him to reassure them that they had nothing to fear.

"Let me tell you how to really be strong," said Elenn. "If one of you finds one day that you have been weak, and you have broken your oath, that will be the time to be really strong and put your hood on again and try to believe in yourself."

The young outfield workers were not encouraged at all by these words. For one thing, Master Elenn, a guard on the hood squad, was telling them that he himself had done that despicable thing that they didn't even want to mention out loud.

"You only let it happen one time, right? You were so curious that you let it happen one time," said Serka, hopefully.

Elenn let his silence answer the question.

"It didn't happen any time when we were going around the capital together, did it?" asked Nula with dread.

"No, Master Nula. It didn't happen any time after the squadron was formed. It happened before we took hood." This detail seemed to appease the young masters somewhat.

"That's why our hoods and our oath are so important," said Serka.

Elenn could see how loyal these young fieldworkers were to their oath. "Yes, our hoods and our oath are very important," he said. "And I'm glad that you young masters are so dedicated. You will be a great help to one another."

For a while, there was a lull in the conversation as they all silently watched the fire. Then Serka spoke again. "Master Elenn, I know it's not possible for us all to be guards, but would it be all right if we tried to help the squadron sometimes?"

"You want to help?" asked Elenn.

"I know how we could help," said Serka. "If we see barren breaking their oath near the western gate, or along the drystreams that go up around to the north side of the capital, we could make them stop. And then we'll tell you about it."

"I don't think you'll see them," said Elenn. "They won't do it right in front of you."

"But if we see hooded masters roaming about either of those places, we'll know what they're up to," said Jeber.

"How would you make them stop?" asked Elenn.

"We'd tell them to be strong and remember their oath," said Serka, "just like you do."

Even Nula saw the naivete in this idea. He wondered how Elenn would answer.

"Let me be honest with you, young masters. There is a reason why the members of the squadron never work alone. You may not think that you'll ever be tempted to break your oath, you may think that you'll never want to take off your hood. But I'm afraid I must tell you that that day will come. If you start to keep watch around the western gate or the drystream along the wall, it's very important that you don't go there alone. If you go alone, it will only be a matter of time before you do the thing that you are there to stop. You must always go together. All three of you together would be best, but sometimes if two of you are together, it may be all right. Never alone, though. Do you understand?"

The three outfield workers were embarrassed by the suggestion that they would ever remove their hoods, and Nula was embarrassed as well. There was an awkward moment of silence. Finally, Serka said, "We understand. We'll never go around those places alone."

"We'd want to go together anyway," said Leol, "I'd be too scared to say anything to anybody if I were by myself."

"We can't be hood squadron guards, but we can be oath keepers," said Serka.

Nula thought to himself about the innocent manner of these young outfield workers. Either they were very good at covering up their true feelings, or else they were genuinely free of temptation. It was hard for him to imagine that they never experienced it at all. If that were the case, he envied them. But he was glad that he wasn't living with them in the workhouse. Whether they were covering up their feelings or were genuinely innocent, he didn't think he would fit in with them. They were too pure-acting. He wondered if they would stay that way.

"Do you want to hear one of our songs?" asked Leol.

"Yes, we would like that very much," answered Elenn.

"Which one should we sing?" Leol asked his fellow workers.

"How about 'The Lern is With Us'?" suggested Jeber.

And so they sang, their youthful faces bobbing in the firelight as they sang:

> *The Lern is with us when we wake,*
> *Wake, wake, workermaster, wake in the outfield!*
> *Wake with a heart that's ready to wake,*
> *And the Lern will be happy to find us awake.*
>
> *The Lern is with us when we work,*
> *Work, work, workermaster, work in the outfield!*
> *Work with a heart that's ready to work,*
> *And the Lern will be happy to find us working.*
>
> *The Lern is with us when we plow,*
> *Plow, plow, workermaster, plow in the outfield!*
> *Plow with a heart that's ready to plow,*
> *And the Lern will be happy to find us plowing.*
>
> *The Lern is with us when we sow,*
> *Sow, sow, workermaster, sow in the outfield!*
> *Sow with a heart that's ready to sow,*
> *And the Lern will be happy to find us sowing.*

The Lern is with us when we harvest,
Harvest, workermaster, harvest the outfield!
Work with a heart that's ready to harvest,
And the Lern will be happy to find us harvesting.

Elenn and Nula cheered and clapped, and the fire crackled as the night wore on.

Later, after the fire was all burned up and the group retired to the workhouse to bed down for the night, Elenn and Nula were given bedding right alongside their new friends. The two guards avoided one another's eye contact as they stepped around the figures of Serka, Leol, and Jeber who lay face-down on their wheel-shaped pillows to sleep. They both had the same thought. They were very glad that hoods were in place to hide the neckstraps and catheters of the strong, young fieldworkers.

More Hooded Masters Break Oath

Nula was now to the point at which he no longer had to follow Elenn around like a child-uedin; he would separate from Elenn, staying within earshot, and check the areas off path where feeding barren sometimes hid their activity. They were patrolling an area around the slopes that led to the Haka Cliffs. Nula knew it was a critical time for the squadron and no team of hood guards could afford not to both work at full capacity and total engagement. He recalled the last meeting of what was now a very strong alliance between the hood guards and the caretakers to barren. Discussion of the fact that barren were breaking their oath in large numbers caused the meeting to last so long that finally Master Benar had had a small temper tantrum and insisted that the meeting had gone on long enough. Nula had mixed feelings about Master Benar, but Master Elenn had reassured him that he was a fine uedin once you got used to him.

The pressure was certainly on from the masters council. Signs of symptomatic large body development and derangement among certain masters had led the council to call all operations into question. Nula knew that for him, the daily routine had become extremely stressful, and knew that Master Elenn felt the same way. The first few times they caught syndrome uedin in the act of feeding, the shock of seeing it was the most unpleasant aspect of the arrest. That was no longer the case. Nula was actually almost used to seeing uedin with their heads bent over one another. The worst thing now was the interrogation. He hated doing it. He hated getting confrontational in order to determine the identity of a uedin. Then they had to escort them. That was awful too. And then there was reporting to counselors and supervisors. Sometimes the apprehended uedin were angry, but usually they were just in such a panic that he felt like he needed to reassure them, but he absolutely did not know how to do so, no matter how much he wanted to.

It was a time for thinking about the meaning of duty. Nula was miserable about his work, but he was a guard. Asked to serve on the squadron, he knew it was his duty to report, and that meant it was his duty to protect the oath. That was what he thought about when an hour or two passed without any encounters if Master Elenn was not in a talkative mood. The oath. On this particular day, he was feeling less sure about it. His doubts left him feeling lost and insecure, since there would be nothing in which to place his confidence should the oath prove to be a total vanity.

Nula was walking swiftly on the small side paths when he heard Elenn jogging up behind him.

"This time, when we come upon a two of them feeding, we're going to try something different," said Elenn. Nula, despite his doubts, had complete and total respect for Elenn and his dedication to the work of the squadron. He nodded in agreement as Elenn explained, "We're going to confiscate their hoods before they recover from their intoxication. They will have to take us to their counselors in order to get them back."

"Take their hoods? And hold on to them?"

"We must force them to help themselves, Master Nula," said Elenn.

"Very well," said Nula.

"I know you must think it's harsh," said Elenn.

"It's harsh, but I understand, it's necessary."

"Also, we have to stop calling back and forth so much when we're trying to talk them into cooperating. We can't talk them into anything when we're shouting about them back and forth."

"That makes sense," said Nula. "We'll keep our same routine, though, right? You start talking to one first, and then I'll talk to the other."

"That's right. Just remember now, I'm going to talk only to my uedin until I have his cooperation, and then I'll talk to you."

"I'll do the same," said Nula. Nula always tried to get his uedin to relax by telling him that he was not going to be punished, he was just going to be required to talk to his counselor. Sometimes that was enough to calm them down. Then he thought of a question. "What will we do if one of them runs away from us without his hood?"

"I've been thinking about that," said Elenn. "We could just turn the hoods over to the caretakers and let them figure out who they belong to."

"That shouldn't be too hard for them," said Nula. He had to admit, he saw a benefit in this hood-stealing strategy. Any feeding barren who ran away without his hood would be confronted later by his counselor. Nula and Elenn wouldn't have to confront him. In that case, Nula wouldn't mind if they all ran away and left their hoods behind.

Elenn then left him to scout his side of the path, and it wasn't until a while later that Nula heard Elenn talking and knew he had encountered someone. Nula went over to see. Elenn was speaking to a single hooded uedin. He was delivering the message that they used with solitary barren encountered in places with high incidence of feeding. "There is support for you if you talk with your counselor. . ." Nula heard him say. The hooded master, whoever it was, listened and nodded politely, but then he just raised hands to face and then turned and walked back toward the capital. They let him go.

After he was gone, Elenn turned to Nula and said, "I wonder if he'll go all the way back to the capital, or will he wait till we're out of sight and go right back to looking for another barren to feed with."

"Well, Master Elenn, you've told me enough times that you were in the habit at one time," said Nula.

"That's why I don't feel sorry for them as much as you do," Elenn answered.

They had gone as far as they intended to go and were on their way back to the eastern gate. The same rock formations that they had already passed by now looked completely different because of the darker shadows of late afternoon.

Nula heard Elenn's footsteps halt. He looked across at him. It took Nula a moment to see the two feeding masters just off the path on Elenn's side. One had his head bent forward while the other leaned over him, his face down in the first one's neck, just at the base of his skullwomb. They were motionless, their eyes closed. Their hoods were on the ground, just as Elenn and Nula had seen them on the ground many times when this scene had appeared. Nula watched with admiration as Elenn walked up to them with no hint of nervousness or anxiety, stood there for a moment to give them a chance to notice him, and then, without any haste, reached down and picked up one hood, then the other.

"Masters,. . ." he said, trying to get their attention.

The one bearing his neck opened his eyes. He jerked a little, and the other one lifted his head. Elenn turned and looked at Nula with a resigned expression and tossed him one of the hoods.

"We're here to help you," said Elenn. The two finally sat up straight, looking somewhat confused but not quite ready to respond. Nula waited for Elenn to initiate a conversation with one of them. Elenn said it again, "We're here to help you," and then stood close to the one who had been leaning over the top of the other to feed and reached for his hand to help him up. He took Elenn's hand and let Elenn guide him a few steps toward the path.

"We are hood squadron guards," Elenn started to speak to him, and Nula knew he had to talk to the other one.

"Please, come and talk to me," said Nula to the other uedin, who still had his neckstrap undone.

"Give me my hood," said the uedin to Nula, regaining his wits, "Give it to me now!"

"What is your name, master?" asked Nula.

"I will not tell you my name!" he answered angrily.

"Please don't be upset," said Nula gently. "No one is going to hurt you. But we will have to escort you back to speak with your counselor."

"My counselor already knows I do this," cried the master, reaching for his hood. Nula felt sure that he was talking to a uedin of his own generation, but he could see that he was large. He didn't doubt that this uedin had been in the habit of feeding.

"If your counselor already knows, then it shouldn't be too difficult for you to tell him about this happening. But we do have to tell him that we found you here, doing this. We can't just let you go. What district are you from?"

"I don't want to tell you. Please, give me back my hood!"

"I can't give you back your hood until after we have escorted you all the way back."

"Then I won't go back to the capital!" cried the distraught uedin. He broke away and started running, but instead of running toward the eastern gate, he ran away from the capital, further into the slopes. Nula ran after him. Elenn put his arm around the other barren uedin and kept talking to him.

Nula wasn't sure how far he should pursue the runaway master. When he looked back over his shoulder, Elenn looked up and yelled, "Let him go!" Nula took a few more steps and then stopped and turned back around. He had the barren's hood in his hand. It would be up to the caretakers to find the unhooded barren uedin and talk to him about what had happened. This was the way it was going to work now. Still, he felt horrible.

He slowly walked back to where Elenn was still talking to the other one. He decided to keep a distance and let Elenn keep talking privately to him. Nula could hear their conversation. The unhooded master was trying to negotiate with Elenn. He would go back to the capital with him, and he would take him to his counselor, but he wanted to wear his hood. He didn't want to walk unhooded through the streets of the capital with his neck-strap exposed. He was ashamed.

"But this is too important. Your counselor must know what is happening. We can't risk letting you run off."

"What about the other barren? He's run off. I won't run off if you just let me wear my hood."

"No, master," said Elenn sternly. "You are not in a position to negotiate. Come with us now."

The uedin looked at Nula now, and then back at Elenn.

"Come," repeated Elenn. When the uedin showed no signs of following, Elenn started walking away. "Come on, Master Nula. We're going back."

"No wait!" said the uedin. "I'll come." He started walking with them, though he did not walk quickly, and they had to slow down to allow him to follow them.

"Where are we going?" Elenn asked the uedin when they got to the eastern gate. He hesitated, and Elenn said, "We will either be giving this to the senior caretaker, or we will give it to your counselor. It's your choice."

"We're going to Bramble," said the uedin.

Nula looked back in the direction the other barren had run away. He was long gone now. "I'm sorry the other one ran away," he said to Elenn. "I tried to stop him, but I couldn't."

"There was nothing you could do," said Elenn. "We'll take his hood to Master Yenca. He'll know what to do." Elenn held the apprehended master's hood up and motioned for Nula to come and take it. "Put this in your pack together with the other one," he said.

When they got to the eastern gate, Elenn turned and spoke to the uedin. "If you are embarrassed to be seen walking with us, you may walk ahead. We will follow you back to Bramble."

Nobody spoke as they walked through the capital. It was close to the hour for evening meal, and few masters were in the streets.

Nobody noticed him at all. But his avoidance of the humiliation of having been caught ended when they arrived at Bramble.

One of the Bramble masters saw him as soon as he arrived and said, "What—Master Hemi. . ." He looked at Elenn and Nula in their guard's garb and quickly understood what had happened.

Now they knew that the uedin they were escorting was named Hemi. He said nothing to the master who had identified him and walked right past him. He took them to a hut which they found unoccupied.

"This is my counselor's hut, but he's not here."

"What is his name? We'll have the hood delivered to him as soon as we return to our station," said Elenn.

"No! You must let me have it! I'm here now! Isn't that enough?"

"No, Master Hemi," said Elenn, and he shook his head. "Your counselor must know."

"I will tell him!"

"We will send it," said Elenn.

"He's in the meal hall, with all the other masters. I don't want to go in there in front of all of them!"

Nula spoke up, "Master Elenn, why don't you take it into the meal hall and give it to Master Hemi's counselor and explain this to him. I'll wait outside the meal hall with Master Hemi."

"If we do that for you, will you tell us your counselor's name?" asked Elenn.

"Master Mebok is my counselor," said Hemi. He led them to the meal hall and stopped outside the door. Nula put down his pack, opened it, and took out the two hoods.

"Which one is yours, Master Hemi? Can you tell which one is yours?"

"May I see them?" asked Hemi. Nula looked at Elenn, and Elenn nodded. He handed both hoods to Hemi. Hemi looked at both of them closely and then held them to his nose.

"This one is mine," he said, and handed it to Elenn. The other he gave back to Nula who returned it to his pack.

"This may take a few minutes," said Elenn, and he entered the meal hall. Nula waited with Hemi and listened to the noise and chatter coming from the inside. It got quiet, and Nula could hear Elenn's voice, be he couldn't make out what he was saying. Then they heard them coming to the door. Elenn came out, followed by a fourth or fifth generation master in caretaker robe.

"Master Hemi," he said. "You'll be all right. Here." He immediately handed the hood to Hemi.

"I didn't say your name in front of the other masters," said Elenn to Hemi. "They only know that it's one of Master Mebok's counselees, but they don't know which one."

"They'll all know soon enough," said Hemi.

"They might not, young master," said Mebok.

"Someone saw us coming in," said Hemi.

"Oh," Mebok said, seeing that there would be no way to spare Hemi the humiliation.

"We will leave you to talk," said Elenn, and signaled to Nula that they should go now.

As they were leaving Bramble, Elenn said to Nula, "You can go home. Give me the other hood, and I'll take it to Master Yenca."

Nula thought that maybe he should offer to go along with Elenn so that he could explain what had happened with the runaway, but he was tired and hungry. "Are you sure? I'll go if I'm needed."

"You're fine. Go on home to Crafting and eat something and get a good rest. I'll see you at Flatpools Station in the morning."

Nula got the runaway's hood from his pack, gave it to Elenn, and raised hands to face to thank Elenn for letting him go. He then turned and headed back to Crafting.

It was dark by now, and Elenn wasn't sure if he should bother Yenca in the evening hours, but he decided it was important enough to go speak with him.

Though Benar was still the senior caretaker to the syndrome-afflicted, Yenca had taken over many of the less pleasant responsibilities of caretaker supervision. He was very busy. When Elenn found that Yenca's residence at Quarterhouse was empty, he imagined that Yenca was probably meeting with one of his own counselees.

He saw one of the younger caretakers and asked him, "Have you seen Master Yenca?"

The caretaker looked at him with the most serious expression and said, "Master Yenca was called to Southgate District guard station for an emergency. Don't you know about it?"

"No. What sort of emergency?" asked Elenn.

"I don't know, but Master Yenca left very suddenly. He even left his plate on the table in the meal hall. Perhaps you should go to the Southgate District guard station."

Southgate District Station was on the opposite side of the capital, and Elenn was already exhausted, but he walked at a brisk pace to get there as soon as he could. He arrived to find the district station office full of uedin. Yenca was there along with other caretakers from Southgate. Onnek and Posha, the Southgate squadron team, were being questioned. A body, wrapped in wax-cloth and lying on a stretcher, occupied the space in the middle of the room. As soon as Elenn saw the general shape of the large figure, he knew what had happened.

"We knew he was barren when we saw the tan line around his face where he wore his hood. But we don't know what happened, and there was no sign of his hood."

"I have his hood," said Elenn, and everyone in the room turned to look at him.

"So you know what happened?" asked a Southgate ro-guard.

"Was he found in the Haka Cliffs?" asked Elenn.

"Yes, at the base of the cliffs," said Posha. "He apparently threw himself over."

"Are you the one who found him?" asked Elenn.

"Yes, well, Onnek and I were just taking a look around, outside the eastern gate. Another hooded master came to us, and he was very upset. He said that someone had jumped off the Haka Cliffs. We followed him to the cliffs and found this body there."

"May I see his face?" asked Elenn.

The ro-guard pulled away part of the wax-cloth to show his face. He had struck hard at the base of the cliffs, his jaw was mashed in, and his mouth was severely gashed, revealing a bloody hole of broken teeth. Elenn recognized him nonetheless.

"Yes, that is him. We tried to be as gentle as we could with them. . ."

"He was not alone, then?" asked Yenca.

"Master Nula and I found him feeding with another barren in the slopes," said Elenn. "This is his hood." He took the hood from his pack and handed it to the ro-guard.

"Were you chasing him, Master Elenn?" asked Yenca.

"No. Nula tried to go after him when he first ran, but I told him to let him go."

"Why do you have his hood?" asked Yenca.

"He was with a Bramble master by the name of Hemi. We took both of their hoods when we found them feeding. We actually took their hoods to stop them from running away."

"The other master gave you his name?"

"No. We didn't know his name until we followed him back to Bramble."

"We'll question Master Hemi to help us identify the body," suggested one of the Southgate guards.

"I don't think that will work," said Posha. "They don't even exchange names."

"They're too ashamed," said Yenca. "Anyhow, I'll put the word out to all the caretakers that an unidentified hooded master has died at Haka Cliffs. Someone will show up missing tomorrow, and we'll determine who this is."

Elenn looked down at the wrapped body. He couldn't see how mangled and broken it was from the fall, and he had no interest in lifting the wax-cloth to see. What couldn't be denied was the largeness of the body. Whoever this was, it was fair to say that he had been feeding enough to bring about an advanced case of syndrome. Perhaps he was already in derangement when he threw himself from the Haka Cliffs. Even so, it was horrible to think that catching him in the act of feeding had prompted his suicide.

"Master Elenn, are you walking back to Flatpools?" asked Yenca.

"Yes. I've had a terribly long day," answered Elenn.

"May I walk with you?"

"I would like that very much, Master Yenca."

By now, the streets of the capital were dark and quiet. Elenn and Yenca walked quietly until they reached the central plaza. While they were crossing the plaza, they saw a hooded master sitting on the steps of the sunken courtyard. He regarded them nervously and then got up and walked away. It appeared that even in the center of the capital, barren uedin were looking for opportunities to break their oath.

"The hood statute is failing, isn't it?" said Yenca.

"It seems that way," answered Elenn.

"It must be terribly hard for all of you on the squadron."

"It is hard, but we have no choice."

"Maybe we do," said Yenca. "Some of the caretakers think that we should abandon the hoods."

"What good would that do?" Elenn had thought about it before himself, but he wanted to hear what Yenca would say.

"Do you think that master would have run away and thrown himself over the Haka Cliffs if there were no hoods?"

"I don't know. Maybe not. But you had to notice that his body was growing large. Since you're not a guard, you probably have never seen what happens to us when we get to an advanced stage of barren syndrome."

"I'm aware of the danger, and I understand why the council passed the hood statute. But if it's not working, don't we need to think about whether the hoods are doing more harm than good?"

"That is a question that I ask myself every day, Master Yenca," said Elenn. And then, he unwittingly added, "I have my own struggle to remind me." After he said it, he realized it was saying too much, but he was so tired he didn't have the energy to worry about it.

"My counselees all talk about loving and hating their hoods at the same time," commented Yenca.

"I'm not sure if 'love' is the right word, but I know how much I need my hood," said Elenn.

"Master Benar is your counselor, isn't he, Master Elenn?"

"Yes," said Elenn, wondering why Yenca had asked.

"He is very popular with all our hooded masters. But if you ever feel that you need a different perspective, please feel free to come to me."

"Thank you, but Master Benar is just right for me," answered Elenn. "I feel very comfortable with him. There are questions that have no answers. He doesn't ask me those questions. And he helps me to stop asking them myself."

As they continued walking throughout the dark capital streets, Elenn thought about Yenca's good intentions. He couldn't truly appreciate the conflict that the barren dealt with because he wasn't one of them. A good caretaker, he made it his duty to understand, but his understanding would always be limited. Only other barren really understood. And that was part of the problem causing them to break their oath. The desire to share necks with another barren uedin was not just to experience pleasure and satiation. It was also to relieve the awful solitude of carrying such a conflict all alone. Though he had not shared his neck since taking hood, Elenn keenly remembered what it felt like to submerge himself in surrender with another uedin. It was a moment of relief that reached the full depth of the conflict and rendered it momentarily null. But this knowledge was not something he would ever speak about.

Nula Takes Ill

Morning fog lay around Flatpool Station. Elenn was used to Nula's occasional tardiness, but it was rare for the other guards to clear out before he got there. Elenn considered that the fog might be thick around the whole capital, and that that might be what was slowing him down. After the last guard on assignment left, leaving only Elenn and Deben in the station house, Elenn began to worry.

Whenever Nula was unaccounted for, for any substantial amount of time, Elenn couldn't help wondering if he might be exploring on his own, perhaps flirting with temptation. A fog might just invite such a thing. But wouldn't Nula, even if he did decide to roam, be more careful about getting to Flatpools at a reasonable time so as not to raise questions? On the other hand, if he did find someone to feed with, he could be intoxicated by the experience and not be thinking clearly. Elenn expected him to come walking in out of the fog any minute with some kind of excuse. How much should he play along and pretend that everything was normal? Elenn decided that when Nula arrived, he would act as if nothing were out of the ordinary. It would be up to Nula to tell him if he was having any kind of difficulty. Elenn had noticed that Nula had grown slightly larger in the last moon cycle. Though it was not exactly the growth pattern Elenn usually associated with the syndrome, there was indeed a visible weight gain. Elenn was certainly in no position to judge him or anyone; he only wanted to support Nula in the best way possible. But Nula didn't come, and when the morning fog began to burn off, Elenn decided that he might need to start walking toward Crafting to see if he could find him.

Before he could grab his cloak, a messenger came to the door of the station house. "Guardmaster Elenn here?" a distribution master called from behind the door tarp.

Elenn reached up and drew aside the door tarp, saying, "Yes, I'm Ele—"

"A message from Crafting District Station." It was Pavis holding the folded note for Elenn. He looked at Elenn with an absolutely neutral expression.

"Master Pavis," said Elenn, taken aback. "What a surprise to see you." When Deben heard Elenn say this, he turned around and looked. Pavis neither smiled nor acknowledged the greeting.

"Shall I wait while you read it, in case you want to send an immediate response?"

His adherence to service speech told Elenn that Pavis did not want to talk socially with him. He took the note. "Thank you, that would be very helpful," he said with polite distance. Then he opened the note and read it.

> To Master Elenn of Flatpools District Guards:
> Master Nula was very ill this morning and could not get up from his bedding. We have taken him to infirmary. They don't know what is wrong with him yet. He is currently under the care of Medic Master Goril. This is to notify you that Master Nula will not be reporting for duty today, and we don't know how long he will be ill.

*Please let us know if any of us at Crafting District can
assist you in any way.*
Huma, senior guard, Crafting District.

Elenn looked up and said, "Yes, I will send a short response."

"Is it about Master Nula?" asked Deben.

"Yes. He's in the infirmary." Elenn went to the storage room
and looked for paper and ink.

"Some kind of accident?"

"No. He's ill. The note says he couldn't get up from his bedding
this morning." He took paper and ink to the table and wrote a
brief thank-you note in a hurried hand. He gave it to Pavis, who
took it, quickly raised hand to face, and left.

"Do you think it's something serious?" Deben asked.

"I don't know. The note from Crafting just says he won't be able
to report for duty."

"Master Ippal has no assignment today. Perhaps he can go with
you on your rounds."

"I want to go check on Master Nula at the infirmary, then I'll
come back and get Master Ippal if he's available."

"I'll let him know. Please give Master Nula our regards."

Walking to the infirmary, Elenn thought about how he had
suspected that Nula might have been looking for an opportunity
to break his oath. He was ashamed for thinking that. In all proba-
bility, it was he, not Nula, who was more likely to break oath. He
silently chided himself as he walked briskly through the streets.

He got to the infirmary and asked for Goril.

"Wait here," said the apprentice medic. "I'll see if Master Goril
can speak with you."

Goril appeared a few minutes later. "I'm Goril," he said, raising one hand to face.

"I'm Elenn of the Flatpools District Guards," said Elenn.

"How can I help you, guardmaster?" Goril asked.

"You have a young guard here from Crafting?"

"Yes. Master Nula. He was brought in this morning."

"We are partners on the hood squadron," said Elenn. "I got a message from Crafting that Master Nula was brought here."

Goril looked serious. "Sit down, Master Elenn. Let's talk first, then I can take you to see your partner guard." Elenn didn't like the sound of Goril's tone.

"The message I got said Master Nula couldn't get up this morning."

"Yes, he woke up with great difficulty breathing and felt too weak to rise. It's a good thing they brought him here."

"Do you know what his problem is?"

"I want to confer with Master Feril. We'll need to observe him for a few days."

"Is there anything else wrong with him besides difficulty breathing?"

"Master Nula's legs are swollen, his abdomen is enlarged around the middle, and his heartbeat is very irregular."

"Does it have anything to do with the syndrome?" he asked.

"Right now, I don't see any connection between barren syndrome and Master Nula's symptoms," answered Goril. "Tell me, Master Elenn, have you noticed that Master Nula gets tired easily?"

"No, not at all. Master Nula has been strong and energetic as long as we've been working together."

"Well, he's very weak right now."

"Do you think he's in any danger?"

"Difficulty breathing almost always indicates problems with the lungs and the heart. That is dangerous."

Elenn felt afraid. "Is his life at risk?" he asked.

"Master Elenn, there isn't any more I can tell you right now. Master Ferin and I will observe Master Nula for a few days, and maybe we'll know more by then. All I can tell you now is that Master Nula will not be able to report for duty until further notice. Would you like to see him now?"

"Yes, please," Elenn said, raising hands to face.

Goril led Elenn to the infirmary courtyard where Nula was seated on a special drop-back chair leaning back.

"Well at least you got out of bed!" said Elenn in a loud, teasing voice when he saw Nula. He tried to act casual even though he was terribly worried.

"Master Elenn! I'm sorry I couldn't report to Flatpools this morning."

"Well the fact that you couldn't breathe makes it somewhat excusable," kidded Elenn, continuing the cheerful act.

"The medic masters want to keep me here for three days! I'm so bored already!" Nula seemed to be completely unaware that his condition was serious.

"Use your guard discipline. Or just imagine yourself sitting through a very long squadron meeting with the caretakers." He wondered if Nula could tell that he was trying to cover up his worry. He didn't usually joke so much.

"That reminds me, I wonder if my counselor knows I'm here. How did you find out?"

"I got a message from Master Huma."

"I don't know if he would have sent a message to my counselor at Bramble or not," said Nula, ". . .probably not."

"I can go over to Bramble today and tell Master Yinob."

"You remember him?" asked Nula.

"Of course I remember Master Yinob," said Elenn. Nula had introduced Elenn to Yinob one day when they had happened upon him in the bartering yards. Elenn also remembered Benar talking about Yinob.

"Well, you only met him that once when we saw him in the Central District."

"He's about fourth generation, right? Very nice master."

"Yes, he's fourth," said Nula.

"I'll go see him after I leave here. I'll let him know that you're here for a few days."

"What are you going to do today? Are you going to patrol by yourself?"

"One of my Flatpools comrades has no assigned duty today. I'm going to ask him to walk with me."

"Who is that?" asked Nula.

"Master Ippal. Have you met Master Ippal?"

"I think I might have talked with him once when I was waiting for you at the station."

"Well, we need help from the non-hooded guards," said Elenn. "We can't keep a watch on the whole capital by ourselves anymore. There aren't enough of us. I think Master Ippal will be able to handle it."

"I don't know why they need three days to do their observation. I'm sure I could be getting back to work right away," said Nula.

Elenn didn't comment.

"I do need to send a message to Master Yinob to let him know that I'm here," said Nula.

"I can go to Bramble after I leave here. I'll let him know what's going on. I imagine he will come to see you as soon as he can. As far as your not being able to do guard duty, I'll have Master Ippal with me today. Tomorrow, we'll just have to see how it works out."

Elenn asked Nula to describe what had happened that morning and what kind of tests he had been given. After this had been shared and assessed with considerate optimism, and after other small talk had been exhausted, Elenn stood up straight and smiled at Nula, signaling that he was going to leave.

"Thank you for coming, Master Elenn. Look for me in about three days. I'll come to Flatpools at our regular time."

"I will come to say hello each day, if you don't mind," said Elenn.

"That's very kind of you," said Nula.

"Oh, by the way, Master Deben told me to send you regards on behalf of Flatpools."

"Please tell him I said thank you, and I'll see them again soon." Nula smiled back with a face that reflected little worry. Elenn had a feeling that Master Goril had as of yet made no mention to Nula about his heart and lungs.

Elenn excused himself with a quick hand to face and left the courtyard. He found his way to the infirmary main door, gave a polite nod to the apprentice medic, and stepped out into the busy, midday street. What a morning it had been. Elenn was in a somber mood now. For how long had he been caught up in the frustrations of duty with the squadron? He had gotten so used to it that it seemed almost a surprise that something else like this could even happen. Nula could be seriously ill. Walking to Bramble, he thought about how much he should tell Master Yinob. Maybe it would be better to say very little about Nula's condition. After all, Goril needed a few days to observe him and confer with Ferin. Maybe Nula had nothing wrong with him. Maybe his trouble that morning was just an isolated event.

When Elenn neared Bramble, he could hear child-uedin playing. He approached one of the apprentice caretakers, asked for Master Yinob, and was taken to a kitchen where Yinob was washing out jars.

"Master Yinob, a guard to see you," said the apprentice.

Yinob stopped and dried his hands with a towel before bringing one hand to face. "Guard Master Elenn, good morning," he said, recognizing Elenn right away. There was some odd look in Yinob's eye that suggested to Elenn that Yinob knew him better than he knew Yinob. "What brings you to Bramble? Isn't Master Nula with you today?"

"Master Nula is in the infirmary," said Elenn.

"What?" Yinob's face changed immediately to concern. "What happened? Was there an accident?"

"No accident. When he woke up this morning, Master Nula was having trouble breathing and was so weak that he couldn't get out of bed. He was taken to the infirmary. I just came from there. He seems fine now, but they're keeping him there for a few days for observation. He wanted me to tell you that he's there."

"What's wrong with him?"

"The medic masters don't seem to know yet," said Elenn.

"Well I'm glad you came to tell me," said Yinob. "I'll go see him today. You say he seems fine now?"

"Yes, he's just bored because he's stuck there. But he was smiling and talking with me as if nothing were wrong."

"Maybe I'll bring him a book of verses," said Yinob.

"That would be very nice. I'm sure he would be glad to have something to read."

"Master Nula talks about you very often, you know," said Yinob. "He is grateful to have you as his partner guard."

"We get along very well," said Elenn. Elenn wondered what Nula might be saying about him. He felt a little strange, learning that Yinob knew much more of him than he knew of Yinob.

Yinob noticed Elenn's discomfort. "You seem very worried, Master Elenn. Is Master Nula's condition quite serious?"

"I don't know how serious it is," Elenn said. "I plan to check in every day at the infirmary while he's there."

"I will be seeing him too. And if you are around here in the coming days, please stop in," said Yinob.

"I will," said Elenn.

"Thank you for coming."

Elenn brought hands to face and excused himself. Walking out from Bramble, he encountered some child-uedin at play. They looked at him curiously, very aware of his hood.

"Master Nula. . ." one of them said. He obviously reminded them of Nula because of his hood and green guard's garb. Nula might even be the only hooded master they had seen before.

Another child-uedin said, "No, it's not. It's not Master Nula. Somebody else."

When Elenn got back to Flatpools, Deben was gone, but Ippal was waiting for him.

"Guardmaster Elenn, I was told I could step in for Master Nula today. He's sick?"

"Yes, he's in the infirmary."

"I'm so used to seeing his face here every morning, I forget he's from Crafting."

"He's probably more at home here than at Crafting. He only apprenticed just before the squadron was formed."

"I hope Master Nula is all right, whatever's the matter with him," said Ippal.

"How do you feel about going with me on my rounds? You know what we're doing these days?"

"Yes, I have an idea. I don't know if I can be of any help. I definitely don't want to get in the way."

Elenn sensed Ippal's reluctance to patrol hooded masters around the capital, and he couldn't blame him. It was already a terribly uncomfortable job for Elenn and the hooded guards on the squadron. It was no surprise that the regular guards didn't want to go near it. "I could use the help, if you don't mind. You definitely won't be in the way. It is our job, anyhow, to get in the way."

Ippal looked at him unsure, interpreting the comment. "You mean you guards on the hood squad have to get in the way and stop hooded masters from sharing neck?"

"Yes, that is what I mean."

Ippal shook his head to convey that he felt unprepared. "Oh, Master Elenn, you're going to have to help me a lot with this. I'm completely out of my element here."

"That's okay. We'll keep it very easy today. We won't go outside the walls. We'll just walk around and try to get a nod from whatever hooded masters we see."

"I guess I can handle that," said Ippal.

Elenn thought that a joke might lighten the mood and help Ippal relax. He decided to play a trick on his comrade guard. "Oh, there's just one more thing," he said, "We have to stop at Master Benar's hut and get you a hood."

"What? What do you mean, 'get me a hood'?"

"Well, you need to be hooded so that all the hooded masters will trust you," said Elenn, maintaining a serious face.

Ippal looked at him, astounded. ". . .But, but. . .I'm not—I don't have the syndrome," he stammered.

Elenn's face cracked into laughter. "Master Ippal, don't worry, you don't have to wear a hood! I'm joking!"

Ippal smiled, with just a bit of disapproval on his face. "Master Elenn, that was not very nice," he said.

"Come on, get your pack," said Elenn, and he led Ippal out of the station house. They made their way to Crafting Station, where Elenn thanked Huma for the morning's message. They spent a little time at the central courtyard and the bartering yards. Ippal followed Elenn around the capital. Hooded masters were indeed in the habit of nodding to Elenn when they saw him, a kind of brief reassurance that yes, they knew his message to them. The nod was a way of saying, "Yes, I'm being strong, and yes, I'm remembering my oath and being faithful to it." However, Elenn knew, and all the hooded guards knew, that the nod was coming to mean something different. It was coming to mean, "We're doing the best we can, all of us."

Elenn said little more about Nula, but he could hardly get him out of his mind. It was such a complexity of feelings he had. It would have been good if Ippal would have been chatty to distract Elenn from his worries, but Ippal was nervous about patrolling hooded masters and said very little.

They encountered another squad team, Umat and Cebik, walking in the Bells neighborhood.

"Master Elenn, hello!" said Umat. "Someone substituting for Master Nula today?"

"Yes, this is Master Ippal," said Elenn, "This is Master Umat, and this is Master Cebik." The guards gave one another casual one-handed greetings.

"Master Nula have a special appointment today?" asked Cebik. The hooded guards all knew one another by now from attending meetings of the alliance.

"Master Nula is in the infirmary," said Elenn. "He awoke ill this morning. But I saw him a while ago, and he seems to be doing well." Elenn thought that was enough to reveal at this point.

"Well I hope he's all right," said Cebik. "So, isn't Master Ippal the lucky one! He gets to be on the hood squadron today."

"I must admit, it *is* more walking than I'm used to," said Ippal.

"I'm breaking him in slowly," said Elenn.

"Good idea. Stay away from the drystreams. Poor Master Ippal will have nightmares," said Cebik.

"I hear that Masters Posha and Onnek are getting a lot of help from the other Southgate guards," commented Umat.

"Yes, non-hooded guards are going to have to get involved. I think we'll be talking about that at our next squad meeting," said Elenn.

"All right, well, we'll see you there!" said Cebik, and the two of them raised a hand and went in their own direction.

Ippal asked Elenn, "You say non-hooded guards are probably going to be asked to help more with the squadron work? On-going?"

"The situation is not getting any easier, and with only six of us on the squadron, we can't keep up with it," said Elenn.

"You know it's not something the guards are eager to take on," said Ippal.

"I know. But I also know that the guards are dedicated to the welfare of the capital."

"Yes, we'll all do what we must," agreed Ippal.

"Master Ippal, it looks like Nula is going to have to stay in the infirmary for a few days. Would it be all right if I asked Master Wanba to reassign you to work with me until he's back?"

"That would be fine," he said. After a moment he added, "I know that your other squadron comrade was joking about staying away from the drystreams or I'll have nightmares,. . .but what am I going to see?"

"Oh, it's not anything too awful," said Elenn. "You know why we have these hoods on. The worst thing you'll see is what happens when they come off."

"Well, that's something I don't look forward to seeing."

"Have you ever seen a deranged barren?"

"I did once," said Ippal. "when I was an apprentice guard. That was before the hoods."

"Well, if you saw that, you can be assured that *that* was much worse than seeing two barren feeding." Elenn meant what he said. Encountering a barren uedin in derangement was more of a problem than happening upon two who were feeding. But he could see that Ippal was not particularly reassured.

". . .'two barren feeding'. . .that's how the non-hooded guards talk. I'm surprised you talk about it that way."

"Whatever you want to call it, it's not as bad as dealing with someone deranged," answered Elenn.

At the end of the day, when Elenn and Ippal got back to Flatpools Station, they found that the rest of the guards had mostly all finished their duties and signed out. Elenn sat at a table to write a note to Wanba. "Thank you for going with me today, Master Ippal," he said. "I'm writing to Master Wanba to ask if you can fill in for Master Nula until he's out of the infirmary. I'll let you know what he says in the morning."

Ippal knew that he was free to go, but he pulled up a chair and sat beside Elenn.

"Tell him that you played a very cruel joke on me, making me think you were going to require me to wear a hood," said Ippal.

Elenn was writing now, and he murmured the words as he wrote, "'. . .*Master. . .Ippal. . .has graciously. . .agreed to do so,. . .if you. . .approve.'* There. What were you saying?"

"Oh, nothing," said Ippal. Then he leaned over to speak in a low voice lest anyone entering the station should hear. "Master Elenn, I have something I want to show you," he said.

Elenn smiled, aware that he was being let in on a secret. "What is it?" he asked.

Ippal looked at the doorway to make sure no one was coming. "Wait just a moment," he said. He went to the storage room and came back with a small box, usually used for holding brushes. It had a lid that slid open and shut along grooved slots. In his other hand, Ippal had a few pieces of dried mola.

"Look," he whispered, setting the box on the table. Elenn was fascinated. What could it be?

Ippal slid open the lid. Inside, a little straw-colored mouse huddled in the corner beside a small ceramic cup that held a tiny bit of water. Ippal dropped in a piece of the mola, and the mouse went to it and started nibbling.

"A mouse?" said Elenn, a bit too loudly.

"Shhh!"

"Where did *that* come from?"

"The other day, I was emptying the small waste bin. This mouse had somehow gotten in there and couldn't get out. It was scurrying around the bottom of the bin, trying to climb up the sides, but it was too slippery and the little thing was trapped. I know I should have just killed it, but I couldn't! So I put it in this brush box."

"And you're giving it food and water!" said Elenn, giggling.

The mouse was rather cute. Its little eyes were intent on the piece of mola as it nibbled.

"What are you going to do with it? You can't keep it!"

"I have an idea. I just thought of it today when you were telling me about what I could expect to see if we go around the drystreams. I've been waiting for a chance to get outside the capital walls to set this little mouse free. But I wouldn't be able to do it without letting you know what I'm up to."

"That's fine," said Elenn with a smile, "We can go up to the north gate in the morning, as long as Master Wanba says you can join me. You'll need to put it in your pack so nobody asks what you have in the box."

"Then I think I'll put the box in my pack now, so I don't have to answer any questions in the morning. This is a secret between us, Master Elenn," said Ippal. "I don't want to get teased by all the other guards."

"I won't tell anyone," said Elenn.

"Hey there, little friend," cooed Ippal, looking down at the mouse. "You're going to be free tomorrow!" Then he slid the lid shut, put the box in his pack, and carefully carried it out.

After Ippal left, Elenn folded up the note to Wanba and left it on his desk where he would see it first thing in the morning. Then he sat down again and stared at the wall. He wasn't ready to go have evening meal. Everyone would be asking him what he knew about Master Nula. He had to appear cool-minded about the situation. Nula was foremost his comrade guard. It would be unseemly for him to get too emotional.

Painful Events and Realizations

The next morning, Ippal quietly checked on the mouse in the brush box in the top of his pack before he and Elenn left the station. He was glad to have this chance to set the mouse free outside the capital, but he was also nervous about the possibility of seeing barren uedin feeding out there. He would never think of letting Elenn know how much he dreaded seeing such a thing, since he wasn't sure how Elenn would feel about his disgust.

"I think we'll go over to the infirmary after this, so we can see how Master Nula is doing," said Elenn.

"That will be fine," said Ippal.

"The streams appear dry these days, but they have moisture in them. The mouse will do much better there than it would being kept in that box in the storage room at Flatpools. So long as a snake or something doesn't get him."

"Cover your ears, little friend," Ippal said jokingly to the top of his pack. The two guards laughed together.

They exited the capital through the north gate and started walking along the wall. The northwest corner was not actually a square corner, but a rounded section of the capital where the stream had encroached many generations back and the wall was rebuilt to allow its course. That spot was the easiest place to climb down into the drystream so that they could let the mouse go among the weeds that grew thick in the dampest sections.

They got to the place where the wall was rebuilt and climbed down. The stream bottom was wider and cooler than Ippal had imagined it would be. He thought it was practically nice enough to come there sometime for a picnic of yeastdrink.

"I didn't even know this place existed," said Ippal.

"Few masters do. That's why it's a favorite spot for barren to feed," said Elenn, reminding Ippal of the thing he dreaded to encounter.

"This spot looks as good as any," said Ippal, and he took the pack from his back and opened it to retrieve the brush box.

"That poor mouse is probably dizzy from getting tossed about in that box," said Elenn.

They crouched around the box as Ippal slid open the lid. The mouse was in the corner, it's little sides pulsing.

"Good luck, little friend," said Ippal. He held the box all the way down to the ground, and tipped it a little to let the mouse spill onto the ground. It didn't move.

"Go on!" coaxed Ippal. But the mouse had apparently been tossed about too much. It didn't want to move.

The sun was on their backs, and they were looking at the mouse resting on the sunlit patch of ground between their two shadows. Suddenly the patch went dark as a shadow appeared from another figure coming up right behind them. They spun around and looked. The glare of the sun made it hard to see any face, but it was clear that they were looking at the enlarged figure of a uedin in an advanced stage of barren syndrome. He was not wearing any hood.

"Hello, Master!" said Elenn loudly.

"Lern Beyana doesn't like mice!" cried the barren uedin in a very strange voice. His face, now somewhat discernable, looked crazed. He took two large steps forward and stomped hard to kill the mouse. Ippal gasped, hearing the sound of the mouse being crushed under the barren's foot.

Elenn made eye contact with Ippal and said in a measured voice, "Master Ippal, be on your guard. This uedin is deranged."

Ippal looked at the squashed mouse for a second before coming to his senses. He greeted the uedin as Elenn had done, acting friendly to de-escalate the confrontation. Ignoring the barren's brutal action, he called out, "Hello, Master!" The large uedin looked at them both with a vacant expression and said nothing.

"What is your name, Master?" asked Elenn.

The barren hesitated, looking back and forth between them. "You are guards," he said.

"Yes, we are Flatpools District guards," said Elenn. "Will you tell me your name?"

"*I AM YU-NET!*" yelled the barren, a self-announcing that sounded like the manner in which a newly-named presents himself to the capital at Namesgiving.

"Master Yunet, where are you from?" asked Elenn.

"*I AM YU-NET!*" repeated the barren.

"Master Yunet, you need help," said Elenn sternly. "Can we take you to your counselor?"

"You are both guards, but only *you* are hooded," said the barren, indicating Elenn.

"Come with us. Come." Elenn gently reached for the barren's arm.

"You guards try to stop us. But you can't. It's too late," said the barren Yunet. He let Elenn put his hand on his shoulder.

"Will you come with us?" asked Elenn. "We want to help you."

"It's too late," he said, in a weaker, exhausted voice.

"We'll take you to your counselor," said Ippal, trying to help. "What's your counselor's name? Where is he?"

Elenn could tell that this Yunet, though deranged, wasn't presenting any danger to them at the moment. He didn't seem to be driven by craving, and he was showing some capacity for communication. Elenn took the risk of drawing close to him and putting his arm around him to lead him away. The barren acquiesced.

"Come, Master Yunet," said Elenn gently. "It's all right if you can't tell us who your counselor is right now. We'll go to the station, and we'll get you some water. You look like you need water,"

"Yes," said the hulking Yunet, and suddenly his face broke into crying. "I'm very thirsty," he sobbed.

"Master Ippal, I'm going to take him to Northgate because it's closest. Master Yunet and I are going to take our time getting over there. Will you run ahead and tell whoever's on duty at Northgate that we're coming?"

"Won't you need help climbing up the bank?" asked Ippal.

"No, we'll be fine."

Ippal picked up the empty brush box and put it in his pack, then turned and ran across the flat drystream bottom to the bank and climbed up quickly. Behind him, he heard the barren sobbing.

Elenn was very patient with the barren and led him slowly, a little at a time, up and out of the drystream, back to the gate, and into the capital. On the way to the station, when they crossed paths with other masters, Elenn kept his arm around Yunet and said, "Never mind, don't worry, come along," and kept going. Before they reached the station, Ippal came running back to meet them, accompanied by another guard.

"Our senior guardmaster says you are welcome to bring the afflicted uedin to Northgate Station, but there is nobody there to assist at this time. He suggests you bypass the station and take him directly to the infirmary," said the Northgate guard.

"That's fine," said Elenn. "We'll go straight to the infirmary. Come, Master Yunet, we're going straight to the infirmary. You'll get water, and food, and you can rest. Later they will help you take a nice bath. You've been outside for a long time. It will feel very good." Yunet followed obediently.

"I'll run ahead to let the medic masters know that you're coming," said the Northgate guard.

"Thank you, master," said Elenn. "Everything will be fine now," and he patted Yunet on the shoulder as the guard ran off.

When they reached the infirmary, the Northgate guard was there waiting with Ferin and some apprentice medics. They had a sedative tea ready. Yunet was admitted with no questions. He drank the tea eagerly, and they gave him more water. He was already so exhausted that the sedative effect of the tea worked within minutes. One of the apprentices led him to bedding, and he immediately lay face down in the manner of a proper uedin.

"Thank you, guards, for your help," said Ferin.

"I'll have messages sent to all the senior caretakers," said Elenn. "We should know who works with Master Yunet within a day."

The Northgate guard addressed Elenn. "We at Northgate know that we're the closest station to the drystreams. We want to help the squadron whenever we're needed. Don't hesitate to call on us."

"Thank you for all your help," said Elenn.

The guard raised hands to face to excuse himself and left.

Ippal quietly said to Elenn, "Master Elenn, since we're here, shall we check on Master Nula?"

"Yes," said Elenn, and then addressed Ferin. "Master Ferin, you have another guard here as a patient. A Crafting guard by the name of Nula."

"Yes. Master Nula is here."

"Master Nula is my partner guard on the hood squadron," said Elenn. "Master Ippal here is his substitute while he's here in the infirmary."

"Master Goril and I have observed him."

"Do you have a better idea of what his problem is?"

"We think we know what it is," said Ferin. He frowned.

"If there's anything you can tell me, I'd be very grateful," said Elenn.

"It looks like Bilmin's Condition," said Ferin. "It's something that occurs very rarely. Master Nula has had this all his life, but it is only showing up now."

"What is Bilmin's Condition?"

"It's a disease of the heart muscle. The heart becomes large and doesn't pump correctly."

Goril had told Elenn that it might be something related to the heart and lungs, and that as such it was probably serious. "Can you treat it?"

"There is no treatment, but we try to keep it from getting worse by prohibiting any hard physical exertion. There are a few records of uedin with Bilmin's Condition living long enough to go to their passing-of-life."

Elenn looked at Ferin squarely and waited for him to remember that he was talking about a barren uedin. After an instant, his face registered awkwardness, but he did not venture to ask for pardon.

"Uedin with Bilmin's Condition sometimes die young?" Elenn finally asked.

"They usually do, I'm sorry to say."

"I see," said Elenn.

"Oh, no! Poor Master Nula!" said Ippal, and he looked at Elenn, but Elenn did not make eye contact with him or the medic master.

"Does Master Nula know all this?" he asked.

"We told him this morning. Of course we could be wrong, but his symptoms are very consistent with what we know about Bilmin's Condition."

"May we see Master Nula?" asked Elenn.

"Yes, of course. He needs his comrades right now." He signaled for one of the apprentice medics to escort the guards to Nula's room.

Nula heard them come, but postponed looking up by concentrating on the book of verses that Yinob had brought the day before. He was not ready to look Master Elenn in the eye. He had never been so terrified in his entire life. After hearing his diagnosis from Masters Ferin and Goril, he had spent a miserable morning thinking about what would happen to his body after he died. This was even worse than the days leading up to the taking of hood ceremony, when he was told that he was barren. Then, at least, he had been with others who shared the same fate. This time, he felt completely alone.

"Master Nula, your comrade guards are here to see you," said the apprentice medic.

Nula slowly closed the book and looked up, but did not speak.

"I see Master Yinob brought a book for you," said Elenn.

Nula cast his eyes down at the book and ran his hand over the cover, but still remained silent.

"I'm going to wait in the front room," said Ippal, and then to Nula in a kind voice, "All the guards at Flatpools send their regards, Master Nula."

"Thank you, Master Ippal," said Nula quietly. After Ippal left them alone, Nula said, "How is Master Ippal doing? Is he all right filling in for me?"

"We just brought a deranged solitary from the drystream at the northwest corner here to the infirmary. I was planning to come later, but since I was here, I asked to see you."

"Was it a solitary seeking to feed?"

"I don't think he was actually seeking to feed anymore. I think he was confused and lost."

"Pretty deranged, then?"

"Yes, but docile."

"I must find some way to thank Master Ippal for taking my place," said Nula.

"It's only temporary. You'll be back with us soon." Elenn knew that wasn't necessarily true, but he spoke to encourage Nula.

Nula didn't answer for a long time. Then, finally, he looked Elenn in the eye. "Didn't Master Ferin tell you? About me?" His face was tense as he looked to Elenn for his answer.

Elenn reached down and took Nula's hand. "Yes, he did. But he also told me that a uedin with your condition still might live a long life."

"And why would I want to live a long life?" asked Nula, choking back his tears.

Elenn wanted to tell him that his work was important; that he should live long to serve the capital. But since Nula was probably not going to be able to keep up with the physical routine of the squadron, it was unclear how he would even continue as a guard. Elenn searched his mind for some kind of encouragement to give. Finally, he drew his face close to Nula's, looked at him with great compassion, and said simply, "Be strong, Master Nula!"

"Be strong, and what? And protect the oath?" Nula's voice was filled with anger and frustration. He looked in Elenn's eyes for a moment and then buried his head in his arm. Elenn let him remain with his head down for a long time.

Neither of them spoke. Elenn thought about the difficulty of protecting the oath, especially as it grew more meaningless by the day. It was failing, and the squadron's work appeared to be all in vain. But there was no walking away from it. They had to protect the oath until the masters council told them to stop. They were guards. Perhaps it was wrong to choose "be strong" as his encouragement to Nula, but what else could he say? What else was there to do but be strong? Nula *was* strong, and Elenn knew it. Nula just needed time.

Finally, Elenn broke the silence and spoke. "Master Nula, you have only just received this news, and of course you're upset. But we never know what will come. The medic masters aren't always right about everything. And however much life there is ahead of you, you must live it with courage, and find purpose in every day. I'm sorry if those words are no comfort to you. They're all I have to offer."

Nula sat up and tried to recover his composure. Elenn saw that his words had solicited the response he hoped for. Nula took a deep breath, nodded and looked up with appreciation. Elenn felt the honor of this, knowing that Nula was primarily accepting the encouragement because he valued Elenn's words.

"You're right," said Nula. "Master Yinob would say the same thing." He calmed his breathing and sat up straight to reclaim his dignity.

"Master Yinob is a wise uedin, isn't he?" said Elenn.

"Yes. I remember something he told me once, back when I first learned that I was barren. He told me that one should always identify something to hope for, no matter how small, then treat it as if it were the last seed of a plant that has to be given great attention in order to sprout and grow. It has to be planted in good soil, in a place where it will neither lack sun nor be burned by it, and it has to have the right amount of water every day."

"Has that worked for you before?" asked Elenn.

Nula looked down at his guard's garb. "My hope was to be a fine guard. . ."

"And you *have* been," Elenn assured him.

"But now I need a different hope."

"What do you hope for, Master Nula?" asked Elenn with a gentle voice.

"I hope for a life of friendship with you," answered Nula. "It may not be a long life, but I hope it will be a life built on our friendship."

"Of course you will have me as a friend," said Elenn. "Not only me, but all the guards. We're all concerned about you." Elenn noticed Nula's smile fade a bit. Nula seemed interested in some kind of exclusive friendship. Elenn thought of how Yinob had regarded him with a curious interest, suggesting that he had been a topic of their private discussions.

Fortunately, Nula seemed to be getting a grip on himself and redirected the conversation. "Master Yinob was so worried when he came to see me yesterday," he said, "I wish I didn't have to tell him that the diagnosis is bad."

"He seems like a very supportive counselor," said Elenn. He thought about asking Nula if in fact they had talked about him as he suspected, but it was not the right time to ask.

"I've been reading the book of verses he brought me. It gives me something good to focus on."

"Does it have some good poems?"

"It does. Would you like me to read you one?"

"Yes, that would be nice!"

"I marked one that I like. Let me see. . ." He opened the book where a page was marked with a piece of straw. "Here it is. It's by Galbi." He read,

> "A silver streamfish followed one
> Clear from the Lake Ceulan
> But when one stopped here to take leg
> The streamfish just swam on.
> If one had chosen not to stop
> But go where the streamfish go,
> One wonders where one might would be
> What nowheres one doesn't know!"

"That's nice," said Elenn. "I haven't heard it before."

"I marked it to show Master Yinob when he comes back," said Nula.

"I'm glad that you were able to have something to read."

"It's a good thing I had that book of verses," said Nula. "It has given me something to think about besides myself."

"And you'll tell Yinob everything—about your condition?"

"I am in the habit of telling Master Yinob everything."

"Do you know how long they will keep you in the infirmary?" asked Elenn.

"I think it might be just till tomorrow. The medic masters have to consult with my superiors at Crafting Station," said Nula. "I don't think I'll be able to stay on the hood squadron. They'll want me to have a very easy job."

Elenn looked at Nula with seriousness. They both knew this meant that they might not work together again.

"Thank you for coming, Master Elenn, but I don't want to keep Master Ippal waiting too long."

"I'll come back," said Elenn. "Maybe this evening, after evening meal."

"I'll look forward to seeing you," said Nula.

Walking towards Flatpools, Elenn said, "Master Ippal, it's been quite a day, and we're not even finished with our shift."

"I'll tell you one thing," said Ippal, "I know now that the hood squadron is the hardest of all guard assignments."

"It was a shame about the little mouse. I'm sorry that happened, Master Ippal," said Elenn.

"Well it was just a mouse that showed up, and I thought it would be nice to set it free instead of killing it." said Ippal, "But I was just so surprised when that uedin stomped on it like that. It was so unexpected."

"Yes, it was an ugly moment."

"I hope you didn't tell Master Nula about all that," said Ippal. "I'd rather just forget about it now."

"No, I didn't mention it. I guess there's no point in telling anyone about it."

"It was strange though, when that Master Yunet said 'Lern Beyana doesn't like mice.' I've heard that before," said Ippal thoughtfully.

"That master has really gone far into derangement," said Elenn. "I wonder how many days he was outside the capital."

"What do you think will happen to him, Master Elenn?"

"I think the medic masters will find his counselor quickly and work closely with him. They'll make sure his catheter is functioning, then they'll get him another hood. He could recover very well from his derangement if he doesn't feed again. I'm sure they won't leave him alone for a long time."

Elenn noticed how Ippal thoughtfully nodded, making a mental note of this information. It was the sort of thing that a squadron guard needed to know, and Ippal was apparently accepting, on some level, that he was going to be serving the squadron for at least some period of time. Elenn sadly considered that Ippal would likely have to remain in Nula's place for a long time to come.

A Fateful Decision

Elenn took his evening meal a little early and left quickly to go back to the infirmary. When he got to Nula's room, Yinob was there. Food had been brought in for both of them, and they were eating.

"Oh, Master Yinob, I'm sorry to interrupt," said Elenn.

"Stay, Master Elenn. I'm just going to finish eating and go back to Bramble," said Yinob. "The apprentice medics were kind enough to bring enough food for both of us."

"Are you tired, Master Nula?" Elenn asked, but he knew Nula was waiting for him.

"No, I even fell asleep for a while, while Master Yinob sat with me."

Yinob finished his meal quickly and stood to leave. "Tomorrow, I know you'll be going back to Crafting Station," he said to Nula. "It's probably better if you don't do a lot of walking for a while. I'll come to Crafting to see you. Should I come tomorrow, or shall we wait a day or two?"

"You don't have to come tomorrow. I'll send you a message after I get back to Crafting and get settled," said Nula.

"Very well. Have a nice visit with Master Elenn, and then I hope you get a good night's sleep."

"Thank you, Master Yinob."

Yinob raised hands to face, smiled at both of them, and took his leave.

"The guards all wish you well and said to say hello," said Elenn.

"As soon as I'm strong enough, I want to go to Flatpools and thank them for making me feel welcome while I was reporting there for the squadron."

"They'll all be glad to know you're strong enough to visit," said Elenn.

An awkward moment passed with neither of them knowing what to say next.

"They will all miss you," said Elenn. It was a way of acknowledging that they both knew Nula's work with the squadron was over.

"I will miss all of them, too," said Nula.

"But I plan to come to see you often. I hope it's all right if I come often to Crafting."

"You should come," said Nula. "I hope you do."

"Did Master Yinob help you today?" asked Elenn.

"Yes. He gave me some very wise advice. He said that even though life is more complicated than the mind of Lern Beyana, sometimes it may help to recite the Names when trouble seems great."

"That's very good advice," said Elenn.

"Yes, and we did recite the names together."

"Did that make you feel better?"

"I felt better *while* we were reciting the Names," said Nula. "The worry came back as soon as we were done, but at least I know it does make me feel better for a short while when I recite them."

"Do you want to recite the names right now, together?" asked Elenn.

Nula hesitated, and answered, "No, not now, thank you. Maybe another time."

"Have the meals here been good?" asked Elenn.

"The food is fine," said Nula, but he didn't want to talk about the food at the infirmary. It was not worth talking about. He didn't want to make small talk with Master Elenn. They might not have another chance to talk alone. Finally he said, "Master Elenn, there's something bothering me that I'd like to tell you, but I'm afraid you will be offended."

Elenn hesitated. He hoped Nula knew that there were some things that were better left unsaid. "Master Nula, if it's about feeling a temptation to break our oath, I want you to know that every one of us who wears a hood struggles with that."

"The point of the oath is to stop us from getting deranged like that uedin you found this morning. I know that. What I don't know is what it feels like to do the thing that I'm not supposed to do. *You* know what it feels like, but *I* don't."

"Believe me, it's not worth the disaster that it brings," said Elenn.

Nula thought carefully before speaking, then said, "Master Onnek told me that he shared neck before." Onnek was Nula's generation.

"Master Onnek from Southgate?"

"That's one of the reasons the Southgate squadron guards are asking for help from the non-hooded guards."

"When did you hear this?"

"I went and found Onnek after that master threw himself off the Haka Cliffs. I was very troubled by that. I felt like I should have run after him when he took off towards the cliffs."

"I'm the one who told you to let him go. You were just doing what I told you. We didn't know what he was going to do."

"But I wanted to talk to Master Onnek and Master Posha. They were the ones who found him, and I just wanted to hear what they had to say. I found out that shortly after that incident, they stopped patrolling together. Master Onnek and I went for a long walk, and he told me that he had broken his oath, and he was trying to be very careful not to bring shame to the squadron. He prefers to partner with a non-hooded guard."

Elenn thought about this for a moment. "I can see the logic in that," he said.

"I asked Master Onnek what it was like to share necks," said Nula.

"That was probably not a good idea. Not when Master Onnek is trying hard to keep his oath."

"I know," said Nula. "It was a bad idea to ask. But Onnek is the only person I could ask."

"Why couldn't you ask me?" said Elenn, but after he said it, he realized it was not the right thing to say. Nula's reason for not asking Elenn might be that he felt tempted by Elenn. Elenn wasn't prepared to talk about that.

Fortunately, Nula didn't answer the question. He continued, "Master Onnek told me that some of the hooded masters refer to feeding as 'passing-of-life.' Can you imagine that?"

"I know where *that* came from," said Elenn with a bit of disgust.

"What do you mean?" asked Nula.

"Do you remember when I told you about that distribution master, Pavis, who used to be a server?"

"Yes, I remember something about a Master Pavis," said Nula.

"Well, he referred to feeding as 'passing-of-life.' He didn't want to take hood. He had to be convinced," said Elenn. "I'm sure he's the one who started that. I just saw him, too. He's well established with the distribution masters now. He delivered the message from Huma about you being brought here."

Nula wasn't distracted by the mention of Pavis. He pressed Elenn, "Is it true, though? When you share necks, is it like passing-of-life?"

"Oh, I don't know about that, Master Nula. Only those who go to the Lake can ever know what passing-of-life is really like."

"But you and I won't *ever* go to the Lake," argued Nula. "Just now, when I told you that I asked Master Onnek about sharing necks, you said, 'Why couldn't you ask me?' So I'm asking you now. What is it like to share necks? Is it amazing?"

Elenn took a deep breath. "It's not an experience we need to have," he said.

"Master Elenn, I don't think you understand what it's like to be in my situation. You *know* there's a chance that I'm going to have an early death."

Elenn thought about the times when he had been near death himself. The first time was when he almost let himself drown when he was swept into a Great Rains river shortly after he had joined the guards. The second time was when he was attacked by wasps with Master Hela and the child-uedin at Redrock. For a normal uedin, the fear of an early demise was, at its core, a fear of losing one's passing-of-life. For the barren, passing-of-life was already lost to them, but that only made the finality of death all the more dreadful to think about.

"Death is a great worry to all of us in hood, Master Nula," said Elenn.

"I don't want to die without experiencing whatever it is that makes hooded masters call it 'passing-of-life'—whether that's a proper way to refer to it or not," whimpered Nula.

"Master Nula, you know that no good can come from sharing necks. Besides, you don't need to think so much about dying! You're not going to die any time soon!"

Nula took a moment to summon his courage to say what he wanted to say. "I want to share necks one time in my life. I want to know what it feels like." Then he leaned forward and clutched the sleeve of Elenn's robe. "Please, Master Elenn, can we? I don't know anyone else in hood that I can ask. I don't want to go looking for it outside the capital walls like the hooded masters we see every day." Nula looked at Elenn with pleading eyes.

"Oh, Master Nula, please don't ask me for that," said Elenn miserably. Nula had done exactly what Elenn had hoped he wouldn't do. He had brought Elenn to that terrible point at which he had to choose which side of himself to deny. For indeed, to some degree, he wanted to let Nula have the experience of sharing necks. Granted, he had caught himself looking at Nula with desire more than once, but that was something he could suppress. What he couldn't suppress was the sadness he felt, thinking about Nula's lonely life and the dreadful fact that he could die. If Nula died, would Elenn someday regret that he had insisted on acting only as the proper guard, and denying him this favor?

"You're ill," said Elenn. "It would be dangerous to do such a thing when your heart is weak."

"Master Goril had me doing exercise this morning," argued Nula. "I did shifting exercises in the courtyard. I'm strong! They think it's just when I'm reclining that my heart is very weak!" He leaned forward from the drop-back chair and stood up.

"It's not a good idea," said Elenn, though he felt himself faltering.

"You don't desire it," said Nula, realizing that he was being refused. "I'm very sorry. How disgusting I must seem."

"That's not true," said Elenn. He felt lost. At this moment, he actually felt no desire to share necks with Nula. Many times in the past he had felt it. He had watched Nula from behind and imagined seeing his bare neck, strap undone. He had fought with himself to keep from thinking about it at night. But now it was not desire that moved him; it was love for his comrade. He wanted to give him this momentary comfort and pleasure. He wanted Nula to know he cared about him enough to do something that didn't necessarily make sense.

"Master Nula," Elenn finally said in a cautious, whispering voice, "I will."

Nula looked at him with wide eyes. He was filled with excitement, but also a little afraid.

"Now?" asked Nula.

"Now might be best," said Elenn. "It's quiet. No one is here."

"You will have to show me how," said Nula, apologizing for his innocence.

"Yes. I want you to know that you may not feel good about it later, but at least you will know what it is, this thing that you are afraid you're going to miss."

"Master Elenn, please don't if you don't want to," said Nula.

"I want to give you what you want. I want that the most," said Elenn. He reached with one hand to get the flap of his hood out from under the shoulder of his own robe.

"Have you ever thought about doing this before?" asked Nula. "With me?"

"Many times," said Elenn.

"I have thought of it so many times, Master Elenn. Sometimes it was very hard to work with you."

Elenn took out the flap from his other shoulder and then reached back and pulled the hood from his head. To Nula he looked calm and strong with his head naked. Nula remembered seeing Elenn like this before they were introduced, when Elenn appeared as the first master to receive hood at the hood-taking ceremony. Now he was seeing him with it off for the first time since that day, and he thought Elenn was the most beautiful ue-din he had ever seen. He got suddenly very nervous and started to tremble.

"Shhh. . . It's okay, Master Nula. I will help you." He put out the lamp so that they were in near darkness. Then he quietly reached under Nula's plain robe, removed the flaps of his hood, and carefully lifted it from around his head.

"I don't know what to do," said Nula timidly.

"I will put my mouth on your neck, and then you will understand how I do it, and you can do the same thing to me," Elenn whispered. Now it was happening, and there was no more to think about. He drew one of the regular chairs up beside Nula's drop-back chair. "Sit again, and lean forward," he said. They sat, and Nula leaned far forward, his face nearly to his knees. He placed one hand on Nula's bare head and the other on his back. As he breathed, Nula's back rose and fell under Elenn's hand. Then Elenn leaned way over and ran the tip of his nose slowly around the edge of Nula's neckstrap, finally wiggling his nose in the side as if trying to nuzzle his way under the strap. Nula exhaled heavily. Elenn could smell the scent of Nula's skullsap; there was no way he was going to stop now. He rubbed the middle of Nula's back with one hand and ran a finger along his ear with the other. Nula moved his body ticklishly under these touches. He loved the feel of Elenn's hands.

"Master Elenn, I want to take off my neckstrap, but I want to do it myself. I want to remove the pouch myself," Nula said.

"Go ahead," said Elenn, and sat up to let Nula undo his neckstrap. Nula fumbled momentarily with the pouch, then removed it and placed it carefully on the table by the lamp so that it would not leak out. They paused and looked at one another, but it was dark and they couldn't see each other's eyes well.

"Are you all right? Do you want to stop?" asked Elenn.

"No. Show me how to do it, then I will do it to you," said Nula, and he leaned forward once again.

"Master Nula, I want you to promise me just one thing," said Elenn.

"What?" asked Nula.

"If, later, you are disgusted by having done this, please don't try to pretend that everything is just fine. Tell me if you don't want me to visit you at Crafting after you go back. I'll stay away if you don't want to see me," said Elenn.

"That won't happen, Master Elenn. I'm very grateful to you for doing this."

"But will you promise me that, in case you are disgusted?"

"I promise," said Nula.

"All right. I do care very much about you, Master Nula," said Elenn. He leaned over and touched his cheek to the base of Nula's neck. Then he put his mouth over the protruding stub of glass catheter that came out just below the hard edge of his skullwomb. He let Nula feel his lips and tongue around the catheter. When Nula carelessly let out a moan, he caressed his back to calm him. He drew a bit of the warm viscous ooze into his mouth. In seconds, he felt its intoxicating effect. A great wave of dreamy ecstasy rushed over him.

"Ahh, Master Elenn. . ." whispered Nula. "If normal uedin knew what this felt like, they would all put catheters in their necks."

Elenn thought the words, *"You think that already, and you haven't even had anything from my neck yet,"* but he was too deep in pleasure to speak out loud. He reached behind his head to undo his own neckstrap for Nula.

Part 4

IN THE MIDST OF FIASCO

Controversy in the
High Server Assembly

Nekur nearly chuckled at the thought that crossed his mind as he sat with the assembly of high servers waiting for the Most High to arrive. The thought was that they would probably have a much better meeting and a better discussion if he didn't show up! They needed to unify their approach to him. He was obviously lost in his own world. A few of the high servers could see it, and Nekur was one of them. It wasn't even necessarily a problem that the Most High was lost in his own world; that, perhaps, was to be expected. But too many in the assembly seemed to want to follow the Most High right into his mental miasma. What would happen if the whole assembly got taken in, swallowed up in their admiration for the young prodigy who had come along and led them all to this so-called "new level of communion"? Who would oversee the operations of the temple? He knew the answer to that question. The temple would have to be overseen by those who *didn't* get taken in. Nekur knew that he was unlikely to become one of the Most High's dumb admirers. He never did quite trust the server who sat in the chair of the Most High. Since that young server had first come to the assembly of high servers, and then quickly distinguished himself, Nekur suspected that there was something less than genuine about his remarkable unnameliness. He was so "naked" about his devotion. Can one really be unnamely and still set himself apart by demonstrating such unique devotion? Anyway, at the very least, it was time to start thinking of the Most High as someone they had to take care of instead of someone to follow.

He heard the door tarp being lifted and the shuffling of feet as the Most High arrived. The high servers sat up in attention, but out of politeness, they all refrained from ogling him. He came in and sat at the head of the room, where finally the assembly greeted him with their eyes. It was the Most High who would have to speak first, and unless certain among them were smart and spoke carefully, the meeting could come to nothing, and they would all just continue in their downward slide.

They waited for him to speak. His gaze floated dispassionately around, neither making nor avoiding eye contact with the high servers. He seemed completely unconcerned about the fact that everyone was waiting for him. Of course, this was to be interpreted as apathy born from the fact that only the Soft One received his attention. After a certain length of time passed with no word, Nekur felt a flash of aggravation. Was this Most High really so wrapped up in his communion with the Soft One that he couldn't even speak and open the meeting? Somehow it seemed a little fake.

The Most High sat quietly, furrowed his brow, and tilted his head slightly as if trying to figure something out. He wore this perplexed expression for a long while. All eyes were on him.

"We will begin with a mind-stilling," he finally said. A few of the high servers glanced around to see if any of the others shared their impatience. A mind-stilling could take half the night, and nothing would be settled. But the Most High didn't look to see who approved; he appeared very confident that a mind-stilling was best. Nekur knew that there was a faction of the assembly who would be very impressed by the instruction to commence with mindstilling. They were the ones forever reminding their fellow servers not to behave like masters, not to argue about anything, not to hold opinions, lest it upset the Soft One.

So oil was allowed to burn in the lamp for a long hour while the high servers sat in silence for the mind-stilling. But Nekur did not admonish himself too much for allowing his mind to wander wherever it wanted. Mostly he thought about how to get the Most High to delegate responsibilities to himself and other cool-minded members of the assembly so that they could get the temple operating as usual again.

Finally the Most High picked up the small mallet that was sitting on a hollow block in front of him and lightly tapped the block, calling the mind-stilling to a close. The high servers in the assembly opened their eyes.

The Most High spoke softly and slowly. "You wish to voice your concerns," he said.

Oh, thank goodness! Nekur was not only relieved to be over with that mind-stilling—it had been getting a bit tedious for him—but what a relief to hear that the Most High was directly inviting them to voice their concerns. He didn't hesitate, for he had already practiced what he wanted to say. He raised hands to face, but it was another high server who caught the eye of the Most High and was given the nod to speak first.

Oh no, thought Nekur, seeing who was first. That one is completely taken in by all this "new level of communion" nonsense. What kind of idiocy were they about to hear?

In a whisper, the server asked, "Most High, would it please the Soft One if we made greater dietary restrictions for the temple?" It was customary to whisper to the Most High in his own residence, but some of the more dedicated high servers whispered even at the assembly meetings, which Nekur found irritating.

"What did you have in mind?" asked the Most High.

"We could eliminate all sweets, all forms of yeastdrink, and eat our meals cold," the high server explained, still whispering.

"And how do you believe this would please the Soft One?" asked the Most High.

"We will pay less attention to our food and more attention to our exercises, and to the Soft One," whispered the high server eagerly.

The Most High almost seemed not to be listening to this explanation. He was looking at the wall on the opposite side of the room. But after a considerable pause, he said, "Such restrictions are not necessary. When you are so attentive to your exercises, and to the Soft One, that eating doesn't interest you, *then* will be the time to pass over sweets, because you simply won't want them."

The high server tried to hide his disappointment. Nekur knew exactly what he must be thinking. *"But we want to be in a high level of communion with the Soft One, too!"* How pathetic and stupid they were!

The one who wanted the restriction looked around to see what kind of reactions there were on the assembly to this response from the Most High. He was hoping to see some disappointed looks. Instead, almost everyone on the assembly seemed to be pondering what the Most High had said—that the only time to pass over sweets was when you didn't want them. Only Nekur was looking at him, and it was with a rather smug and unsympathetic smile.

"Are there other concerns?" asked the Most High.

"Yes," Nekur said in a normal voice, "There is something else we might discuss."

"Please speak. Have no regard for me, but please remember the Soft One is awake."

That was exactly the kind of talk that Nekur despised. Before this Most High came around, nobody ever talked about the Soft One being awake. She was always said to be asleep, and the server tradition was to aid her in having the most peaceful slumber. But those were things that could not be said out loud, for it would only invite a long and confusing explanation from the Most High that went on and on and made no sense to him.

"For many of us, it is precisely our regard for *you* that gives us concern," said Nekur.

"What is your concern, high server?" asked the Most High calmly.

"Some of us feel that you should come out of your isolation. We feel sure that the Soft One wants you to be healthy and strong. You should start eating with us and joining us in exercises again. That is my concern." Nekur felt that this was the best way to nudge the conversation in the right direction to address whether the Most High was really fit to be making decisions for the entire community.

The Most High again let a long moment pass before responding. He said, "High server, I do not know why the Soft One has fixated on me." He stared at Nekur for a long time, as if trying to help him see his point. "Does that answer your question?" he finally asked.

Nekur was a little taken aback. The Most High had not answered his question at all, but instead, he had answered another question, and perhaps a more important one. Why, indeed, had the Soft One fixated on this high server, even before he became Most High? But he had to come back with a strategic response. "I think we understand that the Soft One doesn't tell us *why anything*," said Nekur. "But if your communion is sound, it will not lead to your physical decline." It was a bold and risky thing to say, but Nekur was going to use this point to gain an advantage with his intentions. The Most High's physical decline was already in evidence.

Nekur scrutinized the reaction of the Most High, watching for any sign of agitation, but the Most High remained perfectly relaxed.

"I have told you before that the Soft One needs us very much right now," said the Most High. "That is why she has drawn me away from regular practice. But for it to be a sound communion, it's true I must remain in good health."

"So will you eat with us and join us in exercises once again?" asked Nekur.

"I will take the question to the Soft One, and I believe she will lead me to accept your suggestion," said the Most High.

It was not a concession that Nekur was hoping for. He wanted the Most High to react negatively to the suggestion, which would illustrate to the rest of the assembly that they needed to start acting more independently and work around the Most High and his total preoccupation with communion. By agreeing to reconsider his isolation, the Most High averted the intervention that Nekur wanted. His little attempt was unsuccessful, and he felt a tiny bit of frustration. The high server who had asked for food restrictions was now looking at him to return the offensive smile. And so it was unlikely that the assembly was going to be able to wrest any decision-making power from the Most High—at least until he deteriorated more. . . but how long would that take? And how unbalanced and divorced from the realities of orderly administration would things get before these other high servers might wake up and see that the Most High was not fit to do anything but lounge on pillows and ponder his own communion?

Later, back in his chamber, Tilke sat in stillness with eyes closed. *Health is an indicator of a sound communion.* This was on Tilke's mind. He was wrapped around it tightly, trying to absorb the thought. The high server's point had quite penetrated him. It did not matter what things lay around its source, be those things master-like or not. As a server, his whole purpose was to give all of his attention to the Soft One. And he had known before this that in the interest of serving her in his best capacity, self-care was important. But just how important was it? That was the question that had come to him at the meeting of the assembly.

One can never know the real importance of self-care when attending to the Soft One. This was his next thought. It was followed by a flash of understanding in which he saw himself as he appeared to the Soft One—as a timid and small being in a bubble of his own humility. The Soft One needed a server whom she could rely upon completely, and the conditions for that seemed to involve a yielding and recessive nature, even on the physical level. In this case, she needed him to gain strength. Tilke knew that the Soft One generally shielded him from problems that she faced, but this seemed to be one that she was allowing him to know. It energized him to think that he could serve her in this unanticipated way by being more attentive to his own self-care.

I will remember the importance of self-care, and I will always invite you to remind me when I need to give attention to my own health.

This made very good sense, and he let the words repeat over and over in his mind to let the Soft One receive them. *I will always invite you to remind me. . .I will always invite you to remind me. . .I will always invite you to remind me.* The Most High didn't expect to receive an immediate response.

"THIS IS MY FIRST REMINDER. YOU MUST ATTEND TO YOUR OWN HEALTH FIRST, EVEN BEFORE YOU INVITE ME TO BE WITH YOU."

Unlike the usual flashes and inferences, it came as a chain of words forming a complete thought, a thought not his own. Tilke opened his eyes in amazement and stared at the blank wall. Two attendants were sitting silently by the door. They obviously had heard nothing. This was the second time Tilke had experienced such a thing. The first communication from the Soft One, some moon cycles ago, had been, *"LET US BE AT PEACE."* That simple phrase, perfectly consistent with all his mind-melding and experience with the Soft One, had been the first time actual words had come into Tilke's head that seemed not to be his own words. It was followed by a time of great self-doubt for the Most High, as he had asked himself—was he sure it wasn't just *him*, the one the temple had chosen to act as the Most High, saying the words "Let us be at peace" in his head? Was it *he*, the Most High, proposing peace to the Soft One? No, it definitely was not. He had concluded, based on his certainty that he would never be so presumptuous as to suggest anything to the Soft One, that it had been the Soft One saying it to *him*.

In all uedin tradition, whether inside the temple or not, it was understood that the Soft One did not speak. The Most High had already created considerable disturbance by telling the high servers that the Soft One was awake. So the first time he had received an actual message of words from her, he had chosen not to tell them, lest the event create too much upset.

He tried to remain calm about the fact that the Soft One had again *spoken* to him by placing an actual sequence of words in his head, and now he needed to comprehend the instruction that he was being given. He had invited her to remind him when self-care was needed, and she had immediately given him the message that it was needed as a prerequisite to any communion at all! Tilke's physical health must be of great importance to the Soft One!

The Most High turned his head and raised an arm to summon one of the two attendants who were sitting by the door. The older attendant, the one with the large nose and timid eyes came to hear what the Most High wanted.

"I would like to send a message to the assembly about today's meeting," he said quietly.

The attendant nodded and responded, leaning forward to whisper in his ear, "We could prepare ink for the Most High to hold the brush himself, or we could transcribe for the Most High."

"I will hold the brush myself, thank you server," He looked lovingly at the attendant, and the attendant smiled back reservedly.

The attendant went back to speak with the other server, who then left immediately to get supplies for writing. While the supplies were brought and ink was prepared, the Most High continued to ponder this development. He was to make his health a great priority, just as he had been told by that high server in the assembly. He would send a message to all of them to let them know that he would begin to take meals and exercises with them starting tomorrow.

Master Benar Receives a Visit from Master Elenn

Benar had taken a sealed jar of yeastdrink from the Quarterhouse kitchen and was planning to offer Master Elenn a drink. When it got close to the time for the visit and Benar was waiting for Elenn's arrival, he decided to open the jar early and have a sip while he waited. But when he went to get a cup, he realized that all three of his cups were in the washbucket, which was otherwise dry. The cups would have to be taken to the kitchen for washing. This created quite a dilemma. He had to have clean cups in order to invite Master Elenn to enjoy a drink, but if he went to the kitchen to wash the cups, Master Elenn might show up and find him not at home. There was only one thing to do. Benar had clean soup bowls, and they would have to have their yeastdrink out of those. Master Elenn was always so agreeable to anything; he would certainly not mind.

Pleased with having resolved that matter, Benar went to the shelf and took down two soup bowls. He still had a hankering for an early sip of yeastdrink while he waited, so he chose one of the bowls for himself and poured a bit from the jar. It was just a swallow. He found the flavor very agreeable. Perhaps just a bit more... When he tilted the jar to pour a little more into his bowl, quite a bit more came out than he meant to pour, but he shrugged and decided that he would simply have to drink it quickly before his guest arrived. He lifted the bowl to his mouth and took a good sip. It was fine yeastdrink. He wondered how long the jar he had found had been sitting there in a forgotten cupboard corner of the Quarterhouse kitchen. When he went to take a second sip, some of the yeastdrink splashed against his cheeks and dribbled down onto his caretaker robe. The brown liquid formed two wet stains on either side of his chest. Holding the bowl off to the side, he peered down his nose at the stains. How aggravating! Now his robe had these stains, and he didn't have time to clean it! Oh, well. . . He drank the rest of the drink in his bowl.

Just then, Master Elenn came to his door. Benar shouted, "Welcome, Master Elenn, please come in!" As Elenn ducked under the door tarp to enter, Benar rose to greet his counselee. He noticed Elenn's cautious expression and felt a momentary embarrassment. He was, after all, holding a *bowl* filled with yeastdrink and had two brown stains on his robe. But rather than digging himself deeper with apologies, he chose to ignore the awkwardness of the situation and just invite Elenn to join him. "Master Elenn, before we talk about anything serious, we're going to have a cup of yeastdrink together."

To Benar's relief, Elenn smiled and refrained from asking the obvious questions.

"Oh, yes, that's right—I don't have any clean cups right now, so I hope you don't mind if I serve the yeastdrink in these bowls."

"I see you've given it a taste," said Elenn.

"I had to make sure it was good enough to serve," explained Benar, smiling at his own half-fib. "But be careful drinking from the bowl. It drips!" He poured some into Elenn's cup first and then refilled his own.

Benar quickly surmised that Elenn was in no mood for a party. Perhaps a drink would loosen him up. It was starting to give Benar a pleasant and tipsy feeling.

"I can only have one," said Elenn. "From here, I'm going on to Crafting to see Master Nula."

"Wait till you have a cup and see how good it is. Then you can decide."

"Well, Master Nula is expecting me," said Elenn.

"I'm so sorry to hear about Master Nula's illness," said Benar. He tried to achieve the right look of sympathetic concern, but it was hard to do because he was feeling the effect of the drink.

"The medic masters have said that he may remain healthy for a very long time; he just can't endure hard physical activity."

"That's good to hear," answered Benar, taking the comment as a show of optimism. He wanted to make this a pleasant visit, not a depressing one. "And now you'll partner with one of the non-hooded guards from Flatpools Station?"

"Yes, with Master Ippal. He went with me while Master Nula was at the infirmary. He's agreed to join the squadron."

"So I'll meet him at our next alliance meeting?"

"Yes, I suppose so."

"Good, I'll look forward to that. So far, the non-hooded guards have worked very well with the squadron, don't you think?" Benar smiled to convey his optimism.

"It's true," said Elenn. He wasn't looking very cheerful. Granted, Elenn's partner had taken ill—that was very unfortunate—but there was nothing that either of them could do about it.

"We must keep on smiling, never feel sorry for ourselves," said Benar. Elenn did not smile, and Benar knew that his choice of words had missed the mark. Hoping to get the conversation back on track, he said, "Well, it's very nice that you're planning to pay a visit to Master Nula, and I'm sure he'll be glad to hear that your fellow guard from Flatpools has agreed to take over his position."

"Yes, he knows Master Ippal will do a good job."

"That's the important thing. The hooded masters are counting on the squadron to coach them."

"Coach them?"

"Yes," said Benar. "Wouldn't you say that you squadron guards coach the hooded masters?"

"I suppose," said Elenn.

"By the way," said Benar, "I want to prepare you; Master Yenca has an astonishing proposal that he's going to bring up at the next squadron meeting." This was not the sort of gossip to share with a counselee, but the drink had him feeling buoyant, and he felt like discarding his reservations.

"What's the proposal?"

"Some of the caretakers wish to construct a hut outside the capital walls so that they can work with syndrome uedin who are out of hood and needing attention. They want the squadron to help oversee the project and be a part of the operation, once it's in place. I'm not sure how all that will work." Benar shrugged and took another good sip from his cup.

"They want to build a permanent hut outside the walls—and staff it all the time? I'm not sure if there's a need for that at this point," commented Elenn.

"That's exactly what I think," said Benar. He swirled the remaining bit in his bowl, finished it up, and poured himself another. "Apparently the proposal comes from Master Jutef. He's convinced that the hood statute is bound for widespread failure. I think he's just expressing a lack of confidence in something that was his own idea. Anyhow, he convinced Master Yenca, and now Master Yenca has decided to bring the proposal to the alliance to see if there is agreement, and then they will take it to the masters council. I'm telling you because I suspect that you'll be dragged into it. . . Sorry, old friend." Benar picked up the jar. "Are you sure you won't have more than one cup?"

"No more for me," said Elenn. "Master Benar, I'm also worried that the hood statute may fail. Aren't you?"

Benar frowned. "Well, it sometimes fails on an individual level, we know that, but overall there's no reason to abandon the statute. Our syndrome masters are quite capable of keeping their oath."

"What makes you say that?"

"Why, *you*, of course." Benar sat himself up straight as he said it, and he felt a little woozy. "Me? What do you mean?"

"You are proof that a responsible uedin with the syndrome can keep the oath." Benar smiled, pleased with himself for taking the opportunity to pay his counselee this compliment. But then he noticed the blank stare of horror on Elenn's face.

It took him but a moment to figure it out. "Master Elenn, you've broken your oath," he said without emotion. He hiccupped, and then he watched carefully for Elenn's response. What is possible he was misunderstanding? But Elenn's look of defeat put away any doubts. Elenn gazed down at his bowl of yeastdrink. He looked forlorn.

"Oh, the bowls," said Benar. "I'm very sorry I don't have my cups clean. . ." He wanted to provide an escape for his counselee, should he prefer not to talk about his mistake. Once a mistake is made, there is nothing to do but avoid it in the future. Perhaps Elenn didn't need to say anything about it.

But as Benar noticed the pleading, lost look in Elenn's eyes, he understood that Elenn was not interested in light-heartedly changing the subject. Benar thought about what sort of reassuring thing he could say. Finally, he did his best to look calm and unconcerned, and wiping a drip of yeastdrink from the tabletop, he commented, "But you have not been taking off your hood outside the capital walls, I'm sure. It must have happened just once. . . Am I right?"

"Just once," said Elenn.

"There you are. It was just once, and it can remain just once," said Benar assuringly, "So please don't waste any time being miserable about it. You're a fine guard, Master Elenn."

Elenn kept looking at him. "It was with Master Nula,"

"Master Nula. . ." repeated Benar with a slow nod. "I suppose I shouldn't be too surprised."

"He wanted to experience. . ." Elenn's face finally showed a quiver of emotion. "I'm so sorry, Master Benar," he said.

"It's all right," said Benar, "But see the difficulty it's causing you. I hope it won't happen any more."

"I think it's most likely that it won't," said Elenn,

Benar was glad to hear that Elenn was at least thinking properly. "Given your position with the hood squadron, I'm sure you won't want others to know about it. I will certainly say nothing about it to anyone."

"Master Benar, do you ever wonder what it is like to crave the sharing of necks, as we with the syndrome do?"

"My only understanding of the craving is that I know it must be tremendously powerful; otherwise it would not have caused you to take off your hood, Master Elenn. Being the fine guard that you are, I'm sure you did not give into it easily."

"Thank you," said Elenn. Benar thought that he saw a bit of recovered pride in Elenn's expression, and he was glad that he had said the right thing. Then Elenn said, "It's impossible to know who, if any, is keeping the oath. For all I know, all of us in hood are breaking it."

"No, no, no, no, no, don't say that!" Benar shook his head emphatically, "We mustn't ever let that become the common assumption. You and the other squadron guards are very important role models for all the hooded masters, especially the second generation hooded."

"I recognize that," said Elenn. "Master Nula and I have befriended three hooded masters of the western outfields who are all second generation. We certainly wouldn't want them to know that we've broken our oath." He seemed to ponder the matter for a moment before adding, "Well, they may not be as innocent as we think they are, but there would be no point in their knowing."

"Of course, the senior caretakers know that you hooded guards have no easier time of it than any of the others. One of the Southgate squadron guards has requested a non-hooded partner, and rumor has it he's going to be recommending the whole squadron be reorganized similarly with non-hooded partners."

"You're talking about Master Onnek," said Elenn.

"You know about Master Onnek?"

"Yes. I heard that he had requested a non-hooded partner."

"Do you know why?"

"He broke his oath."

"Yes, but it wasn't with Master Posha. It was with some other hooded master. It seems he requested a non-hooded partner because he became convinced that he couldn't trust himself working closely with a hooded guard any longer."

"But if we can't trust ourselves, how can we be effective as a squadron?" asked Elenn.

"To be very honest with you, Master Elenn, I have always suspected that regular non-hooded guards would eventually have to take on the greater responsibility of monitoring the hooded masters. Master Yenca and I discussed it before he ever spoke with Master Wanba. We knew that the guards would not want to do it." He knew that he was being very candid with Elenn, and maybe the yeastdrink was loosening his tongue more than it should be loosened, but as Elenn had been very honest with him, he felt he owed him that much candor.

"Master Benar, if we were to recruit hooded masters of other professions and have them change their whole lives to become guards, and if we were to have a very large squadron of hooded guards, do you think it might be unnecessary to depend on the regular guards?"

Benar was uncomfortable with this question. It put him on the spot. His counselee might be offended, but the idea of building up the squadron to a huge force was a terrible idea, and he couldn't let him run away with it. "That would be greatly disruptive to the capital," said Benar, and lowered his eyes to convey that he didn't want to encourage such a plan.

"It's because we can't control ourselves," said Elenn sadly.

"Well, Master Elenn, if you had to take off your hood, then I don't expect very many of my other counselees to keep theirs on." Benar meant it as a compliment, but he hoped he wasn't too drunk and saying all the wrong things.

"You may be giving me too much credit, Master Benar," said Elenn. He finished the tiny bit of yeastdrink at the bottom of his bowl and put it down.

"Are you quite sure you won't have more than one?" asked Benar.

"No, thank you Master Benar. I must be off." He stood up to signal that he was leaving. "But I will see you at the next alliance meeting. I'm sure it's going to be an interesting one, with all these new proposals."

Benar didn't notice that Elenn was standing to leave, and he kept talking, "For the first time, we'll have regular guards there as squadron members. The ones that step in now, like your Master Ippal, will eventually have a very important role to play."

"Yes. Well, Master Ippal is an excellent guard. If we get more like him for the squadron, I will have no regrets about it. I'll see you again soon, Master Benar."

Benar gestured to emphasize that he was about to offer his true opinion. "Master Ippal and the other few non-hooded guards who are stepping up may turn out to become very prominent figures in the capital one day," he said.

"He's a fine guard. Farewell, Master Benar."

". . .because they will be the best trained in dealing with the hooded masters," said Benar. He was a little drunk and slow to notice that his guest wanted to leave. "They'll be leading the way for all the other guards."

"Good-bye, Master Benar," said Elenn, and raised hands to face in a very pronounced manner.

Benar smiled widely. "Good-bye, Master Elenn. It was very good talking with you. I'll see you at the next squadron meeting."

He stood at the doorway and watched as Elenn walked off, then he turned to pick up the bowls. "Shield the lern," he said to himself, "If Guardmaster Elenn can't manage to keep his hood on, I don't suppose any of them can. . ." He noticed that Elenn had left a small amount of yeastdrink in his bowl. No sense letting that go to waste. He swished it around once and then drank it, belched loudly, and let the bowls drop with a clatter into the bucket.

A Shift in the Wind

When Elenn reached the station, one of the Crafting guards was reading alone by the window, but Nula wasn't there.

"Has Master Nula finished his shift today?" asked Elenn.

"Yes, he's in the courtyard," said the guard. "We all know that he's not supposed to strain his heart, but he insists on doing shiftings."

Elenn found Nula attempting a flat form. His effort struck Elenn as particularly pathetic—not because his shoulders and buttocks stuck up way too much, but because his skullwomb, which is supposed to rise from the plane of the body and be exalted, was covered by his hood. The centerpiece of the form was under cover. Of course, he would never say that out loud. What really needed to be expressed was that Nula had no business attempting this extremely difficult pose with his heart condition. He waited, however, for Nula to hold the form for a short while and slowly come out of it.

Nula had heard footsteps but did not interrupt the process by turning his head to see who was there until he was pushing himself back up onto his feet. When his eyes caught sight of Elenn, they revealed a hint of surprise. It was an unannounced visit.

"Oh, Master Elenn," he said respectfully, quickly withdrawing from the focused attention of shifting and raising hands to face with slight clumsiness. Though they had shared necks, Nula still regarded Elenn as his senior guard.

Elenn spoke in a disapproving tone, "Master Nula, you haven't been out of the infirmary three days, and you're doing shifting exercises? Is that wise?"

"I feel fine. I feel as strong as ever," said Nula.

"Well, I hope you are following the advice of the medic masters," said Elenn.

"All I do is waste time at the station. I used to walk all over the capital multiple times a day. A few shifting exercises is nothing compared to that."

"You might start with the rock form or something, instead of going straight away for the flat form—the hardest one!"

"I know I'm not getting very far with it. I can't seem to release my shoulders and hips from their joints."

"Leave that to the servers," said Elenn.

"Was anyone at the station office? You want some tea?"

"No tea. I just had yeastdrink," said Elenn. "I was visiting Master Benar."

"How is Master Benar?"

"Oh, he's just fine. . . He drank three cups for my one."

"Did he say anything about the alliance meeting next lesser moon? I'm not planning to stop attending, you know."

"Yes, there are some new developments coming up," said Elenn. "For one thing, the caretakers want to build a hut outside the capital walls to tend to barren who are out of hood."

"Really? They believe that's necessary?"

"They do," said Elenn. Nula apparently did not want to enter a discussion about the increase of oath-breaking. He didn't press for any more details. "Also, what you told me about Master On-nek was confirmed, and now he's recommending we should all be partnered with non-hooded guards."

Nula maintained a neutral and passive expression. This was clearly more about which he didn't want to talk. "Come back with me to the station office," he said. "You don't have to drink tea with me, but I'd like to have some myself."

Elenn followed Nula back to the office where the bored guard looked up from his book of codes and said, "Master Nula, will you be here for a little while? Until Master Huma comes back?"

"Yes, I'll be here. You can go ahead if you have something to do," Nula offered. He flashed a smile at Elenn, and it made Elenn very uncomfortable with the thought that Nula might actually want to share necks with him again right there! Nula noticed that Elenn did not return his smile and awkwardly resumed his serious face. The guard excused himself with hand to face for Elenn and left them alone. Nula went to the small burner at the back of the office, stirred the smoldering charcoal, and put on a kettle of water.

Elenn saw that there was a comfortable chair, probably the one that Master Huma usually sat in, and a hard wooden bench beside it. On impulse, he sat in the comfortable chair, even though as a guest he would ordinarily wait for Nula to invite him to sit in it. "Master Benar said that the caretakers always anticipated that non-hooded would end up taking over the squad," he said, loudly enough for Nula to hear from the other side of the station office.

"Maybe it's just Master Benar who always anticipated it," said Nula.

"That's true. Master Yenca seems to believe in us," said Elenn.

"So Master Benar doesn't have confidence in us. . ." commented Nula, walking back. Elenn wanted to see the look on his face when he saw him sitting in Huma's chair. He expected Nula to take it as a sign that he was acting like a senior guard—something that would point out the distance between them. But Nula looked happy to see him there, as though it were a sign, instead, of their mutual ease with one another.

"As I was leaving him, he kept on telling me about how the regular guards were going to need to be well-trained so that they could 'deal with the hooded masters.'"

"The whole point of the squadron is that it's made up of hooded guards!" said Nula.

"That could change suddenly. . . Though, I suppose you won't be on duty with us anyway. . ." said Elenn, thinking it fine to speak frankly and openly. He immediately regretted his choice of words.

Nula let out a little inscrutable laugh, turned around, and walked back over to the charcoal burner. He lifted the kettle and swirled it so that the bit of water inside sizzled on the sides of the kettle. It was hot enough. He poured it over a strainer of milk-grass into his cup.

"Well, I suppose Master Benar isn't the only one who doesn't have faith in the squadron," said Nula.

Elenn thought about saying outright that he didn't have faith in the squadron either, or faith in barren of any ilk, for that matter. But he was afraid he might have already offended Nula enough.

Nula carried his cup to the table and seated himself on a bench. "So, some uedin don't trust us hooded guards. So what? I respect the ones who do. Master Yenca doesn't doubt us. Master

Yinob doesn't. I don't think we need to worry that the caretakers as a group are losing confidence in us."

Now Elenn drew a bit closer and spoke more quietly, lest any approaching guard hear what he was about to say. "Master Nula, we can't act like there's no reason to doubt the hooded guards. After all, we ourselves have *done it*."

Nula stared at Elenn with a disappointed look in his eyes. "Master Elenn, just because we shared necks does not mean that we are any less effective as guards on the hood squad," he said.

Elenn did not want to disappoint Nula, but he had to be honest. "It was a mistake to do the thing that we are there to stop," he said.

"There is such a thing as recovery from derangement," argued Nula, even as emotion brought a quiver to his voice. "You said it yourself—you told me before that when we take deranged barren to the infirmary they usually recover in time."

Elenn frowned sympathetically at Nula. He understood that Nula was distraught about where his life was going and wasn't thinking straight. "That has nothing to do with the fact that we made a mistake," he said, trying to be sensitive to Nula's unwillingness to hear such a thing.

"Some sharing of necks is going to happen. It's just when it gets out of control that it has to be stopped," countered Nula, sounding desperate.

"We both know, it's only controllable if we keep the oath."

"We did control it, didn't we? We controlled it until we both learned that I may not live," said Nula.

Elenn was quiet for a moment as he pondered the thought. It indeed had been a choice to give Nula something he longed for, in light of his condition. "You're right, Master Nula, and I don't mean that I completely regret what we did, but as a guard of the capital. . ." Elenn shook his head hopelessly, ". . .I know it was a mistake."

Nula looked grimly into Elenn's eyes. "Master Elenn," he said, with a doomed sound to his voice, "Are you saying we will we never do it again?"

With all the respect he could summon, Elenn answered, "No, Master Nula. Never."

He watched Nula give a hint of a nod, the habit of a junior guard. But he didn't like the faraway and hopeless look on Nula's face, and he searched his mind for something to say. Feeling greatly conflicted, he unconsciously brought a hand to face and simply said, ". . .But Nula —"

Then he was embarrassed for saying it. Nula's name without the honorific 'master' would normally never be used except by Nula when he introduced himself. He hadn't planned to say it; it had just come out. He quickly corrected himself, "Master Nula, I must tell you something."

Nula looked at him, mystified by this odd manner of being addressed, and seemed eager to hear what special thing Elenn was going to say.

"We will never share necks, but. . ., but. . ." What would they share? They would not share the squadron any more. They would not share quite the same fates. They would not share mornings at Quarterhouse and days walking around the capital. But something bound them together. It was their troubled lives and their determination to endure the trouble. It was their deep sense of duty, made heavier by the truths they encountered every day.

And it was hope in the face of despair, not a hope for some specific outcome, but simply a hope in the greater balance of the capital, that it would benefit from their efforts and survive the syndrome. But Nula didn't want to hear any of those things, and Elenn knew it. Then it came to him, what he could say.

"We will share hearts," he said to his junior guard. "I will share my heart with you, and your sick heart will be my sick heart as well."

Nula's face revealed his wonder at Elenn's words. Elenn likewise knew that this was not the way any uedin, let alone guards, spoke to one another. When Nula's eyes suddenly filled with tears, Elenn worried for a moment that his strange choice of words had upset Nula, possibly offended him in some way.

"Oh, Master Elenn,. . ." he said in a stunned voice, ". . .if that is what we will have, it will be the honor of my life."

They both brought hands to face at the same time. Awkward and embarrassed as they both felt, they kept their hands up, cupping the space between their eyes and framing their views of one another. Nula lowered his arms first. Elenn lowered his, then, and regarded his young comrade with an unusually long and sad smile. When he looked into Nula's eyes, what he saw was another barren uedin like himself. But along with the pain of being barren and facing some unknown demise that was not the passing-of-life, Elenn saw in Nula also a beautiful bravery.

"We are barren, Nula."

"Yes, we are," answered Nula. "All we can do is try to be happy in spite of it. We can only try."

"We will try, and we will succeed," said Elenn with wistful eyes. "We'll help each other."

For a moment, the earnest emotion seemed to corner them in self-consciousness. Elenn noticed Nula's awkward expression and felt it mirror his own embarrassment. Then, thankfully, Nula assumed an exaggerated look of mock concern. "There is just one more thing that I must ask of you," he said, his jest obvious.

"Oh yes? And what exactly is *that*, Master Nula?"

"You must switch places with me."

Elenn was a bit perplexed.

". . . This bench is too hard to sit on, and I want to finish my tea sitting in Master Huma's chair!" Nula broke into laughter just as he got the words out, and Elenn attempted to make a scolding face through his smiles.

Nula Helps Yinob Sew Socks
for the Unnamed

Yinob was alone in the Bramble sitting room with a basket of small pieces of cut cloth that he was sewing into socks for the unnamed. The unnamed were getting big, and the whole domicile was busy with them. During these busy times in the fifth year of a novade, hardly anyone even used the sitting room. No other masters were likely to come around, and it was a good spot for a meeting with young Master Nula. Nula was very fine young uedin, and Yinob had grown fond of him, but he did not look forward to this meeting. Counseling hooded masters who had no passing-of-life ahead of them was one thing. Counseling a young uedin who might not even live to the end of the novade was quite another. The challenge was made all the more difficult by the fact that young Nula and he shared an exceptional level of candor. Nula had fully confided in him about his temptations to feed, and Yinob, in turn, had shared his own history of craving yeastdrink. He understood full well how hard it was to struggle with a destructive desire.

It was when he was just about the same age as Nula that he had developed a yeastdrinker habit of some severity. After his apprenticeship, the older masters who like the drink had invited him into their circles, and it had been a time of much fun and daring.

But while occasional yeastdrink seemed to suit most of the masters, Yinob found himself wanting it all the time. He met the most shameful and devastating experience of his life the day that he was caught stealing it. It became horrendously clear to him then that yeastdrink would always be a problem for him. Since that time, he had gone through many episodes of succumbing and drinking again, coming to bad consequences, and resolving to resist it for long periods. That was the story of his life, and his deep aggravation with it yielded one consolation: it informed him about struggle in such a way that he could be an effective counselor to others.

Yinob picked out one of the heavier cloth soles to start sewing another sock together. He poked a hole through the tough cloth with his needle and drew a thread through it. He suddenly heard little feet on the floor and looked around to see a child-uedin loitering under the door tarp. The child was alone, holding one arm up to hang onto the tarp and looking at Yinob.

"Oh, hello there, little one," said Yinob. "Did one wander all the way over here?"

"What is one doing?" asked the child-uedin.

"One is sewing. One's making socks for one and many unnamed like oneself."

"One *make* socks?"

"Well yes, of course. Where does one think they come from?"

The child-uedin giggled and came in to see more closely.

"This is the bottom part of the sock," explained Yinob. "See? One is sewing on this other piece that will go up over the toes and the top of the foot, and then one will sew on the sides."

The child-uedin looked up at Yinob with happy eyes, pleased to have this explanation.

An apprentice caretaker to unnamed lifted the door tarp and looked in. "Oh, little one, one was looking for one! One left one's puzzle on the floor. One must put it away when one is finished playing with it."

"One learn about socks," said the child.

The apprentice spoke to Yinob. "Master Yinob, may I bother you for a favor?"

"What can I do for you?" asked Yinob.

"I just need to use the toilet. Then I'll come right back for the little one."

"Go right ahead. He's fine with me. He can play with the puzzle right here."

"Thank you, Master!" said the apprentice. He came in and gave the puzzle to the child-uedin, gave him a little pat on the back, and quickly left.

"One can do *whole puzzle!*" boasted the child-uedin with delight.

"Show me," said Yinob, and the unnamed sat beside the basket and took the puzzle all apart in order to put it back together again. The little one was a bit more confident than capable, and he quickly saw that he was not as sure about the puzzle as he had thought.

There was another hand pulling aside the door-tarp, and Yinob was just thinking that the apprentice was certainly back very quickly, but it was one of the tutors with Nula in tow.

"You have a visitor, Master Yinob," said the tutor.

Nula entered the room, breathing heavily, obviously from a jog across the capital. He smiled at the child-uedin and caught his breath. "Hello there, little one," Nula said, even before greeting his counselor. Yinob looked up from his sewing. Nula was trying to engage the unnamed, and Yinob waited to see if the child would speak.

The unnamed looked up, but quickly returned to his puzzle and worked on it a few seconds to see if they would ignore him. When he realized that they were not ignoring him, but waiting for him to speak, he said, "This pieces all good, but this pieces not good." A single chunk remained to put in place.

"Let me see," said Nula, and he bent to look closely at the gourd puzzle in the child's hands. "Turn it backwards," he said, "maybe it will fit that way."

The child-uedin turned the gourd piece around and then slid it perfectly into place. He looked at Nula with surprise and delight, and said, "Hey! Look! The pieces fits!"

The apprentice caretaker came back in and spoke to the child-uedin, "Come, little one, bring the gourd puzzle. Let's show the others."

The child stood, holding the puzzle together with both hands, and went to his caretaker.

The tutor raised hands to face for Yinob and Nula, and then bent over to speak to the child again. "Are you going to carry it?"

"Yes."

"All right then, come along," he said. He lifted the door tarp to exit the room, and the child followed him out.

"What a joy it must be to live with the unnamed," said Nula.

It suddenly occurred to Yinob that there might be a way for Nula to come and live with them at Bramble. Could Nula become a caretaker? Would it be permitted? He hesitated before making the suggestion, considering whether it would work. He couldn't think of any reason why it wouldn't.

"Master Nula, why don't you become a caretaker and come to live with us at Bramble? You're not happy at the guard station where you can't do what you used to do."

Nula was surprised to hear his counselor suggest such a move. "Master Yinob, I know you feel sorry for me, but. . ."

"I'm sure the masters council would let you transfer without hesitation."

"I don't have the skills to be a caretaker."

"You would learn. Here. Help me with these socks." Yinob handed Nula a set of small pieces of cut cloth to be sewn together. "You can thread a needle, can't you?"

Nula looked at Yinob with reluctance.

"What?" said Yinob, then "Oh, I see. I'm sorry. Of course you wouldn't want to become a caretaker after you've been a guard. I suppose it would be terribly boring for you." Yinob laughed.

"No, I don't mean that," said Nula. "I'm already terribly bored at Crafting Station. It's just that. . . I don't know if I could do it."

"Of course you could do it!" said Yinob. "Here. Take this."

Nula took the pieces of cloth and handled them to see how they fitted together, then reached for needle and thread.

"Master Yinob," said Nula cautiously, "Much has happened since I saw you last."

Yinob looked up from his work and nodded slowly, giving Nula permission to continue.

"Have you received more news from the medic masters?"

"No, it's not that. My condition is stable. I just can't exert myself physically."

"I hope you didn't overwork yourself coming here," said Yinob. "You didn't run did you?"

Nula didn't answer, and Yinob scolded him seriously, "Master Nula! The guards at both Crafting and Quarterhouse are surely worried about you, as are the medic masters, as am I. Is it your wish to cause us even more worry?"

"I didn't run fast, but I had to move! I'm so tired of sitting!"

"Well, you can discuss that with the medic masters. Don't just ignore their instructions." Then he asked, "What has happened since I saw you last?"

"Well, one thing happened while I was still in the infirmary. . ."

"Yes?"

"You know that I was having a hard time with temptations."

"Yes, I know that."

"I was specifically troubled by my temptations when I was working with Master Elenn. . ."

"We talked about that, yes."

"When I learned that I had Bilmin's Condition and that I would probably not live a long life, my feelings about the temptation changed."

Yinob nodded slowly. "How did they change?"

"I didn't want to die without experiencing the thing that I have resisted all along."

Yinob put down the pieces of cloth that he was sewing and gave Nula his serious attention. "You asked Master Elenn to share necks with you."

Nula didn't answer, and his silence told Yinob that it was true.

"He refused your request, I hope."

Again Nula was silent.

Yinob did not try to hide his disappointment. "Many of the caretakers are reporting that their counselees are losing hope in the hoods. But Master Nula, you must think about Master Elenn, not just yourself. He has a great responsibility."

"I know. And he has already told me that he will not share necks with me again."

Yinob tried to read the emotion of Nula's statement, not sure if it made him sad or not. If Nula was sad about never having a chance to share necks again, he would have to pardon him for it. Yinob understood the pain of letting go of a strong want. But Nula seemed not particularly sad reporting that Elenn had seen the error in feeding. Yinob was relieved to see this.

"You, as a guard, have seen what happens to uedin who become deranged from sharing necks," he said.

"This time it wasn't just desire that made me want to share necks," said Nula. "I was afraid. I knew that I had Bilmin's Condition, and I was afraid of dying without ever knowing what it was like to have the experience."

"Well, now you've had it. But you say Master Elenn has already told you he will not do it again, so let's be thankful that one of you came to his senses."

"I am thankful. But I don't regret doing it."

"I suppose if it was going to happen, it's good that it happened with Master Elenn. He has been a very good mentor for you."

"I will miss working with him, but I believe we will always be good friends. Master Elenn has actually promised his friendship to me."

Yinob waited for Nula to explain.

"Master Elenn has promised me a friendship for life, like no friendship I could have anticipated."

Yinob thought quietly about this for a moment, and then reached over and touched Nula's forearm. "Master Nula, I am glad to hear this. It is a little unusual—it is my job as your counselor to be a caretaker to you, but I can see that Master Elenn will be more important than a caretaker."

"The most difficult thing is that we can't work on the squad together anymore."

"Master Elenn visits you at Crafting Station, doesn't he?"

"Yes, but that is possible only when we're both finished with our duties. And, I'm afraid of what the guards will think when he keeps coming."

"The guards all know that you have Bilman's Condition, don't they?"

"Yes, but we are two hooded masters who no longer work together on the squadron. Won't they suspect that we are sharing necks?"

Yinob thought about this. "As long as you do not actually share necks, it doesn't matter if they worry about you. But will you be able to resist temptation in the future, now that you have done it once?"

Yinob quickly perceived Nula's discomfort. It looked as though if there were going to be any resistance to temptation, it would be incumbent upon Master Elenn to demonstrate it.

"Do you think you could say no to him?" asked Yinob gently, with no judgment in his voice.

"I don't think I will have to," said Nula. Yinob sensed that Nula spoke these words with sadness and that he wished he would be given the opportunity to say yes or no.

"Either way, I'm sorry that you have this burden on top of everything else," said Yinob.

"I asked for it," said Nula sadly.

"You may be tempted to ask for it again," commented Yinob, again without judgment.

"There may be temptation. I'll have to live with it, just as I live with my barren syndrome, and just as I live with Bilmin's Condition. I will need your good counsel, Master Yinob."

"You will have it. And if Master Elenn has said that he will not share necks with you again, he will probably keep this promise. He is a fine uedin and a fine guard. Whatever choices the two of you have made, I think you will be very good friends for one another."

"If only I were at Flatpools, or if Master Elenn were at Crafting. Then we could be together more. I feel very alone sorting papers and sweeping the floor at the station house day after day. It's so tiresome."

"I don't think either guard station would support a transfer between stations. But if you are unhappy with your limited duty as a guard, you could seriously pursue a transition to caretaker. Then you could request to go to Quarterhouse. Of course, I would love to have you here at Bramble."

"Seriously, Master Yinob, I have no training as a caretaker. Do you think I would be able to contribute?"

"I'm sure you would. The unnamed are getting big. We can always use a master who's good at showing authority and keeping them in line, and as a former guard, you'd be good at that."

"I never imagined that I would wear anything but a guard's robe," said Nula, looking at the green sleeve of his guard's garb. "But it might offer the best future for me."

"Well, you have time. You can think about it. If you decide to try it, you can discuss it with your seniors at Crafting. Just let me know so I can talk to Master Benar and find out what I can about the situation at Quarterhouse. Will you be going to the next squadron meeting?"

"I was hoping I would be welcome, even though I can't do the work of the squadron guards anymore."

"I'm sure you will be welcome," said Yinob. He picked up the half-sewn sock that he was working on and looked closely to see where he had left off.

"I see what you mean about the unnamed getting big," said Nula, picking up his own pieces of cloth and reaching for a needle and some thread. "Are their feet really this big already?"

"You should see how much they're eating! Even though we have a small generation, the kitchen is busy as it ever was to keep their bellies full," said Yinob with a glad smile. Nula smiled back through his teeth as he bit of a length of thread for threading his needle.

Plans for a Caretaker Hut
Outside the Capital Wall

"We must have a hut. We can't do it without the hooded guards. It would have been an insult to the squadron if we had made the proposal to the masters council without going through them first. If the hooded guards believe that one of them should be assigned to the hut along with the caretaker, they must be given our confidence," said Jutef, his hand on Yenca's shoulder as they walked a quiet back alley to avoid the noise of the bartering yards. They were on their way to Central Station for the meeting of the hood squadron.

"But how can we ask a hooded guard to reside outside the walls, with so much feeding going on these days? He'll be overwhelmed!" said Yenca.

"There are a few unhooded guards on the squadron now," said Jutef. "Masters Onnek and Posha have been working with regular guards at Southgate. And Master Ippal has replaced Master Nula now."

Yenca thought for a moment and then responded, "We cannot ask the only unhooded guards in the squadron and not ask all of them, but neither can we put a master with the syndrome alone outside the walls. Why must there be a guard? Why can't a caretaker or a team of caretakers reside alone in the hut? The hooded are not a danger to us."

"Master Yenca, I hope you won't try to dissuade me, but I will tell you what I have in mind. You see, I was hoping that *I* might be able to live in the hut." Jutef was actually terrified of ever being alone outside the capital walls, a world where his blindness made him feel miserably lost. "But I must admit that with my blindness, I would want one other master there with me, and I know it can't be you. As long as it's not going to be you, I'm thinking I would be more secure with a guard. I hope that doesn't offend you as a caretaker."

Yenca hesitated because he had to sort out everything he was being told. "I'm not offended, but it's true I could not live with you in the hut. I could not live outside the capital. I am dedicated to the welfare of the hooded masters, but that I cannot do. And to be very honest, you cannot do it either. Your work is with us at Quarterhouse." Yenca knew it would insult Jutef to tell him directly that he would be much too helpless outside the walls. He hoped what he had said was enough to discourage him.

"But we must have a hut with a resident caretaker, or there is no reason to build the hut. . . And we've already agreed that we absolutely must have one to care for the syndrome masters who are feeding," said Jutef. "Who is going to do it if not me?"

They were nearing Central Station from the back streets, and Yenca had to slow down to remember the way to get there the back way. "That's why we're going to discuss it at this meeting. Master Benar will probably have some suggestions. I'm sorry, but I don't think you would do well outside the walls."

Jutef didn't have a chance to respond because they arrived at the station house. Once inside, he heard the voices of Benar and someone from the masters council. He couldn't ask Yenca to tell him who all were there, so he would have to wait to determine who were present as they spoke one by one. He focused on listening for voices, but just then Benar called out and addressed all the attendants.

"Masters. . .Masters. . ." he called to get their attention. "If everyone will find his place. . . to begin with, we will recite the Names, then we will have a few introductions. Master Umat, you have such an excellent voice, will you kindly lead us in the recitation?"

Jutef heard Umat pushing back his chair to stand. As he heard the others in the room do the same, he stood up with them and waited for Umat to commence.

"*Lehera Beyana yana ya. . .,*" chanted Umat, and Jutef noticed that indeed he had a beautiful voice.

They all repeated, "*Lehera Beyana yana ya. . .*"

"*Lerna Beyana ulrana uedina. . .*" chanted Umat.

"*Lerna Beyana ulrana uedina. . .*"

As the recitation proceeded, Jutef listened for specific voices. He could make out Yenca, Benar, Elenn, Posha, and who else?

"*Lern Beyan kiman kiman uedin olorrr. . .*"

Master Nula. Master Nula was there too. Jutef was a little surprised that he was there. He had recently heard that Nula was diagnosed with a serious heart condition and would not be able to continue as a hooded guard. Jutef had assumed that Nula would be absent. Well, it was good that Nula was there. Nula might not be able to work with the squadron any more, but why shouldn't he come to the meetings? Besides, the fact that he was strong enough to attend was a good sign.

The recitation ended, and the masters in attendance remained quiet until someone spoke, a voice Jutef had never heard before. "Masters, this is the twenty-seventh meeting of the hooded guards and senior caretakers to the syndrome-afflicted. For those of you who are here for the first time, I am Master Amit, senior guard at Central. I want to welcome Master Ippal of the Flatpools Station, and Masters Rorik and Ulaf of Southgate Station." Jutef understood that these were the unhooded guards who were currently working with the squadron. He reasoned that there would probably be considerable discussion of this new development in addition to his proposal for a caretaker hut outside the capital walls. There might even be a long agenda of other items, but since it was also his first time attending a squadron meeting, he had no idea what they might be. Suddenly he heard his name being spoken.

"Master Jutef, thank you also for coming, and we're looking forward to hearing from you." Jutef knew that the masters in the room were looking at him, so he raised hands to face. He thought he was going to be asked to say something to introduce himself, but was relieved when Master Benar jumped in and spoke to Master Nula.

"Master Nula, we're all very glad to see you looking strong," said Benar. "Can you tell us how you've been doing?"

"I'm doing well, thank you all—guards and caretakers," said Nula. "Thanks for all your kind messages when I was in the infirmary, and I've even gotten some since I've been back at Crafting."

Amit said, "Master Nula, many of us know a little bit about your situation, but could you please fill us in?"

"Well, I've been a second generation guard from Crafting, and after I learned of my syndrome status and took hood, I was asked to be on the squadron. I've been partners with Master Elenn since the squadron formed, but now I have a diagnosis for a serious health problem. I have something called Bilmin's Condition, a heart ailment. It strains my heart if I do anything too physical. If I kept working with the squadron, I would be putting my life at risk."

"You can still consider yourself a member of the squadron, even if you are limited to work duty at Crafting Station," said Amit.

"I regret that I won't be able to continue as an active guard, but I hope you will allow me to attend meetings. I still care very much about the work of the squadron and the caretakers."

"By all means," said Amit.

"You should come whenever you like, and you should feel free to participate," said Yenca.

Benar said, "Master Nula, I spoke with your counselor, Master Yinob, the other day. He told me that you may be asking the masters council to approve a transfer for you?"

"Yes," said Nula. "I may be leaving the guards completely. If the masters council gives me their approval, I will be transitioning to a caretaker position, though I'm not sure which domicile I'll join."

Well, thought Jutef, this was an interesting development. He heard other murmurings of interest and surprise.

"Master Yinob said that they might welcome you at Bramble," said Benar.

"Yes, but I have to consider the other domiciles and go where there is greatest need."

Yenca spoke again. "Well, we certainly wish you the best, Master Nula. And you are welcome to continue to join us here and be part of our efforts on behalf of our hooded masters."

"I want to thank Master Ippal for taking my place on the squadron," said Nula.

Benar interjected, "Yes, we want to recognize both Master Ippal of Flatpools and Masters Rorik and Ulaf of Southgate for accepting permanent assignments working with the hooded guards. Masters Rorik and Ulaf, you were the first to work with our hooded guards. How is everything going? Do you have any questions about the squadron?"

There was a pause, and Jutef thought about what he was hearing. He knew that Ippal, a regular guard, was working with Master Elenn, and there were other regular guards working with the Southgate squad members, but he had not considered what it would mean if they took permanent positions. It would change the nature of the hood squad to have non-hooded guards. The Southgate guards took a very long time before one of them responded. Jutef heard one of them clear his throat and finally speak.

"I'm Rorik. Our senior guard, Master Emel, came to me and told me that our two hooded guards were being separated." Jutef noticed the discomfort in his voice. "We both agreed to work with them. I work with Master Onnek, and Master Ulaf works with Master Posha. This is the first we're hearing that the assignment is meant to be permanent."

This was one of those times when Jutef wished he could see how people were reacting when they didn't speak. The room was silent. It sounded like Rorik and the other guard didn't even know that they were being recruited for permanent positions on the squadron. Rorik didn't seem very eager to embrace the role.

"May I speak, Master Benar?" asked Onnek.

"Please do," said Benar.

"We hooded guards can't work with each other anymore. And we need help. Masters Rorik and Ulaf, and now Master Ippal, might not want to belong to a squadron of hooded guards when they are not hooded. I want to propose that all hooded guards be partnered with regular guards, as we have done at Southgate. But in order to do that, we can no longer consider ourselves as a squadron of hooded guards."

Jutef was appalled by this suggestion. Since he couldn't see if anyone else had stood up to speak, he might be interrupting someone, but he felt he had to speak up. "But Master Onnek, we must avoid a situation in which the hooded are policed by non-hooded. The hooded must be given the opportunity to police themselves."

"And I'm telling you we have proven that we *can't* adequately police ourselves," said Onnek. It was a shocking thing to say, and nobody responded for a moment.

Finally, Benar said, "Master Onnek, the transition must be gradual." He sounded aggravated.

"What transition must be gradual?" asked Jutef.

"The transition to a new partnering system for the squadron," said Benar. "We do need more help from the regular guards. No one can deny that. But it's going to be an adjustment for everyone."

Jutef was still thinking about what Onnek had said. "Master Onnek, you may feel that the hooded masters are ready to be monitored by regular guards, but you are only one. As a caretaker, I feel strongly that our hooded will be humiliated by such an arrangement."

Elenn spoke up. "We may be able to adequately police ourselves with support from the regular guards; we don't have to turn the squadron over to them completely."

"No one was saying we should," said Onnek.

Then Elenn spoke directly to Jutef. "Master Jutef, I was there when you told the masters council that you wanted to disassociate yourself from the hood statute because it was too much to ask of us syndrome-afflicted. Do you remember?"

"Of course I remember," said Jutef. It had taken all his courage to make such a statement before the masters council.

"And my response was that we have no choice," said Elenn. "Again we are in a situation in which we have no choice."

Though this hardly constituted an argument, hearing it from Master Elenn, whom Jutef highly respected, made him seriously reconsider his position. Perhaps the hooded guards really were unable to manage the situation on their own. Perhaps the hood squad could not carry on as it had been doing.

Benar tried to undo the controversy he had created by his reference to the regular guards' assignment as being permanent. "When I spoke with Master Emel, the senior guard at Southgate, we didn't exactly say that the assignments would be *permanent*—just that the regular guards would work with us as long as necessary. Master Ippal, that goes for you too. The hood statute is very threatened right now, but many things could change. We could recruit many more hooded masters into the squadron after the next Namesgiving. Please don't overreact to my careless choice of words!" Benar laughed.

"I'm sorry, I didn't mean it to sound like I don't respect the hood squad," said Rorik, "It's just that—we didn't know the assignment might be considered permanent. . ."

"And it needn't be considered permanent just yet. Again, please pardon my mistake," said Benar

Yenca spoke next. "We have only had six active hooded guards on the squad, and now, because of Master Nula's resignation, we are down to five. Only two are still working as a team. Masters Cebik and Umat, you are still working together and reporting to the caretakers at Bells, is that right?"

"Yes, Master," said Cebik, "but we both have comrades at Northgate that we have in mind to ask, if it is decided that we need to separate."

Hearing this, Jutef understood that everyone on the squadron had obviously heard some warning of a new partnering with regular guards. He felt that the Northgate guards should be able to decide for themselves whether they wanted to separate, but he no longer had the confidence to speak up about it. He waited for another master to comment.

"There are two advantages to partnering with regular guards," said Onnek. "One is that it brings more guards into the squadron. The other is that it keeps us in check with regard to our own struggles with keeping the oath. I broke my oath once. I never want to do it again."

Some time back, Jutef had overheard Benar talking to Yenca about a hooded guard at Southgate who had confessed to sharing necks with another hooded master. Jutef realized Onnek must have been the one they were talking about.

"Masters Cebik and Umat, we would never presume to suggest that either of you may or may not be struggling with the oath, but we do need more guards on the squadron," said Amit.

"We've been anticipating this," said Cebik. "We'll speak to our senior guards tomorrow about it."

"Meanwhile, Masters Rorik and Ulaf, please speak openly about anything that concerns you, and even if you don't remain with the squadron, we will appreciate all your input."

Jutef knew that they would be calling on him soon to share his proposal for a caretaker hut outside the capital walls, but he was glad when Benar first asked all the guards to talk about their interactions with hooded masters in all their varying degrees of adherence to the oath. His mind wandered while Posha talked about the difference between the second and third generation hooded masters.

He thought about the conversation with Master Yenca that had been cut short when they'd arrived at the station house. Had he had more time to talk with Master Yenca, he might have told him things that he could never tell a whole group of people such as were present for the squadron meeting. Jutef was afraid to be outside the capital walls, but he felt he must face that fear in order to address an even greater and more terrifying fear. Even as far back as the time when he had decided to become a caretaker to the barren, Jutef had felt a great foreboding that he would never make it to the Lake of Ceulan when his time came for the passing-of-life. In fact, that was his secret reason for caring so deeply about the barren. Jutef had always imagined meeting a miserable demise in the wilderness as he wandered blindly, unable to find his way to the lake. He thus shared the sorrow of the barren. However, recently, Jutef had experienced a growing sense of the living embryo in his skullwomb. Jutef, of course, was *not* barren. Sorrow was a sufficient response to the doom he felt he was facing, but the uedin life he carried deserved more than despair. He felt he must somehow build his courage and make a life-long commitment to prepare for a pilgrimage, as hard as it might be. His first step would be simply to try living in the hut outside the capital walls. If he could do that, perhaps he could someday summon the courage to venture northward and hope against hope that he might find his way. Given the opportunity to talk more with Master Yenca, he might have told him that, but Jutef was certainly not prepared to talk about it at this meeting.

". . .and so I'm hoping that we might find other hooded masters who will want to actively support the squadron, even if they can't become guards." Master Elenn was saying.

"Thank you, Master Elenn," said Benar. "And now I'd like to invite Master Jutef to tell us about his proposal for a new caretaker hut."

Jutef heard his name and was quickly brought to attention. He raised hands to face with a jerk and let out a little nervous laugh. "First let me say that the idea for a new caretaker hut outside the capital walls came up when I was talking to some other caretakers at Quarterhouse, and it's not my idea alone. I don't want uedin thinking that all I do is dream up new ideas for things all the time." He was referring to the idea for the barren taking hood, which had, of course, originated with him. He went on to explain further, "We have noticed for some time that when our syndrome-afflicted get themselves into trouble, they usually end up outside the capital walls. They become disoriented out there, and by the time we get them back, they're often in bad shape. We find them dehydrated and malnourished. Sometimes they're sick from exposure, and sometimes they have injuries. Of course, we know that that could all be avoided if they could just keep their hoods on their heads—helping them do that is the main goal of this squadron, and none of us wants to suggest in any way that we don't support that goal completely. But we have to deal with the situation as it stands. A caretaker hut outside the capital walls would allow us to treat those who are disoriented, sometimes even deranged, and we may be able to intervene a little better. I come to the squadron first because we need your help and support for this project, and probably even after the hut is built and functioning. If the squadron is willing to help with it, our next step will be to address the masters council."

"Where would the hut be built?" asked Onnek.

"We don't know. We are open to your suggestions."

"Probably either around the Clay Bridge or in the forest outside the western gate," suggested Posha.

"What about along the north drystream?" countered Cebik. "We're seeing deranged barren there every day."

"We have to consider access to supplies," said Ippal. "If the caretaker hut is going to work closely with a guard station, Northgate Station probably has easiest access to the capital exterior."

"Another serious question we have to consider is who will reside in the hut," said Yenca.

"Do you mean you want to have someone living there all the time?" asked Ulaf.

Jutef paused, thinking that Yenca might answer the question, but when he did not, Jutef replied, "Yes, we will need a permanent resident for the caretaker hut. And I would like to volunteer myself. However, I will need an assistant to be there with me full time."

Jutef waited for someone to respond, but no one spoke, and he felt a great embarrassment overcome him as he realized that none of them considered him a suitable candidate for resident of the hut.

Yenca spoke, "Master Jutef, I told you before. Your work at Quarterhouse is important. That's where you belong."

"I believe this is *more* important," said Jutef.

"Master Jutef, please don't be offended by what I'm going to say," said Benar, "You already need a lot of help at Quarterhouse. If you were to live in a hut outside the capital walls, the other caretakers would have to spend a great deal of time there taking care of *you*. That would not be an ideal arrangement."

"I was hoping one of the guards might stay with me there," said Jutef. "The guards need to increase their presence outside the walls anyhow, and I would be fine with one guard there to assist me from time to time."

"None of this needs to be decided now," said Yenca. "We haven't even given the proposal to the masters council yet."

"But we should have a plan in mind," said Jutef. "How can we proceed otherwise? I just need a guard to agree to reside with me at the hut. The masters council will agree to it if they know we have committed volunteers."

"Our hooded guards are spread thin as it is, and we will certainly not ask our regular guards, new to the squadron, to live outside the capital," said Yenca.

There was a long pause as no one had an easy answer to the problem of finding a housing companion for Jutef. Finally, Amit said, "Master Jutef, perhaps we will need to consider a care station instead of a permanent hut. We won't be able to operate a caretaker hut full time."

"I will do it," said Elenn, "but only on one condition."

Jutef was thrilled to think that Master Elenn might agree to live with him in the new caretaker hut. "What condition?" he asked.

"The hut must be built to accommodate three residents. I will want another caretaker there, both to help Master Jutef and to serve as an additional caretaker to the barren."

"That may be achievable," said Amit. "The caretakers will have to find a candidate for that role."

"I have someone specific in mind," said Elenn.

"Master Elenn, don't look at *me*!" said Benar. "I'm much too old to move away from my hut at Quarterhouse!"

"No, Master Benar, it wasn't you I had in mind. I would like my squadron partner, Master Nula, to join Master Jutef and me. By the time the hut is built, his transition to a caretaker vocation should be complete."

"He won't have much experience as a caretaker, but his time on the squad will prepare him for life outside the walls," commented Yenca.

"Won't it be a physical strain? Living outside the capital?" asked Amit.

"I'm not sure if this is a good idea," said Benar.

Elenn responded slowly. "What is your objection, Master Benar?" he asked, with some kind of obvious concern in his voice.

Benar also hesitated before answering. "Well,. . .Master Nula would definitely have to limit himself," said Benar quietly. "He would need to make a conscious effort *not* to overexert himself."

"Would you be amenable to such an arrangement, Master Nula?" asked Elenn. *Please say yes,* thought Jutef.

"If I might be of use to you and Master Jutef, and if the senior caretakers are in agreement, I would be honored to work at the new caretaker hut," said Nula. Jutef could clearly hear a note of gladness in Nula's voice. Things were falling into place just as Jutef had hoped. But getting his way was also frightening in some respects. He tried to imagine what it would be like to actually live outside the capital walls. The move was bound to turn his life upside down.

*Construction Outside
the Northern Wall*

Nemis was on his way to the building site for the new hut going up outside the northern wall. Two of his comrades from Flatpools were both very involved in the construction, helping the building masters between shifts. He had been surprised when he had heard that Ippal was taking over for Elenn's hooded partner from Crafting. When Ippal accepted the assignment, Nemis had to reconsider his belief that the regular guards had no business in the affairs of hooded uedin. The fact that Ippal had been asked and had agreed to work on the hood squad meant that the work of the squadron didn't depend on its member guards being hooded. At any rate, Master Ippal had invited Nemis to come and see what they were working on, and Nemis thought that since he had a free morning, he might be able to help out. He was particularly interested in construction because he still envisioned an observation deck being built onto the grainhouse at Murro where he had seen the magnificent view of the capital. A temporary repair had been done to the storm-damaged grainhouse while some members of the masters council were considering the possibility of an observation deck. Nemis thought that he might be able to get more involved in the project if he could gain a little experience working with the construction masters.

When he passed through Northgate, he encountered a gusty wind that hadn't been so noticeable inside the capital. Nemis knew that it was too early to find the building masters at work, and the guards wouldn't come around to help at least until the builders got there. But Nemis went early because it had been a while since he had been outside the capital walls, and he thought he might enjoy being out there while the sun was only coming up and things were quiet. He had hoped for a wonderful sunrise, but it was too cloudy a day to even see the direct point of the sun's rising.

He had no trouble finding the half-completed log structure. It was close enough to the drystream that they would easily find chinking clay for between the logs. He sat on the edge of one of the logs that were waiting to be used and took out a cold cooked potato that he had wrapped in a piece of throw-away paper and stuck in his pocket the night before. As he was unwrapping it, he saw a hooded master walking along the edge of the gully that led down to the bottom of the drystream. At first, he thought it might be one of the hooded guards, but the master wasn't wearing guard's garb. Nemis stood up and called to the stranger.

"A cloudy morning!" he called, greeting him.

The stranger looked up, startled. He wore an expression of panic for a moment and then smiled and called back, "Yes, a cloudy morning it is!"

Perhaps the stranger was one of the worker masters coming to help at the building site. Why was he coming from that direction? Nemis waited as he approached. When the hooded stranger got close, he stopped, raised hands to face and said, "I'm Leol, second generation fieldworker from the western outfields."

"I'm Nemis of the Flatpools guards," said Nemis. "Are you here to help with building this morning?"

". . .uh, Yes," said the young master. "I can help a little bit."

"How did you know about the project? Did Master Elenn invite you to come?" Nemis immediately noticed the hooded master's awkward look. Of course! The master was out there along the drystream looking to feed. It was no surprise.

"I did not know about the project. But I do know Master Elenn," he said.

Nemis looked at him with a shrug, "It's ok if you didn't know about it. You don't have to tell me what you're doing here."

The master blushed, clearly embarrassed. Nemis tried to put him at ease by changing the subject. "Master Elenn is my comrade at Flatpools Station. He will probably be here later in the morning."

"Master Elenn will be coming here?"

"Yes, he's very involved in this project. He's going to be living in this hut after it's built."

"Outside the walls?"

"That's the plan."

"Master Elenn and Master Nula came to visit us at western outfields once," said Leol.

"Yes, Master Nula will be living here too," said Nemis. He still had the potato in his hand. He thought it might be nice to offer a piece to this young Master Leol. "I have a potato, but I need something to cut it with," he said.

"I have a knife," said the young master. He reached in his pocket, took out a small case blade, and handed it to Nemis. Nemis opened it and used the knife to cut the potato into two halves, then handed one half to Leol together with his knife back.

"That's wonderful that Masters Elenn and Nula will be living here."

"I think another caretaker will be here too—a caretaker to the hooded masters. Three of them are going to be here."

"I have a counselor, but he doesn't know what I'm doing," he said, trying not to be so embarrassed.

"Well, I guess you don't have to tell him anything you don't want to," said Nemis casually, and then, to further show that he wasn't intent on interrogating this young master, he said, "This potato probably came from your fields. Do you grow potatoes?"

"We grow everything," said Leol. He didn't elaborate. "Master. . . I'm sorry, your name again?"

"I'm Nemis."

"Master Nemis, I shouldn't be here. I don't want to be here when Master Elenn comes."

"He won't be here till after the builders arrive," said Nemis.

"I don't want to be here when they come either. I'm sorry, I won't be able to help today."

"If you need to leave, it's fine. Come back another time."

"I will," said Leol, and he raised hands to face then turned and ran off. He went to the rim of the drystream gully and then descended down into it, and Nemis reasoned that he was going to follow the flat bottom of the streambed around the corner of the capital and back to the western outfields. As he stood and watched the young hooded master disappear, he heard the worker masters arriving behind him.

"Was that a barren?"

"He was a hooded master, yes," said Nemis. "I was just talking to him."

"I hate to see them out here. It makes me sick to think of that thing they do," said the worker.

"It's a very troubled life they live," said Nemis. "I don't think we can imagine what it's like."

Leol ran along the bottom of the drystream, and when the ground started to get rocky, he got on the well-worn path that wove through the rocks. One of the reasons he dreaded seeing Master Elenn was that the three hooded fieldworkers had kept their promise to Master Elenn for a very long time—the promise that they would never go alone to the drystreams or near the walls—and it was Leol who was secretly visiting the dreaded area outside the north wall. He had come close to openly arguing that they were adults and should individually come and go as they pleased. But he had none of Serka's boldness or Jeber's courage, and he knew that anything he said would reveal his real motivation. Now that the thing he dreaded most had come to pass, Leol felt terribly ashamed for breaking the agreement that they had made to follow Master Elenn's advice. The last thing he wanted to do was get caught by Master Elenn. He remembered how Master Elenn had said all that about "put your hood back on and believe in yourself again." But that was so hard to do. Leol could put his hood back on, but he couldn't believe in himself again.

Tired from running, he slowed down to a walk. Then he reached a place where a side path led up the outside bank of the drystream, through the row of trees, and into the western fields. After a short distance, he could see the workhouse and the larder shacks. He could count on Jeber and Serka not to ask him where he had been. They were so kind to him. If only he could be as strong as they were at keeping the oath. The strange thing was, even though they wouldn't ask where he had been, Leol wanted to tell them what he had heard about Masters Elenn and Nula planning to live in a hut up on the outside of the north capital wall. He had to tell them. He would just tell them the truth. He hadn't met anyone that morning except a guard from Flatpools. They wouldn't make him explain what he was doing there. They knew. They knew and didn't treat him badly about it. They were kind enough to pretend they knew nothing, and Leol likewise pretended that his secret was safe. But this time would be different. He wasn't going to be secretive. He was going to tell them exactly what happened, and maybe they would be able to get Master Ghera's permission to go help with the construction one day soon.

He broke into a run again as he approached the domicile and larder shacks that rose from the fields, and went straight for the silkworm cabin. They were supposed to be cleaning it that day, so he was pretty sure he would find them there. He ran past other worker masters pruning fieldpear bushes, went around the side the workhouse, and right to the door of the cabin. It sounded quiet. He pushed in the door tarp and stepped in.

It took him a few seconds to comprehend what he was seeing. Serka's bare shoulders were leaning over an empty crate, his short worker robe gathered around his waist. His hood was off, and his neck strap was resting against the face of Jeber who had his mouth on Serka's neck. Serka turned his head and looked at Leol, and they both wore an expression of shock.

"Master Leol—" said Serka, and Jeber then looked up.

Before anyone could say another word, Leol turned and ran away from the silkworm cabin. He ran to the tool shed, pushed open the door, went in, and huddled by the garden tools. It was dark, except for the line of sunlight around the door frame. His heart was pounding and he felt faint. He felt as if he had fallen from a ladder and landed hard on the ground. He was completely unprepared for what he had just seen. It was so crushing to him! Master Jeber and Master Serka, his dearest friends! He respected the both of them so much. He thought they would never break their oath. It felt to him like a very great disaster. "*Shield the Lern, shield the Lern, shield the Lern, shield the Lern, shield the Lern. . .*" he cried to himself. "*We're all going mad!*"

First Visitor to the New Caretaker Hut

The thing that Elenn liked the least about his new residence was having to carry water from Bells all the way to the hut. Since he was large, it was easy to carry two full buckets at once, but it seemed like such a long distance to him! He had a carrying pole over his shoulders and held both arms up to steady the heavy buckets. He was nearing the hut when he heard a voice inside that was neither Nula nor Jutef. Someone else was there. Elenn, interested in knowing who was visiting, put down the buckets and left them with the carrying pole attached, then pulled the tarp aside and stepped in.

"This is a new piece I'm working on," said Jutef, as Nula and the guest looked down at his work. He was showing the guest some of his weaving. The guest was hooded and had his back to the door, so Elenn couldn't see who it was.

One of the first things Jutef had done after relocating to the hut was to ask Nula to take him down to the bottom of the drystream. He had never been any place like that before. His first reaction was that he loved the feel of the tall reeds that grew in the moist creekbed. It made him remember his days of weaving, and he decided he would start weaving again to have a healthy pastime.

"It's very delicate," said the hooded guest, looking down at Jutef's work. Elenn thought he recognized the voice.

"Hello," said Elenn. When the hooded master looked up, Elenn saw his face and was very surprised to find that it was Pavis. Pavis was someone that Elenn didn't much trust, but he needed to be polite in this situation. "Master Pavis, I should have known it was you. Master Jutef is your counselor, of course! Welcome."

Jutef raised his face toward the wall, smiled, and spoke to Elenn. "Master Elenn, as you know, Master Pavis is a distribution master, and he knows every little street and alley in the capital. He came to get me because he's going to take me for a walk around the Northgate district. I want to get acquainted with it."

"Master Elenn," said Pavis, raising hands to face, "I haven't seen you for a long time. I was telling Masters Jutef and Nula, your new hut is very impressive."

"We want every hooded master to feel welcome here," said Nula, "or any uedin, for that matter."

"I like how you've built a charcoal burner right into the wall there," said Pavis.

"The builder masters suggested it," said Elenn. "I wasn't sure how it would work, but with the vent in the roof, it's very nice, isn't it? Keeps the place warm." They paused to gaze at the glowing charcoal, except for Jutef who wore a smile with his eyes closed as he often did.

"Have you seen Master Jutef's most recent weaving?" Nula asked Elenn.

"No. . . Is that it?"

Jutef handed Elenn the disk of woven reeds, and Elenn studied it closely for a moment. "It is very beautiful, Master Jutef," he said.

"I think it will be the base of a shallow basket," said Jutef.

"I can picture that," said Pavis.

"Master Pavis has a new pastime also. He's learning to play the woodflute," said Jutef. "Master Pavis, did you bring it with you?"

"It's small. I carry it in my pocket," said Pavis. "But I'm just starting to learn how to play it. I can't play anything yet."

"Yes you can," said Jutef. "You can play that song I taught you, the one I learned at Bells when I was unnamed."

"Oh yes, that little tune. . ." said Pavis.

"Let's hear it!" said Nula.

"You must!" said Jutef.

Pavis took the woodflute from his pocket. He held it to his mouth and played a little tune. He played it slowly, wavering a bit on a note here and there, but Elenn thought that he had heard it before.

"Again!" demanded Jutef, and this time, as Pavis played the flute, Jutef sang along. *"Hokey pokey turtle, in his turtle shell,. . .when the puppy comes he does very well,. . .just take a nap and when he wakes up,. . .no more sign of the naughty little pup!"*

"Master Jutef! I heard you sing that when you were a little child-uedin!" said Elenn, "When we went with the Bells unnamed to the moss beds!"

"Did I sing that for you?" said Jutef. "I don't remember. But that little song has always stayed with me."

"I've learned to play the melody on my woodflute, but I always think of the words when I play it. Masters are poets," said Pavis. "Server tradition has no poetry."

"It's not true, Master Pavis. There have been many server poets. You must know some of them—Yemel,. . .who else, Master Elenn?"

"Wimin. Wimin was a server poet."

"I've never heard of either of them," said Pavis. "Who wrote the poem about the turtle?"

"Oh, I don't think that's a poem," said Jutef. "It's just a child's song."

"That's the only thing I can play so far," said Pavis. "I'll have a longer song to play for you the next time I come."

"You're off to a good start," said Nula.

"Master Jutef, let's go take our walk," said Pavis. He got their cloaks that were hanging on pegs beside the door.

As he was putting on his cloak, Jutef said, "Master Pavis brought us sweetpepper biscuits. I put them in the cool pit. Save me one!"

Elenn was a little surprised to hear that Pavis had brought a gift.

"That depends on how good they are," said Nula. Jutef and Pavis chuckled.

"Have a pleasant walk," said Elenn.

Jutef and Pavis exited the hut. Elenn and Nula remained seated for a while, looking again at the glowing charcoal in the burner.

Finally, Nula said, "That was the Master Pavis who you told me was responsible for hooded masters referring to feeding as 'passing-of-life', right?"

"Yes, that was he."

"He seems very decent to me," said Nula.

"I think Jutef has had a great influence on him," said Elenn.

"Master Pavis seems to have had an influence on Jutef as well," said Nula.

"I'm sure he has," said Elenn.

"Do you think Master Pavis still refers to feeding as 'passing-of-life'?"

"I don't know. He might," said Elenn. "I've gotten to where I don't even like the word, 'passing-of-life,' which I know is very un-uedin. It just seems like a word that has no promise for us."

"What about the *sharing-of-life*? That would be a word that has promise for us, wouldn't it?"

"That's a very good thought, Nula. I like your word." It *was* the sharing-of-life that had come to replace passing-of-life for Elenn. The sharing of life not only between the barren, but between all uedin. All of them who balanced a bowl to live each day with each day's trouble. When he thought about this sharing-of-life, it gave him a quiet, easier feeling.

"So you brought water?"

"Yes. It's a bit of a slog carrying it all the way from Bells."

They stepped out of the hut intending to go to the side facing the capital wall where Elenn had left the buckets, but as soon as they were outside and saw the wind making whooshing waves in the reedgrass down in the distant drystream bottom, it stole their attention. The tall, lush reedgrass was swirling as though it had come to life.

"It's like a Great Rains river, but of wind!" said Nula.

Beyond the drystream was a sloping plain with cultivated fields in the west already looking thirsty for the next rainy season. Farther was the hill country that continued to a hazy horizon. They stood to take in the view.

"It is beautiful here," said Elenn.

"I'm grateful that I will live out my life in this place," said Nula.

Elenn looked at him with fondness and acceptance. "Shall we get the water?" he said.

They went to the other side of the hut where Elenn had left the covered buckets still attached to the carrying pole. They each disconnected a bucket. Nula picked one up for just a moment to get a sense of its weight and put it back down. "These are heavy. Too bad there isn't a well closer to the gate," he said.

"It does get heavy when you carry two full buckets at once."

"I could fetch the water sometimes. I don't think it would be too much strain on my heart."

"You better ask one of the medic masters before you do."

"I will ask Master Goril."

"Good. If Master Goril says it's all right, you can get the water every day," said Elenn with a mischievous smile.

"Not every day!"

"Oh yes. That will be your chore. You asked for it."

"I said *sometimes*!" yelled Nula, laughing at Elenn's joke.

"Nula, there's something on my mind right now. . ." said Elenn, with mock seriousness.

"The sweetpepper biscuits, right?" said Nula.

"We're going straight for the sweetpepper biscuits!" said Elenn.

"Master Jutef will be lucky if he gets one," added Nula.

Elenn laughed. "We'll see how good they are. If they're not very good, maybe we'll leave him one or two." The guard and the caretaker lifted their water buckets and carried them into the hut.

◆ ◆

END OF BOOK 2

Preview of Book 3

In *Passing-of-Life: Book 3 of the Barren Trilogy*, Elenn of the Hood Squadron falls into complete derangement, Tilke wastes away in a coma, and the uedin race faces extinction. Barren servers have been responding to the situation by drinking poison to spare the Lern and their community the burden of their presence. Now a controversial new method of self-extermination has been conceived, and it is catching on outside the temple compound. Uedin have always known that Lern Beyana does not speak. How can this quiet being help them now? What will she make them do, and where will she make them go, in order to carve out a pathway to survival? In this third and final book of the series, Elenn must rise above personal conflict and heartbreak as he is called to lead.

www.ingramcontent.com/pod-product-compliance
Lightning Source LLC
Chambersburg PA
CBHW031216120726
47905CB00002B/362